SISTERS OF THE MOON

Books 1-3

by

NINA CROFT

Sisters of the Moon Books 1 – 3

Copyright © 2012 by Nina Croft

All rights reserved. This book or any portion thereof may not be reproduced or used in any manner whatsoever without the express written permission of the author or publisher except for the use of brief quotations in critical articles or reviews.

This is a work of fiction. Names, places, businesses, characters and incidents are either the product of the author's imagination or are used in a fictitious manner. Any resemblance to actual persons living or dead, actual events or locales is purely coincidental.

Contents

Bound to Night
Book 1

1. Prologue — 3
2. Chapter One — 7
3. Chapter Two — 19
4. Chapter Three — 35
5. Chapter Four — 42
6. Chapter Five — 52
7. Chapter Six — 60
8. Chapter Seven — 76
9. Chapter Eight — 89
10. Chapter Nine — 99

Bound to Moonlight
Book 2

1. Chapter One — 107
2. Chapter Two — 112

3.	Chapter Three	119
4.	Chapter Four	128
5.	Chapter Five	139
6.	Chapter Six	146
7.	Chapter Seven	151
8.	Chapter Eight	161
9.	Chapter Nine	170
10.	Chapter Ten	177
11.	Chapter Eleven	185
12.	Chapter Twelve	192
13.	Chapter Thirteen	202
14.	Epilogue	210

Bound to Secrets
Book 3

1.	Chapter One	215
2.	Chapter Two	227
3.	Chapter Three	235
4.	Chapter Four	246
5.	Chapter Five	257
6.	Chapter Six	274
7.	Chapter Seven	283
8.	Chapter Eight	294

9. Chapter Nine	308
10. Chapter Ten	321
11. Chapter Eleven	329
12. Chapter Twelve	340
13. Epilogue	355
Subscribe to my Newsletter.	358
About the Author	359
Also by Nina Croft...	360

BOUND TO NIGHT

Sisters of the Moon
Book 1

by

NINA CROFT

Prologue

8 years ago

A prickle ran down her spine.

"Dad, are you there?" Tasha called out, but the words were thrown back at her, echoing off the stone walls.

She was early that was all. He'd be here. He'd promised.

The sun slipped lower in the sky, finally vanishing behind the huge warehouses. Shadows hugged the edges of the buildings, drawing ever closer to where she stood in the encroaching night.

She swallowed, her throat suddenly dry. Something was out there, watching her from just beyond the edge of the darkness. Out of the corner of her eye, she caught a movement in the dim light. Tendrils of emotion teased at her mind, like nothing she'd felt before. Not a person; there were no conscious thoughts, only raw feelings.

Anticipation. Hunger. Hate.

For a minute, Tasha stood petrified, every muscle locked solid. Then she forced herself to turn slowly and peer into the gloom. She blinked, trying to make sense of what she was seeing. A dog? But it was bigger than any dog she'd ever come across, bigger even than the wolves she'd seen at the zoo.

It took a step closer, clearing the shadows, and an icy wave of dread rolled over her, threatening to suck her under. Her mind screamed to run, but her body wouldn't obey, every muscle clenched tight as her gaze locked with cold yellow eyes.

Another step and the spell was broken. She hurled her backpack at the thing's head, then spun around and ran. She'd only taken a few strides when a heavy weight slammed into her, crashing her to the ground. Stars flashed behind her closed eyes, and the coppery taste of blood filled her mouth.

Tasha rolled onto her back and the beast was on her, pressing her down, hot stinking breath smothering her. She tried to scramble away, but it lunged, taking her shoulder in its huge jaws. Bone crunched loud in her ears. Searing pain flooded her body and mind, filling her with the certainty of her own death.

Maybe not yet.

But soon.

She must have blacked out. When she came to, the beast was gone, and she wasn't dead after all. Her own shuddering breaths were the only sound in the darkness. She tried to roll over, but red-hot spikes of pain pinned her to the ground. Her phone was in her backpack. She could see it lying about ten feet away. It might as well have been a mile.

Her dad would be here soon, all she had to do was hold on.

The beam of an approaching vehicle flooded the area with light. Tears of relief blurred her vision; she'd known he would save her. Always before, she'd balked at using her inner sense, scared it would mean she was accepting the impossible, descending into madness. Now, for the first time she reached out, needing to feel her father's comforting presence. But the minds she encountered were strangers.

She twisted her neck so she could watch. Some sort of dark van pulled up a few feet away, but she didn't recognize the vehicle. Two men stepped out and came toward her.

"She the one?" the closest asked.

"Oh yeah. Let's get her in the van—that thing's still out there."

"Wait. My father—" Tasha clamped her lips on a scream as the first man leaned down and dragged her to her feet. He tossed her over his shoulder, oblivious to the moan of agony wrenched from her throat. The few paces to the van seemed to last a lifetime. She was dropped in the back, and she landed with a jolt and lay staring at the roof, trying to get a grip on a world reduced to nothing but pain.

The rear door slammed, and she was alone. Panic tore at her insides as the vehicle started to move, and quickly picked up speed.

The journey passed in a haze of pain and confusion intermingled with brief respites of unconsciousness. Finally, the door opened, and a dark figure stared down at her.

"Welcome to the Facility."

Chapter One

Present day

Jack raced through the dark forest, weaving between the trees, listening for the sound of his pursuers. When he realized he was leaving them far behind, he slowed his pace. He hadn't spent all this time planning the operation just to elude them so easily.

He halted behind the broad trunk of an oak tree, pulled out his cell phone, and punched in speed dial.

"I'm going in," he said.

"Have fun," Sebastian replied.

"Yeah, right, like that's going to happen." He ended the call, tossed the phone into the undergrowth and peered around. The place was in darkness, no sign of any lights. Presumably, they were using night vision, because he could still hear them heading toward him, smashing through the undergrowth like a herd of blundering elephants.

Finally, when he was about to give up hope and go looking, one of them appeared. Tall, he was dressed all in black, with camouflage makeup darkening his face, and a rifle in his hand. A second man appeared at his side, and then a third—all armed. Jack was guessing the weapons would be loaded with tranquilizers. They wouldn't go to all this bother to get hold of him, and then risk killing him off.

He hoped.

Not that bullets could kill him, but they would hurt like hell.

Time to get this over with.

He stepped out from behind the tree and turned to face them. Then stopped abruptly and plastered a surprised expression on his face.

"Don't move." The first man raised his weapon and pointed it straight at Jack.

He hadn't been planning on moving, though he did snarl, baring the tip of one fang, just so they could be sure they had the right person.

The weapon made no sound as it fired. Jack released his breath and glanced down. A small dart stuck out of his upper arm. He waited to see whether the drug would have any effect.

Nothing.

With a sigh, he closed his eyes, swayed, then toppled to the ground.

He kept his eyes shut and his body limp as they wrapped him in chains. Silver chains. What did they think he was? A bloody werewolf?

They carried him through the forest, slung over someone's shoulder and finally dropped him in the back of a vehicle and slammed the doors shut, leaving him alone.

The journey took over an hour. At long last, they stopped moving and the door opened.

"Welcome to the Facility."

After two long and tedious weeks, Jack was far from impressed by the hospitality at the Facility. He hoped that was about to improve.

He opened his eyes and stretched on the narrow cot.

Someone was approaching.

With any luck, they were bringing him some food. He'd told them he needed sustenance, that he was starving, might even die without it. Though in truth, he was far more likely to die from boredom in this place, than he was from hunger. At over five hundred years old, he could go months without feeding, but they didn't know that. In fact, here at the Facility, they knew fuck all. At least about his kind. And if he had any say in the matter—and he planned to have a great deal—things would stay that way.

But he also needed information. After all, that was the point in his being here. He'd thought to coerce it out of the guards, but his first attempt had resulted in the man having some sort of aneurism and ending up bleeding from the ears. Then dead. Very inconvenient.

The guard must have had some sort of implant in the brain, which had reacted to the compulsion. But Jack had never come across anything like it, and he didn't want to risk it again, at least not yet. Once, they might put down to an accidental occurrence. Twice, and nobody would believe it a coincidence.

That was a week ago. Afterward, he'd decided the best way to get his information was for them to believe he was cooperating. So he'd made them an offer. His "collaboration " in exchange for food, though he was actually telling them a load of bullshit. He'd even managed to convince them he was allergic to garlic, and many a bored hour was spent coming up with even more ludicrous misinformation.

The footsteps came to a halt outside his cell, and he heard the numbers being punched into the keypad locking mechanism. There was also a retinal scan—the security was top of the range and far more advanced than anything out in the general market.

As the door slid open, Jack sat up but didn't get to his feet. He was expecting one of the guards, but instead a small, almost hunched figure, hovered in the open doorway. Someone shoved her hard, and she lurched forward and then turned and snarled at whoever was behind her.

Johnson, one of the less pleasant guards followed her into the cell, and then a second man stepped in behind her. This was someone new, and definitely not a guard. Probably in his forties, with short sandy hair, he studied Jack as though he were some sort of lab rat. Which he supposed he was in a way, though that didn't mean he had to like it.

"I'm Dr. Latham," he said. "I'm in charge of your...case."

Jack didn't answer, just curled his lip revealing the tip of one sharp fang. The guard took a step back. Latham remained where he was, his expression more curious than fearful. He was a fool.

A small gasp came from the girl. He'd almost forgotten she was there; she was so small and quiet. Now he turned to study her.

She was presumably his dinner. Or not. He had few rules, but not feeding from children was one of them. Then she raised her head to look at him. Her intense golden gaze locked with his, and he realized she was no child.

He could see why he'd been mistaken. She was short, maybe just a whisper over five feet, and slender—too slender. Her dark red hair fell in ripples to her waist, and her small, pointed face was pale as though she rarely saw the sun. She was dressed in grey sweatpants and a white vest top. Her small breasts pressed against the cotton, and he felt an unexpected stab of lust.

She'd controlled her initial fear and now was returning his inspection with obvious curiosity.

"So, can you read him?" Latham asked.

"I'm trying," she snapped. "Keep your pants on."

She took a wary step closer. Jack breathed in and caught a wild feral scent, like the forest at full moon.

Wolf?

And what did they mean, "read" him?

Then he felt it, faint tendrils of power, probing at his mind, seeking a way in. He slammed down his defensive walls and saw her eyes widen.

"Ow," she said.

"Well?" Latham prompted.

"No, I can't."

"You mean he's shielded? Like us?"

She studied Jack for a moment, her head cocked to one side. He felt the tentative probing again, but his mind was safely locked away behind his walls. At least he knew now why the guards were shielded. She was a telepath, and the most powerful one he had ever come across. And a wolf? How had she ended up at the Facility? The pack usually looked after their own.

"No," she replied. "Not like you. Different. You feel unnatural, an aberration." There was a distinct sneer in her voice, and he got the impression she wanted them to hear it. She was baiting them—probably unwise if she was a prisoner. "He feels natural. Right. But there's a big wall I can't get through."

"Why am I not surprised?" Latham said. "Yet again you manage to disappoint." He glanced from her to Jack and back to her. "Well, perhaps we can find one thing you're useful for." He turned to leave the room, followed by the guard, but paused at the doorway and spoke directly to Jack. "She's yours. Just don't finish her off. She may yet prove of some use."

"Bastard," she muttered as the door closed behind them. Then she turned slowly to stare at him. Her lower lip caught between her teeth, he suspected to keep it from quivering. Otherwise, there were no outward signs of fear, and he was impressed. Because she was afraid; he could scent her fear in the air.

"How old are you?" he asked. Just in case.

Her brows drew together, but she shrugged and answered. "Twenty-one."

Good.

He didn't need to feed, but that didn't mean he wouldn't enjoy it. She looked and smelled...intriguing. Vampires loved werewolf blood; it was the sweetest. His gums ached at the thought, and his cock twitched in his pants. Maybe the night was improving.

"You know what I am?" he asked.

"Johnson took great pleasure in telling me he was feeding me to the resident vampire. I'm guessing that must be you."

She was very calm, too calm. Was she in some sort of shock? "Do you mind?" he asked.

An expression of disgust flashed across her features. "Since when does it matter what I mind? Never—that's when!"

Shoving her hands in her back pockets, she took a step closer. Jack sat very still, not wanting to scare her further as she came to a halt about a foot away. She didn't have to look down very far to meet his gaze.

"So will it hurt? You know the whole"—she bared her teeth in a grimace—"biting thing?"

Shock ran through him at her words. She was so direct and matter of fact. What had made her like that so young? "How long have you been here?" he asked.

"Eight years." She pursed her lips. "Are you avoiding the question?"

"No."

"No? You mean 'no' you're not avoiding the question, or 'no' it won't hurt?"

"Both."

"Well, that's a relief." She took a deep breath, closed her eyes, and waited.

Jack could see the pulse beating rapidly under the fragile skin of her throat, the tracery of blue veins so close to the surface. His hunger rose. He reined it in, not wanting to frighten her, and savoring the anticipation. He'd never come across anyone like her, and he'd been around a long time and met a whole load of people.

Finally, her lids flicked open, and she glared at him. "Well?"

A small smile tugged at his lips. "Are you in a hurry? Perhaps you have other plans for the evening?"

"Funny man, aren't you." She scowled. "I could say the anticipation is killing me, but that wouldn't be quite correct. Just get it over with, will you?"

Jack chuckled, and her scowl deepened.

"Are you frightened?" he asked.

She stared him in the eye. "Yeah, I'm frightened. But so what? I'm used to it—I've had a lot of practice."

Suddenly he felt guilty for teasing her. He rose to his feet and she took a step back.

"Wow, you're...big."

He stepped around her, rested his hands on her shoulders and felt her tremble beneath his touch. From here, he could look down and see the thrust of her breasts beneath the thin cotton. His balls ached, and he realized with some surprise that he wanted her, and not just because she was here and convenient. He rubbed her shoulders gently, trying to ease her tension, but she stiffened.

"Relax," he murmured. "I can make you forget your fears."

She snorted. "Want to bet on that?"

"I like a challenge."

Looping his fingers in her hair, he lifted the heavy strands to expose her slender throat. He lowered his head into the curve of her neck and breathed in, loving the feral scent of her. This time he didn't fight the hunger building inside him.

He kissed her throat, her pulse point, then the tender spot where her neck met her shoulder. A small moan escaped her lips, and it wasn't a moan of fear. He could have her; he knew it in that moment. With a little care, she would fall into his arms. He grew hard at the thought.

"Did you know vampires find werewolf blood irresistible?" he whispered in her ear.

Her muscles locked, and then she pulled free of his grasp and whirled around to face him. "I am *not* a werewolf." She enunciated each word clearly.

He studied her closely. He wasn't wrong. "Yes, you are."

"No, I'm not."

He frowned, and then breathed in again, filling his nostrils with the musky scent of wolf. He raised an eyebrow.

She shrugged. "They say I'm a werewolf, but I've never changed. I think they made a mistake."

She sounded so hopeful that he hated to disillusion her. But there was no mistake. She was just uninitiated. Shit. There went half his fun. "You're a wolf," he said. "You've just never shifted." But perhaps she wanted to change. Maybe he could help her there. "Do you want to?"

"Are you crazy? My inability to turn doggy for them is the one thing that keeps me going in here." She cast him a narrow-eyed look. "You say I'm a wolf like you know what you're talking about. Do you know why I don't change?"

"Does it matter? If you don't want to, it's best you don't know."

She opened her mouth as if to argue, then clamped her lips closed and nodded. She glanced away, then back again. "Are you sure? That I'm a wolf, I mean?"

He nodded. "You must have been attacked."

"Eight years ago. Afterward, I woke up here." She wrapped her arms around her middle. "They've been trying to make me shift ever since."

Jesus, she'd only been thirteen. He wondered if Sebastian was aware there was a werewolf going around attacking children on his turf. "Trying how?" he asked.

"Different things. But nothing works." She glanced away. "They're not very pleased with me."

Obviously, they didn't know what was needed. Thank God. Jack made a vow then that he wouldn't reveal it, even to her. "So you're also a telepath?"

"I suppose."

Clearly, something else she wasn't happy to talk about. "What's your name?"

"Tasha."

"I'm Jack. Come here, Tasha."

She glanced from him to the camera high on the wall.

"It's broken," he said. Something else he'd convinced them was down to his vampiric powers—he didn't like to be watched.

Her gaze flicked back to him, and he allowed his hunger to show. Her eyes widened, but she took the final step toward him. He slid his hands down her arms, then scooped her up and crossed to the small cot. Sinking down with her in his lap, he silently cursed his erection, which refused to subside despite the fact that sex was now off the menu.

For a few seconds, she was rigid in his arms, every muscle tense.

Jack stroked her hair and she sighed, the stiffness seeping from her. Then as if giving in, she settled against him without comment, like a cat happy to be there, almost snuggling. He reckoned she hadn't been held much in her short life, and a fierce anger rose in him at the people who had kept here, shown her no kindness.

Her lashes flicked open, and she stared up at him with those strange golden eyes. "Are you sure it won't hurt? You weren't lying? You know—lulling me into a false sense of security?"

"It won't hurt. You might even enjoy it."

She swallowed and took a deep breath. "Okay. Go ahead then." And she raised her chin, baring the long line of her throat.

He shifted her slightly so he could reach, then lapped at the pulse with his tongue. A shiver ran through her. Then he bit down. She went instantly still but didn't fight, and he relaxed and savored the sensation as the warm, sweet blood filled his mouth, and he tasted the magic in her.

Her body went soft and pliant in his arms. He glanced down. Her fists were clenched at her side, but her nipples were hard little points clearly visible, and her hips lifted slightly as if straining toward him.

"Holy crap," she murmured. "You weren't lying."

Chapter Two

"**G**et your paws off me, pervert."

Johnson let go of her as though she were something nasty and wiped his hands down the sides of his pants.

"You know, Johnson, if I was the sensitive sort, I'd think you didn't like me."

Johnson ignored the comment. All the guards hated her but especially Johnson. When Tasha had first arrived—before the shielding technology had been developed—she'd been able to read all their minds. And Johnson's was a cesspit. But obviously, he didn't want the rest of the world to know that, so he'd been just a little bit peeved when she'd shared a few of his more bizarre personal fantasies with the rest of the guards.

He was sick, but at least after that, *she* hadn't been part of his fantasies. Not his sexual ones anyway. Though there had been a few things he'd thought about doing to her.

She shuddered. She was glad she could no longer read their minds.

Johnson turned to go but paused at the door. "Did it hurt?" His voice took on a gloating quality.

For a moment, she didn't know what he was referring to. Then she realized he meant the vampire. Her hand went to her throat where she could still feel the wound, though it was closing unnaturally fast.

God, but it had felt good.

Who would have believed it? Weird or what? She reckoned she must be one sad, repressed woman. And was it any wonder? She'd hardly led a normal life.

Johnson was still loitering, waiting for his answer. Probably looking for some details to add to his lurid torture fantasies.

Best not let him see she'd actually enjoyed being bitten by the vampire or he'd make sure she never went near Jack again. "What do you think?" she snarled. "Of course it hurt."

Well, at least that made Johnson happy.

"Maybe one day soon, they'll finally recognize what a waste of space you are, and they'll let that monster suck you dry."

Charming. She supposed it wasn't bad for a parting comment, and she didn't bother trying to come up with a clever answer. She just wanted him gone.

Once he'd left, slamming the cell door behind him, Tasha collapsed on her narrow bed. She stared up at what had been her home for the last eight years.

Ten feet by ten feet.

Bare white walls.

The room was empty but for the cot and a single shelf with her meager pile of books. She only had those because a few years back she'd faked a couple of suicide attempts. They'd taken her to see a shrink and she'd persuaded the woman that she needed some mental stimulation, or she would go seriously insane.

In truth, she hadn't wanted to die then. She still didn't. Most of the time. Occasionally, despair and loneliness would threaten to swamp her. Or they'd think of some new and generally unpleasant way to try and make her shift. But usually she managed to stay optimistic.

One day she would get out of here and go home. She had to believe it.

And now, at least she had something to look forward to.

Jack.

With his long, lithe body, pale skin, and silky black hair, Jack was, without doubt, the most beautiful thing she'd ever seen. She hugged her knees to her chest at the memory of the pleasure.

He'd told her it wouldn't hurt, and she'd been so shocked she'd given in without a fight. No one had ever said something *wouldn't* hurt before. And besides, he was so beautiful, she wasn't sure she could have denied him anything. Like some besotted teenager.

But he'd been right. There had been no pain, just a rhythmic tugging, that had pulled at unknown places deep within her body. His mouth at her throat had woken all sorts of sensations; she could still feel the pulse throbbing between her thighs.

But more than that; it had felt so good just to be held.

Yup. It was official. She was one sad case.

The cell door was in front of them. If she was going to make a move, it had to be now. Tasha cast a quick sideways glance at Johnson. He was a foot taller than her and more than twice her weight.

Still, she took a deep breath, twisted out of his grasp, and launched herself at his throat. Moments later, she hung limp from one huge, meaty hand.

"Goddamn freak," Johnson snarled.

Tasha could see the loathing in his eyes as he raised his fist and punched her in the face. Lightning exploded in her brain, and her mouth flooded with the warm, coppery taste of blood. Wincing at the sharp stab of pain, she swallowed and licked her lip. Time to change tactics.

"Please," she begged. "Don't put me in there. Not with him. Not again."

He smirked as he unlocked the cell door. Tasha started to struggle, was still struggling as he thrust her into the dimly lit cell. She fell to her knees just inside the door.

"Dinner is served," Johnson announced. His sadistic laughter echoed in her ears as the lock clicked shut behind her.

She closed her eyes and breathed in the dark power saturating the room. After a moment, she opened them and peered into the darkness. A pair of emerald eyes glowed in the shadows.

"Is he gone?" she murmured.

"Yes," a soft voice answered, and the hairs rose on the back of her neck. She'd known Jack for over a month now, and he still had the same overwhelming effect on her.

She scrambled to her feet, rubbing her arm where Johnson's thick fingers had bitten into the flesh. Then she grinned. "I was good, wasn't I?"

"Maybe just a little over the top."

"Come on, Jack," she said as his tall figure materialized out of the shadows. "I have to be convincing. You know Johnson would never bring me here if he actually thought I wanted to come. He hates me."

Jack stared down at her, then reached out and stroked the blood from her lip with the pad of his thumb. Tasha's whole body quivered at the touch, and she stared mesmerized as he raised it to his mouth and slowly licked it clean.

"Would you like me to kill him for you?" he asked gently.

"Yeah, I would. And, preferably, very, very, slowly." Then she sighed. "The problem is, Jack, you're as much a prisoner here as I am, so excuse me if I don't hold my breath."

He shrugged. "Then maybe, for the moment, you should try not to wind him up quite so much."

"You're right," Tasha agreed, "I know you're right. Unfortunately, winding up Johnson is just about the only fun I get to have in this place. Still, I should have been a bit more careful today."

"What's different about today?"

"There's a full moon tomorrow night." Tasha shivered. "They always try extra hard when there's a full moon."

He studied her for a moment. "Have you thought that things might be easier for you if you turned?"

"No, I haven't. And you're forgetting one important thing—I can't turn. I don't do this to annoy Johnson—that's just a happy side effect. The fact is I don't know how to turn. Most of the time, I'm not even convinced I am a werewolf."

He shook his head. "You are," he said. "I can taste it in your blood. Besides, even before the attack you were far from normal."

"Yeah, well, a girl can dream." She peered at him through her lashes. "You *do* know why I can't turn, don't you? I know you do."

"Why would you think that?"

"Come on, Jack, you know everything. Why won't you tell me?"

He was silent for a moment, and Tasha couldn't resist reaching out with her mind. She came up against the usual solid wall of his defenses and scowled.

Jack smiled, and she knew he'd sensed her attempt. Then he shrugged. "There is a…" he paused as if unsure of the right word to use, "a ritual which must be performed before you can come into your powers. But, Tasha, you know they've been using mind drugs on you, if you don't want to turn, you're better off not knowing.

Now come here." He held out one hand to her. "I must feed before your friend Johnson comes back for you."

She went to him eagerly, sliding her fingers against the coolness of his palm and lifting her chin to tease him with the smooth flesh of her throat.

He laughed softly with a flash of fangs then pulled her to him, turned her, and backed her toward the small cot in one fluid move. As his fangs pierced her vein, she gave herself up to the sweet sensation of his mouth at her throat, the throbbing at her breasts, between her thighs, the heat pooling at the base of her belly.

Finally, he drew back, licking the last drops of blood from her throat, stroking his tongue across the wound to quicken the healing. He lay back with a sigh, pulling her close, holding her against his hard body. Tasha lay beside him, restless.

"Stop wriggling," he said.

"Why?"

"Because it's distracting, and I don't need it."

She wriggled some more, rubbing her small breasts across his chest, shivering at the delicious friction on her sensitive nipples. Jack lay still, but she knew he wasn't immune to her advances because she could feel his huge erection pressed against her stomach. She'd been thinking about this for weeks now. Some part of her suspected that she would never leave this place alive, and she wanted to experience as much as she could of life while she had the chance. So far, Jack wasn't assisting her plan.

"Jack, why won't you make love to me?"

He stared down at her, a frown on his face. "You're too young."

"I'm twenty-one and all grown up."

"Too immature, then."

"Well, duh! Even you'd be immature if you'd been stuck in this dump for the last eight years."

She looked at him, head tilted to one side. "You know, Jack, you could think of this as an opportunity to help me grow."

He continued to stare at her in that annoying, inscrutable manner.

"It's because I'm scrawny, isn't it?" she said, glancing down at her body. "You can tell me. I can take criticism. It's because I have small breasts and no hips, isn't it?"

His eyes roamed over her body. "You just need to eat a little more," he said. "You're actually quite beautiful."

"Yeah, of course I am. I guess that's why you can't keep your hands off me. Look," she said. "I promise I'll still respect you in the morning."

He laughed, and she scowled. Why wouldn't he just give in and do it? It wasn't as if it was going to hurt him. She was twenty-one, well over the age of consent. She was lying on a bed with the most gorgeous man she could ever imagine, and he refused to cooperate. She propped herself up on her elbows and stared him right in the face.

"You know, Jack," she said, injecting as much pathos into her voice as possible. "It's a full moon tomorrow night. I may not survive. I'll die a virgin, never knowing what being with a man feels like."

He stared back, his eyes half-closed and there was something she couldn't define in his expression.

"I won't take your virginity," he said.

She opened her mouth to argue, and then closed it again. He was telling her what he wouldn't do, but that didn't mean he wouldn't do anything. His eyes were hot on her, and her stomach muscles tightened with a shiver of anticipation.

"Take off your clothes," he ordered.

"What?"

"You heard me. You said you wanted this, so take them off."

Tasha scrambled to her feet. His face had gone blank, but beneath his half-closed lids, his green eyes gleamed. A flicker of nervousness ran through her. She yanked her T-shirt over her head, before he could change his mind, then kicked off her sweatpants to stand before him naked. She couldn't look at him but could feel his gaze running, like fire, over her body.

"Come here." He took her hand and tugged her to the bed, pulling her down alongside him. Tasha let him do whatever he wanted, her body trembling as he took her wrists in his large hands, stretched them upward, and wrapped her fingers around the bars at the head of the bed. "Hold on," he said.

The position thrust her small breasts upwards, and he trailed one long finger over them. A small smile played across his lips as her nipples sprang to instant hardness, straining up toward him. He teased her with his fingers, stroking light patterns over the underside of her breasts. The strangest sensations ran through her, sinking deep into her belly, and the flesh between her legs felt hot and swollen. She needed him to touch her there. Would he?

"Please, Jack," she whispered.

He heard her, his fingers moving to her stiff little nipples. He caught one between finger and thumb, twisting gently, tugging and pulling. She couldn't hold back a whimper of pleasure. It was like nothing she had ever experienced. She peered up through the haze of pleasure to find him watching her, a look of intense concentration on his face. He leaned over her, taking the other nipple between his lips. Electric shocks ran from her breasts to her groin, and her hips rose from the bed.

"Let go and I stop," he murmured against her breasts, and she tightened her grip on the bars.

He spread wet kisses over her skin as his fingers continued to play with her nipples, his teeth nipping her flesh, his fangs grazing the soft swell of her breasts. Then his head moved lower. He licked and kissed his way down over her flat belly, leaving a trail of fire. His tongue dipped into her navel then moved even lower. She needed something, and she pressed her thighs together, her hips coming off the bed at the sensations running through her.

"Open your legs, Tasha."

She let them fall apart and groaned when he moved so his head hovered above the parting of her thighs. She couldn't believe this was happening. She would die if he stopped. She might die if he continued. She didn't care. His breath ruffled the curls of her pubic hair, and she melted, moisture oozing from her. He was taking too long. "Jack!"

Her eyes fluttered closed at the first long, slow lick of his tongue and behind her closed lids, explosions of color burst in her mind. His tongue probed between the folds of her sex, tasting her, slipping inside her, and then gliding wetly up toward her clit. He stopped short, and she bucked against him. He repeated the movement, and she had to bite back a scream of frustration. His hands moved down, slid beneath her to cup her bottom, his thumbs sliding between her legs to part the lips of her sex, so she lay open before him. He paused.

"Please, Jack." She moaned the words over and over, her hands still gripping onto the bars. At last, he touched her, teasing her tight little bud with the tip of his tongue. He stroked lightly across her, and she whimpered. Flames flashed through her, concentrating fire on that one small spot between her legs. He stroked harder, and she went mindless, her head rolling from side to side, her hips bucking against his firm hold. Then he sucked her clit into his mouth, bit down. Without warning, her climax exploded through her. He continued to suckle, and waves of pleasure crashed over her, dragging her under until she blacked out.

When she came to, Jack was lying beside her. She could feel his rhythmic movements. Letting go of the bars, she rolled onto her side. He was on his back, his pants open, his fist wrapped round his rock-hard erection. It was beautiful, arching thick and powerful from a nest of midnight dark curls. Tasha couldn't look away as he thrust his rigid shaft into his own palm. His movements were fierce, and she reached out a trembling hand.

"Don't touch me," he growled.

She lowered her hand and watched, fascinated as he pleasured himself. He was huge, his large hand hardly covering his shaft. The skin was silky pale, the head, purple, swollen, already oozing. The heat rose again in her belly. She licked her lips and heard him groan. Tearing her gaze away, she peered into his face; his eyes were jewel green slits, intent upon her as he thrust himself into his palm. Her body ached for his touch. Without conscious thought, her hand drifted across her breasts, still damp from his kisses.

"More," he said.

Instinct told her what he wanted. Emboldened, she played with a nipple, tugging it between her finger and thumb as he had done, and flames of fire licked through her. Her other hand drifted down, over her stomach, through her pubic hair. She was soft, wet. Opening her legs, she stroked a finger lightly over her swollen clit. It was still sensitive from her orgasm. She gasped, and moved her fingers lower to slide inside herself. Her flesh was hot, slippery with desire, and she moaned as she imagined Jack's huge cock thrusting inside her. She arched her hips, opening her legs wider, pushing another finger into her sopping slit. Jack swore, his movements becoming jerky, until his back arched and his seed shot from him. He collapsed back onto the bed.

A moment later, he rolled onto his side, and his hand brushed hers, one long finger sliding inside her. It felt far better than her own and she gasped as he thrust a second finger into her, while he stroked her to orgasm with the pad of his thumb.

She shuddered against him a second time and heard him chuckle.

He held her as her body trembled, then rolled onto his back and pulled her to him. Tasha relaxed. He was almost warm now from the blood he had taken, and she pressed closer, breathing in the male, musky scent of sex for the first time.

For a while, she was content, and it occurred to her, with a twinge of shock, that lying close to Jack like this was the only time she'd felt safe in long, long years. She wasn't sure what she was to Jack, maybe nothing more than food, but in the five weeks she'd known him, he had become everything to her—friend, confidant, ally. She wished she could somehow crawl inside his body and be safe forever.

But she knew it was a lie. There was no safety for her here.

Johnson would come for her soon, and tomorrow night they would hurt her. She could do nothing to stop them, and the fear shifted deep within her, clawing at her like a living thing.

She'd lied when she'd told Jack she was all grown up. Inside her remained the memory of the child she'd been eight years ago. The child who had woken in this awful place, crying for her mother, pleading with them to let her go, not to hurt her anymore. She'd soon learned the futility of that, but the need was still there, buried deep.

Or maybe not so deep.

Her face was wet, and she realized she was crying silently into Jack's shirt. She bit down hard on her lip and blinked back the tears. Easing her hands between their bodies, she pushed herself up.

Jack's hold on her tightened. His hand reached up to stroke her face, his fingers hesitating as they encountered the dampness of her skin.

"Tasha, what's wrong?" he asked gently.

"Nothing," she muttered. "Johnson will be coming soon. I need to get ready."

She sat up, brushing his hands away. Jack appeared almost shocked, but she ignored him and scrambled off the bed. She pulled on her clothes, and sank to the floor by the cell door, hugging her knees to her chest.

Jack stared at the small figure huddled against the wall, her face hidden by a dark curtain of hair. She lifted her head and looked at him, tears welling up in her eyes as fast as she could blink them away. Watching her was like watching his world collapsing. She was always so strong, so brave, laughing off what they did to her in this evil place.

But what had her life really been like? He'd been here for just over seven weeks, and already he longed for freedom. A miasma of evil hung about the Facility.

What could it have been like being brought here as child? He longed to free her, take her away, but there was more at stake. He had a job to do, and he couldn't leave until he'd done it.

Despite the fact he'd just come, his balls ached, and his cock was rock hard again. He wished he could make love to her, but he knew it wasn't an option if she didn't want to shift. It was her choice. He wouldn't take that from her. Instead, he'd given her what pleasure he could; he could still taste her on his lips. But now she was crying, and he didn't know what to do.

"I've never seen you cry before," he murmured.

She glanced at him and scowled. "I thought I'd make it more realistic for Johnson. I'd hate for him to think I'd been enjoying myself in here.'

Jack rose from the cot and crossed the room to where she sat. He crouched in front of her, and rubbed one long, lean finger down her damp cheek. Then he lifted her chin. "What's wrong, Tasha?" he asked again.

She stared at him, her golden eyes huge in her small face. "What's wrong?" she snarled, and Jack almost smiled at the disbelief in her voice. "What's right would be easier to answer—absolutely nothing!" She shook her head and stared at him through narrowed eyes. "Maybe," she said slowly, "it's that my only friend in the whole wide world is a vampire. And what am I to him? Food! Nothing but bloody dinner."

A shock ran through him at her words. "You're more than food."

"Oh, yeah? Just what am I to you, Jack?"

The question stopped him short. What was she to him? He admitted to a deep craving for her sweet blood. But it was far more than that. From the first moment they'd met, when she'd tried to probe his mind, he'd known she was special. But what did "special" mean? With a sense of surprise, he realized that in all his hundreds of years he'd never wanted a woman the way he wanted Tasha. But he also wanted to protect her, take her out of this place. His brain floundered. A vampire and a werewolf? He'd never heard of such a mating before. The two were natural enemies. Vampires loved were-blood. It was the sweetest and they took it by force when they could. But he'd never needed force with his little red wolf. She gave of herself freely. He stared down at her hunched figure, sensing her tension as she waited for his answer. He searched for a part of himself he could give to her.

"We're friends," he said.

She stared into his face, and he could see a softening in hers. She almost smiled, but then her eyes narrowed in suspicion. "Best friends?" she asked.

Jack smiled. "Of course."

He glanced up, listening.

"What is it?" she asked.

"Your guard's coming."

He stood up and slid into the shadows at the back of the cell. Her eyes never left him until the door opened, and she was taken away.

Chapter Three

Jack!

Jack sat up abruptly, a shrill scream echoing in his mind.

He jumped to his feet. Instinct sending him to the door, but he could see nothing out of the small window. He cursed loudly.

What the hell were they doing to her? She'd said they tried to make her shift. What had she meant by that?

The scream came again, and he banged on the door, though he knew the action was futile. No one would hear him. Closing his eyes, he concentrated hard. His men had orders to stay close by, just in case things went bad. They weren't telepathic like Tasha, but they would sense him.

Come.

He hadn't found out all he'd wanted to in his time here, but they would just have to take the computer hard drives and hope they could pull the information from them.

He didn't care. He had to get her out of here.

If she was still alive.

The screams had died away. The silence was much worse.

Tasha pulled her knees tighter to her chest, whimpering at the pain that ripped through her naked body. The skin of her breasts and belly was on fire where they'd burned her, her wrists and ankles raw from fighting against the restraints. She'd bitten through her lower lip and her mouth was tainted with the sharp metallic taste of her own blood. She swallowed and tried to hold back the tears threatening to overwhelm her. Crying. Twice in two days. She was in trouble.

They always tried extra hard during the full moon. Trying to make her lose control, force her to change. It never did any good, and they were getting desperate, and vicious in their desperation. Whatever ritual Jack had spoken of, her jailors knew nothing of it. And Jack had been right not to tell her. Tonight, she would have done anything to make them stop, told them anything.

For the first time, she wished for an end to all the pain. It would have been better if she had died in the attack and never come to this place. For years, only the thought of one day seeing her family again had kept her going. Now, the certainty gripped her—she would never get out of this place alive, never go home.

She closed her eyes and thought of Jack, but she couldn't see his face anymore. She'd called out to him at some point during the long night, begged him to help her. He'd been there in her mind, and she knew he'd heard her. But how could Jack help? He was as much a prisoner as she was.

Soft footsteps came to a halt outside her cell, and Tasha couldn't hold back the whimper that trickled from her swollen lips. They couldn't be coming back; it was too soon. She couldn't take any more. Not yet. The beam of a flashlight shone through the peephole in the door.

"It's not Jack. It's a girl," a man's voice said, a stranger's voice.

"Leave her," a second man answered.

The light disappeared, and the footsteps carried on down the corridor. Overwhelmed by a wave of relief, Tasha slumped back onto the hard table. She wondered vaguely who they were, but she was finding it difficult to focus her thoughts.

Passing in and out of consciousness, Tasha was in a half-dream state when the door opened. A tall figure stood, framed in the dim light of the corridor.

Jack.

Had he heard her and come? Or was he just part of her dream?

"Jack," she whispered as he crossed the room toward her.

He stood over her, staring down, his eyes fierce.

"Who did this?" he snarled.

Tasha resisted the urge to curl her naked body into a ball. "It looks worse than it is," she said, struggling to sit up.

He shook his head. "I didn't know." He reached out to touch the livid burn marks on her body. "You always made light of what they did. You should have told me."

"Why? What could you have done?"

He opened his mouth to speak, but, at that moment, a man entered the cell behind him, and he turned away from her. "Have we got everything?" Jack asked. "The computer hard drives?"

"Yes, and the place is wired and ready to blow."

"Then let's get out of here."

Despair flooded her mind. He was leaving her. She sank back onto the cold metal of the table. Her eyes closed, only to blink open a moment later as Jack's strong arms slid beneath her, picked her up and cradled her against his chest. She stared up at him and their eyes locked, intense emotion passing between them. Then a third figure appeared in the doorway, breaking the link. He was dragging someone with him.

"Jack, we've got one of the guards and he's alive. Should we take him for questioning?"

It was Johnson, his piggy eyes blank with terror. Tasha hissed, and Jack swung back around to face her, his expression fierce. "He did this?"

Tasha nodded.

"Shall I kill him for you?"

Tasha stared at the guard. Did she hate him enough to see him die?

Oh, yeah.

She nodded.

Jack smiled. "My only regret is we can't take longer to do it. Seth." He waved a hand at the man holding Johnson. Seth grinned with a flash of fangs, and Tasha realized for the first time that Jack's rescuers were vampires.

Seth pulled Johnson to him and grasped his hair, jerking back his head to expose the line of his neck. He lunged, ripping his throat out in one swift move. Johnson squealed, flailed with his hands, and went still.

Seth tossed him away and spat. "Tastes like shit."

Jack stared down at the body, a small frown on his face. "Tasha," he said, "the implant that stops you from reading the guards, do you know where it is?"

"Behind his left ear. I saw the scars when they had the operations."

Seth drew a long, wicked-looking blade from sheath at his thigh and crouched over the body. He probed for a moment.

"Found it." He held up a small silver plate.

"Keep it safe," Jack said. "Now, let's get out of here."

He strode out, the other man falling in behind him.

Tasha wriggled in his arms. "I can walk."

"No you can't. Not fast enough anyway. Besides I want to carry you."

They emerged into the night. Jack paused and took a deep breath; Tasha did the same. The air was crisp, cold, and clean. As they stood in the darkness, the full moon appeared from behind the clouds, and deep within her something stirred to life. It tugged at her consciousness, filling her with a longing to run free through the night, under the moon. She twisted in Jack's hold. "Put me down."

He stared down into her face. "You feel the pull of the full moon?"

"I don't know." She wriggled again. "Please."

His grip tightened for a moment, and then he lowered her to her feet. She wobbled, stiffened her spine, and sniffed the air. "Am I really out of there?"

"Yes."

She wrapped her arms around herself to ward off the chill, and then glanced up. There were more people out here, surrounding her, staring at her. Vampires, from the way the hunger gleamed in their eyes. For the first time, Tasha became aware she was naked. She peered up at Jack.

"I'm not wearing anything," she whispered.

He laughed softly.

"It's not funny."

"No, it's definitely not funny," he agreed, his expression hot and hungry. But he unbuttoned his shirt, shrugged out of it, and offered it to her.

Tasha stared, her mouth falling open. She couldn't help it. He was so beautiful—long and lean, with the smooth swell of muscles under silken skin. All gilded by moonlight.

"Tasha," he murmured, and she could still hear the faint laughter in his voice. "Take the shirt."

She nodded, took the shirt, and put it on. When she glanced up from fastening the buttons, everybody was still watching her.

"They're still staring," she said, tugging the shirt down over her legs.

"That's because you're beautiful," Jack replied. "Besides, they can smell your blood and vampires love were-blood." He smiled down at her. "But don't worry; they've all fed well tonight."

"Jack, your ride's here," Seth said from behind them.

A dark SUV pulled up close, and Jack opened the back door. "Get in," he said to Tasha.

"Why?" she asked. "Where are we going?"

Suddenly, she was terrified. She hated this place, but it was all she'd known for the past eight years. Now a vampire was telling her to get into a van and go God knows where.

She couldn't move.

Jack frowned down at her. "I'll tell you when we're on our way, but we need to leave. This whole place is going to blow any moment."

When she remained frozen in place, he reached over, picked her up, and placed her in the back of the van. He leaped up behind her, closing the doors as the van pulled away. Jack's arms came around her, and he turned her so she could see out of the back window.

"Watch," he said.

A moment later, the night exploded in huge fireball, and a wave of heat radiated through the glass. Tasha sat back, felt Jack's strong arms around her as she watched eight years of misery disappear in flames and darkness.

Chapter Four

"Where are we going?" Tasha asked.

"Where do you want to go?"

An overwhelming longing filled her. "I want to go home."

"Is that wise?"

"Probably not. They told me my mom died in a car crash five years ago, and my dad thinks I'm dead. I'd hate to give him a heart attack." She sighed. "I don't know where to go." Tasha went silent then, not daring to put her hopes into words.

"You can't come with me," Jack said.

"Why?"

He just shook his head and Tasha trembled, the chill of his rejection running through her. Jack pulled her to him, rubbed her arms until the shivers stopped, then wrapped his own around her.

She laid her head on his naked chest and forced herself to relax. "You feel cool," she said.

"I need to feed."

"You didn't feed back there?"

"No. These days, I prefer my food to be willing."

"Oh."

He turned her face up to the light and ran hand over her lips. "You're almost healed."

"I told you I heal fast."

"Yes," Jack said, "it's one of the side effects of being a were."

"What are the others?"

He didn't answer, just contemplated her question for a while. After a minute, he pulled a phone out of his pants pocket. He pressed a button and spoke into it. "Seth, take us to Sebastian's."

"Who's Sebastian?" Tasha asked.

"He's the head of the Lykae—the local werewolf pack."

Tasha shuddered. "You are aware that my last meeting with a werewolf didn't turn out too well." That had to be the understatement of the century; the attack still haunted her nightmares. "I don't want to go," she said in a small voice.

"He'll teach you what you need to know. They look after their own."

"I'm not sure I want to be his. Besides, what if he doesn't want me? And like I said before, I'm not even convinced I am a werewolf—maybe it didn't take or something."

"You are."

"How can you be so sure?"

"Sebastian will be able to explain everything you need to know. It's for the best until you find out what happened and why."

She had to try one last time. "Take me with you."

"No."

She fell silent. She wasn't going to beg. He must have sensed something though because he tightened his hold. "In a lot of ways, you're still a child," he said. "You've been shut away for so long. Give yourself a chance to know this new world before you make any decisions as to where you want to go. Now we'll be arriving soon. Give me your throat."

He shifted her on his lap, lifting her with ease and turning her so she faced him, her knees spread on either side of his lean hips. In this position, she could stare down into his face—see the fierce hunger in his eyes. His hands went to her hips, lowering her onto him. He leaned in close, and she raised her chin, baring the long line of her throat. The sharpness of his fangs grazed her skin and then he was feeding. Her mind floated away, sinking into the sensations. The tugging at her throat caused a deep rhythmic throbbing between her open thighs. She was acutely aware of her bare sex pressed to the rough texture of his pants, of the hardening length of his erection, and a sudden wetness flooded her core. She wriggled, parting the lips of her sex, rubbing her tiny swollen bud over him, whimpering at the delicious friction. Jack went still. His hands tightened on her hips and then he guided her, pressed her down onto the solid length of him, rotating her hips in small teasing circles. As her climax mounted, he pulled her down harder, grinding her to him, so her clit rubbed against his shaft and finally, she exploded.

When she raised her lashes, he'd stopped feeding.

He was watching her through heavy-lidded eyes. His cock was still rock hard, and she shifted just to hear him moan. Then his eyes narrowed further. "Why the hell not?" he said more to himself than her.

His hand slid between their bodies to fondle her bare slippery flesh still sensitive from her orgasm, and a shiver ran through her. With his other hand, he unbuttoned his pants, and pushed the zip down. Tasha stayed motionless. Was he finally going to make love to her fully? Why now, she wondered, when he had refused before?

His erection had sprung free, and Tasha couldn't resist a glance down. It was beautiful. Moist heat welled from her as she thought of all that male power, pushing into her, filling her. She swallowed as he raised her up, parting the lips of her sex with skilled fingers, opening her for his penetration.

A loud banging echoed through the van, and Jack went still. His head fell back, and she could see him fighting for control.

"Shit," he muttered.

The SUV was no longer moving.

Jack lifted her, placed her on the seat beside him, and adjusted his clothing. She didn't have much to adjust. A moment later, the door opened.

"We're here, boss," Seth said. "Actually, we've been here for five minutes. I thought you'd gone to sleep in there."

Jack swore softly. He stepped down, then reached into the van, picked her up and placed her on the ground. She stumbled, her legs weak and shaky.

They'd parked in the drive of a huge house. It was set in a thick, wooded area with a high, stone wall running around the entire perimeter. In the distance, a wolf howled. Tasha shivered and moved closer to Jack.

"I wish I had more clothes on."

"Sebastian will find you something."

"What if he doesn't want me around?"

"I told you they look after their own. Besides, you're beautiful. Believe me, he'll want you." He frowned as if he wasn't entirely happy with the thought then took her arm. "Come on. Let's get the introductions over. And Tasha..."

"Yes?"

"You must promise—no mind reading unless you're asked."

She nodded. "Anything else?"

"Yes. Sebastian may seem very laid-back, but he isn't. So when we meet him, try to keep that smart mouth shut."

She opened her mouth to say something smart, but he'd already moved off. She took a step after him and then winced as the gravel dug into her bare feet. Jack glanced around, came back and picked her up, carrying her toward the enormous front door. It swung open as they approached.

Jack took her across the wide hallway and through another door before putting her on her feet. She peered around. They were in a large, comfortable sitting room, with dark red walls, huge leather sofas, and a fire crackling in the grate.

The room was empty, but at that moment the front door slammed shut and a few seconds later a man entered the room bringing with him the fresh scent of the forest. He paused at the sight of Jack, his eyes wary. At least six foot tall, he was dressed in a pair of faded jeans that hung low on his lean hips. And nothing else. Sweat gleamed on the vast expanse of golden skin and rippling muscle. Wicked blue eyes flicked between the two of them and pale blond hair fell over his forehead, framing the face of a dissipated angel. Tasha's skin prickled as the levels of energy in the room mounted.

"Sebastian," Jack said. "Did we get you out of bed?"

Sebastian snorted. "Funny. Do you know what night this is, vampire? You call me in from the full moon. I thought you weren't supposed to break out until next week. What happened?"

"We had to move the plan ahead."

There was a plan? Tasha glanced at him as she realized he had truly saved her tonight. He'd heard her cry for help, and he'd done what he could.

"So how did it go?" Sebastian asked. "Did you get the information we needed?"

"Not entirely, but we have the hard drives. I'll get my people on it. The names we need are in there somewhere."

"Good."

Sebastian turned toward Tasha, and she found she couldn't look away. A slow smile curved his lips as he strode toward them, moving with the grace of a jungle cat. He halted less than a foot away. Tasha stood slightly behind Jack. Now he tugged her forward, so she hovered in front of the werewolf. This close she could smell him clearly; forest and a faint musky odor of wild animal. The same scent that haunted her nightmares.

His eyes ran over her, lingering over the length of leg shown beneath the hem of the black silk shirt. He whistled under his breath. Tasha was suddenly aware of her bare legs and feet. She was standing in a room with two of the most gorgeous men imaginable and she was very nearly naked. Not that they were wearing much more, a fact that did nothing to cool the heat flushing her skin. Curling her toes into the soft carpet, she forced herself to stand her ground and just hoped she didn't look as flustered as she felt.

"So," Sebastian said. "You've brought me a present. Nice, very nice."

"I've brought you one of your own," Jack replied. "This is Natasha. Natasha, this is Sebastian, the head of the Lykae."

"Hmm, a little red wolf. Where did you find her?"

"Tasha has been an unwilling guest of the Facility for the past eight years."

Sebastian stepped closer. She could see him breathe in, scenting the air. "She smells of sex." He raised one hand. Tasha flinched but forced herself to stand still as he ran a finger down the line of her throat, over the slight scar left from Jack's feeding. A frown twisted his lips. "And you fed the vampire."

She glanced uneasily at Jack. Was that a problem?

Jack shrugged. "I was a little hungry at the time."

They were silent for a moment. Would the wolf refuse to keep her? She almost hoped so. Jack would have to take her with him then. Even vampires must have rules about abandoning their best friends.

"Tasha was attacked by a werewolf eight years ago," Jack said. "When she woke, she was in the Facility. She's been there ever since."

"She must have been a child," Sebastian said.

"Thirteen."

"She was uninitiated?"

"She still is."

"Really?" Sebastian smiled; his eyes gleaming down at her.

"I brought her here for her protection," Jack said.

Tasha glanced at him; she was missing something here.

Sebastian turned his attention from her to Jack. "I do what I will with my own pack."

"You won't force her."

"Do you really think I'll need to use force?" Sebastian held out a hand to her. "Come, sweetheart."

Tasha peered over her shoulder at Jack. He caught her gaze and shrugged so she stayed where she was and ignored the outstretched hand. Sebastian pursed his lips, but the hand dropped to his side.

"There's something else you need to know," Jack said.

"What?"

"You need to find the wolf who attacked her and find out why. I'm sure Tasha can help."

Sebastian frowned. "She can?" He definitely sounded skeptical. Obviously, she hadn't made much of an impression. She hated being little.

"Didn't I mention? Tasha is also a telepath."

Sebastian looked at her, his eyes sharp, his lips drawn back in a snarl. "Are you reading me now?"

"No," Tasha stammered.

"Probably just as well," Jack said from beside her.

Sebastian was still frowning.

"I don't normally," she said. "At the Facility, they taught me how to control it, focus it, only use it when I need to." She paused, then bit her lip. "I don't like to know what people are thinking. Most of the time it's not particularly nice."

Sebastian nodded, but he didn't appear happy. It was like the Facility all over again. She was a freak; she would never escape that stigma.

Jack shifted beside her. "I have to go. It will soon be dawn."

She started to stretch her hand out toward him but let it to fall to her side. "Will I see you again?"

"Of course. I told you, I'll look into your family, find out what's happening." He turned to Sebastian. "I'll be in touch when we've analyzed those hard drives. Keep her safe. And Sebastian, they weren't particularly kind to her at the Facility. Give her time."

Then he was gone, and Tasha stood alone with the werewolf. Jack had been the only person kind to her in over eight years, and he'd left her, just like that. She blinked away the tears before turning back to Sebastian.

He'd taken a seat by the fire and was watching her, a thoughtful expression on his face. "It isn't done, you know."

"What isn't?" she asked.

"Feeding vampires. It's frowned upon in our society."

"Even if it's a matter of life and death?"

"If Jack told you that, then he was taking you for a ride."

Tasha frowned. "What do you mean?"

"Jack's old, very old, which means he's strong. He can go a long time between feedings. It's the reason he volunteered to go into the Facility. No, if he fed from you, it's because he wanted to." His eyes slid over her. "Not that I blame him."

"I didn't know."

"Besides," Sebastian continued. "Vampires are morose bastards, temperamental as hell. You'd be much better off with a wolf."

"I don't want anyone. I just want to go home."

"We'll see." He patted the seat next to him. "Come and sit by the fire while we decide what's to be done with you. Are you hungry?"

"I'm always hungry."

"Hmm, you look half-starved. So, you'll need food and clothes. But maybe first a drink?"

He rose and crossed the room to a small cabinet. He poured her a drink and brought it over. She glanced into his face as she took a sip and saw his almost rueful smile. Then her mind blurred and she fell into a deep sleep.

Chapter Five

The bastard had drugged her.

Tasha's head throbbed, or was it someone banging on the door? A bit of both, she decided. She forced her lids open. The room was in half-light, sunshine filtering through the heavy curtains.

A bedroom, with high ceilings and pale-yellow walls. It was nice, though her standards weren't very high. Most places seemed nice when you'd spent the last eight years in a ten foot by ten foot cell.

At least whoever it was had stopped banging. Instead, the handle turned, and the door opened.

A man stood in the doorway.

Tall, dark and angry. She didn't need to read his mind to know the anger bit. Rage poured off him in waves, though his handsome face was expressionless. He was examining her, his eyes blank, and she had no clue what he was thinking—except they obviously weren't happy thoughts. Was it her? She was used to meeting with distrust, but she'd hoped here would be different, that at least they'd give her the benefit of the doubt. Or maybe he was angry with everyone, not just her.

"You're awake," he said.

As he stepped into the room, Tasha peered under the sheet. She was still dressed in the black shirt—not much, but better than nothing.

"How are you feeling?" His voice was as blank as his expression. He could at least have said hello, introduced himself and made the effort to sound as if he cared.

"That bastard drugged me."

Her teeth ground together at the memory. She'd thought she was escaping from all that, but perhaps she'd just exchanged one prison for another. And how dare Jack leave her with the sort of person who would pretend to be nice, offer a drink, and then drug her.

"I know. He told me. So how do you feel?" He lifted the bag he carried and waved it in her direction. "I'm a doctor."

She wasn't particularly fond of doctors, but then again, he didn't look like any doctor she had ever met. And his bedside manner sucked big time. Which was a pity because the rest of him was stunning. Was it some sort of werewolf thing? You had to be gorgeous, or it didn't take. Maybe that's why she didn't change—she wasn't good-looking enough. Or maybe your appearance changed once you shifted, and you became stunning. She liked that idea much better. Perhaps she might even grow a little.

The doctor's black hair was overlong, clearly, he hadn't bothered to cut it in a while. His skin was olive as though he came from somewhere warmer than here, and his eyes the color of bitter chocolate. He wore black jeans and a grey T-shirt stretched taut over wide shoulders. Breathing in, she caught that same forest scent tinged with the musk she now recognized as wolf.

"You're a werewolf?" she asked.

He shrugged as if it didn't matter, but she could feel the tension radiating off him. "I'm a werewolf doctor. Now, how do you feel?"

She ignored the question, pulled herself up and leaned back against the headboard. "So where's the slimy scumbag who drugged me?"

A smile flickered at his mouth. "Not here. He came in earlier, but you were still out cold. He asked me to check you over, see if there's anything wrong with you that we can treat."

"You mean apart from being a werewolf and a freak. Any cure for those?"

"Nope. The werewolf part at least. Not sure about the freak." He placed the bag on the bottom of the bed and sank down beside her.

"Did he tell you about me?"

"That you're supposed to be telepathic? Yes, he told me." He shrugged again. "Nothing secret on my head—go ahead and try."

A glimmer of curiosity showed in his face—yeah, she was a medical phenomenon. She reached out, touched his mind, sensed the rage, the hatred of what he was, and then backed off quickly. "Ugh! No, thank you." She peered at him "Are you always this angry?"

Surprise flashed in his eyes. "Yes. Now let's examine you."

Tasha hated being examined. All the time at the Facility, she'd been prodded and poked like so much meat. Everything measured and recorded. But at least she was used to it, and she held herself still while he checked her heartbeat, took her blood pressure, drew blood samples.

Finally, he packed everything away and rose to his feet.

"So will I live?" she asked.

"You'll live. A little underweight from the looks of you, but otherwise you're fine. I'll get someone to bring you food."

"Can't I come and get some myself?"

"No."

He turned and left the room and the lock clicked into place behind him.

Yeah, she was still a prisoner, just a nicer prison.

"How's Tasha?" Jack glanced up as Sebastian came into his office.

It was three days since he'd left her with Sebastian. He'd wanted to give her time to settle in before he went back there, but already he felt the pull of her sweet blood and his fangs ached to feed.

He'd kept busy trying to extract the information from the hard drives they'd taken. He was finally getting somewhere. He'd managed to isolate the financial transactions; soon he reckoned he'd be able to tell her something about how she came to be an unwilling guest of the Facility. Though so far, he'd run into a wall on the thing they really wanted to know—who ran the Agency.

A few decades back, Jack had come to the reluctant conclusion that the secrecy of his kind could not last forever. With the advances in technology, he believed it inevitable that man would stumble across them at some point in the not-too-distant future. Also, he'd lived long enough to know that if you didn't adapt—you died. So he'd formed a group, aimed at preparing for that day. Since then, they'd made contacts with government organizations, and they were often called in to help when something happened that might have a paranormal connection.

It was during one of these jobs, a few years back, that they'd first come across the Agency. And they'd been researching them ever since.

The organization was far larger than they'd first suspected. Huge, it spanned the whole globe, infiltrating governments and multinational companies. The Facility, where Tasha had been a prisoner, was only one tiny part of the whole. But they were secretive; Jack would find a lead only to have it come to a dead end. And the Agency was ruthless, quickly eliminating any part of their organization that was exposed.

Jack had also been investigating Tasha's family. Her mother had died as they'd told her. She'd been killed outright in a car crash five years ago, but something felt wrong about the whole thing. Could her mother have been looking into Tasha's disappearance and maybe actually found something? Had the Agency had her killed to keep her quiet? And what about her father? He was still alive and well. Had he accepted Tasha's disappearance?

And how did Tasha's telepathy fit into all this?

Was it pure coincidence? Jack didn't believe in coincidences. Did that mean Tasha had been targeted by the Agency because she was telepathic?

His head hurt—there were too many unknowns and until he'd unraveled them, Tasha was going nowhere near her family.

Sebastian grinned. "She's okay, I believe."

"You believe?" What the hell did that mean? Didn't he know?

"I've been keeping out of the way. I don't think I'm her favorite person right now."

Jack turned his chair and rose slowly to his feet. If the werewolf had harmed her in any way...

"Hey, keep your fangs in," Sebastian said. "I haven't done anything to her... yet. I just gave her a little something to help her sleep after you left the first night."

"You drugged her?" Jack could hear the outrage in his voice.

"Yeah, I drugged her. She's a telepath, and I know next to nothing about her except she's been cozying up to a vampire, and you picked her up at the Facility. Hardly glowing recommendations. For all you know she could be a plant—working for the Agency. No way is she getting inside my head until I'm sure of where her loyalties lie."

"She's no plant."

"Maybe not, but let's be sure about that shall we?"

"They almost killed her. The night I took her out of there, she was nearly dead when I found her."

"Then she must have healed fast—there was no sign of any wounds when you brought her to me."

"She's powerful. I've never tasted so much magic in the blood. Not even you," he added. It wouldn't hurt to remind the werewolf that they had once fought, and that Jack had won and taken the alpha's blood. Since then, they'd vacillated between an uneasy truce and the nearest thing Jack had come to friendship since he'd been changed. Though he knew the werewolf would always put his pack first—it's what made him such a good alpha.

"Piss off," Sebastian replied.

Jack bit back a smile and turned to the computer.

Sebastian leaned over his shoulder to read the screen. "Are you getting anywhere?"

"Yes. I want you to look at these transactions. They're from around the time Tasha was taken. See if you recognize any of the names."

Pushing his chair out of the way, he allowed Sebastian to step closer and scrutinize the screen. Jack curbed his impatience but couldn't shake the uneasy feeling that he wasn't going to like what they found. Something was wrong. The information didn't add up; they were missing a vital piece.

He knew he was going to ask Tasha to stay with him. While he didn't know if it could work out between a vampire and a werewolf, for the first time in his life, he was willing to try at a relationship. But he wanted to give her a decent choice when he made the offer. She'd dreamed of going home through the long years of her imprisonment. And he would give her the chance. But only when he was sure she would be safe.

Sebastian straightened and pointed at the screen. "Got him. Michael Oswald."

"A pack member?" Jack asked.

"No—he's a loner. He works as a freelance assassin. He must be our man."

"Let's go find him, then."

Chapter Six

A finger glided over the bare flesh of her arm. Tasha shivered and turned slowly.

"Tasha," Sebastian said. "You look fantastic."

She glared at him. It had been four days since he'd drugged her, and she still wasn't about to forgive him. Not that he'd given her much opportunity. This was the first she'd seen of him since the night she'd arrived.

In fact, she'd hardly seen anyone. A woman had brought her meals at regular intervals, but she'd obviously been warned not to talk to her. Tasha felt like some sort of pariah, which didn't improve her grouchy mood.

On the second day, the same woman had brought her a pile of parcels. Presents from Jack, clothes, a kindle loaded with books, chocolates—no doubt to fatten up her skinny frame. She would have rather had Jack, but the gifts soothed her a little. It was nice to know he hadn't completely forgotten her.

At first, she'd been content to spend her time eating and sleeping, regaining her strength. Then reading and watching TV, catching up on the last eight years. However, it wasn't long before impatience was gnawing at her. She was supposed to be free, wasn't she? She wanted to get out there and start living. She'd had enough of being caged. So that morning, she'd threatened to smash everything in the room unless they let her out or took her to Sebastian.

It had taken all day, but finally, here she was, back in the sitting room where they had first met.

Now she watched him through narrowed eyes as he circled, coming to a halt in front of her, a slow smile curving his lips. Tasha stared back and saw the smile slide away. Suspicion flickered across his face. "Are you reading me?" he asked.

"No."

"Could you?"

"I don't know," she said. "I can't read Jack, unless he lets me."

"Jack's a vamp. Nobody can read vamps." He studied her for a moment. "Can you control how far you go in? Top level only?"

She nodded.

"Okay, try then."

Tasha looked at him in surprise. "You *want* me to read you?"

"I want you to try." He stared at her; the challenge clear in his voice. "What am I thinking, Tasha?"

She reached out with her mind's eye, sensed the flavor of him, the wolf so close to the surface. She focused on his thoughts and took a step back as intense heat flooded her body. The picture in her head was so graphic, so carnal.

He laughed, but he didn't sound amused. "I guess that answers my question."

He walked away a few paces, giving Tasha a moment to compose herself. When he turned back, his expression was grim. "The pack isn't happy about having a telepath among us."

Despair washed over her; she would never belong. People would always see her as different—a freak as Johnson had enjoyed calling her. "I won't use it. I told you—I don't like to."

He shrugged off her concerns. "Don't worry. I'll sort it out, but it will be better once you've committed to the pack. Once you've run with us, they'll trust you. But for now, we need to decide what to do with you."

"I want to go home," she said.

"That may not be so simple." Sebastian turned away from her. "Jack?"

Tasha swung around as Jack glided out of the shadows at the edge of the room. She didn't try to hide her delight, and Sebastian shook his head in disgust.

Jack was dressed all in black with a holster strapped at his shoulder and a knife strapped to his thigh. His black, silky hair was pulled back in a ponytail, emphasizing the pale beauty of his face, his sharp cheekbones, the long line of his jaw.

He looked dangerous and familiar, and she couldn't prevent herself from taking an involuntary step toward him. He didn't smile at her. He just looked her up and down, his eyes lingering on her throat, then lower, over the soft peaks of her breasts. With a shiver of excitement, her nipples hardened against the thin silk top she wore. Her heart rate increased, and the blood throbbed in her veins.

"Come." Jack smiled. "Sit down."

"I don't need to sit down." She glanced into his face. "Do I?"

"You might as well be comfortable."

She sank into the chair he indicated. "So, why can't I go home?"

Jack sat in the chair opposite, and Sebastian took the seat beside him. "Let me explain a little first," Jack said. "Do you know what the Facility was?"

Tasha frowned. "They told me it was a government organization, research into the paranormal."

Jack shook his head. "They weren't government."

"How do you know?"

"Because we were sent in by the government to find out what was going on there."

"You work for the government, both of you?"

"Let's just say we're sub-contractors." He sat back, searching her face. "Tasha, what do you know of your father's work?"

"Not a lot. I was only thirteen," she said. "I know he was a scientist. He worked for some sort of government organization, but he never spoke about it." She forced herself to concentrate, to think back to the time before she was attacked.

"I did pick up bits and pieces out of his mind, nothing that made any sense." She paused and glanced at Sebastian. "I couldn't control it at first," she explained. "The mind-reading. I'd go up to people and I'd be there, in their heads." She shuddered. "It was horrible. In the end, I told Dad. He said he knew someone who could help me."

"Did he tell you who?" Jack asked. "Or mention any names at all?"

Tasha shook her head. "No, but I suppose he might have worked in the same field himself. Anyway, he was going to organize a meeting, but I was attacked the very next day when I went to meet him." She shrugged. "That's it." She glanced from one to the other, trying to stop the fluttering in her stomach. "Why do you want to know all this? What's it got to do with my father?"

Jack looked at Sebastian, nodded, and then got up and paced the room.

"We found the wolf who attacked you," Sebastian said.

A scalding flood of fear washed over her. Bile rose to the back of her throat, and she swallowed.

"His name is Michael Oswald," Sebastian continued. "We want you to question him."

"Me? How? Why?" She didn't want to go anywhere near him, and she certainly didn't want to get inside his head.

"He's not talking. We need to know who paid him."

"Paid him? Why would you think that?"

Sebastian smiled wryly. "Contrary to popular opinion, we don't make it a habit to attack humans at random. On the other hand, it's not unheard of for weres to act as paid assassins. We don't object as long as it doesn't bring attention to our kind. So, can you do it?"

Suddenly, Tasha longed to be back in her nice yellow bedroom, with her head in a book, or watching TV. She didn't want to confront the creature who had caused all of this misery and confusion in her life—the creature from her nightmares.

"We need to find out why this happened to you," Jack said. "Until we do, there's no going back."

She nodded. "I'll do it," she said, fighting to subdue her fear. "At least I'll try."

"Good." Jack took out a phone and spoke quietly into it, then sat and waited. "So," he said, after a moment's silence. "What was Sebastian thinking?"

At his words, Tasha glanced up. "What?" she asked.

"Sebastian. What was he thinking when you read his mind?"

Tasha flicked a glance at Sebastian, who smiled. She couldn't look away, and her mind was flooded again with the image of that long, golden body poised naked over her own, the sinful expression in his hot blue eyes. She stared down at her hands as heat rose to her cheeks. "Er, nothing important," she mumbled.

Jack raised an eyebrow and opened his mouth to speak, but the door opened behind them. They all turned as two men came in, leading a third, shackled between them, a silver collar around his throat.

Tasha recognized the two guards as the vampires who'd been with Jack the night of their escape, but she didn't recognize the prisoner. He'd been in wolf form the night he attacked her, and she found she could look at him after all.

Compared to the others in the room, he was short, stocky, with cold blue eyes and shaggy, blond hair. He was shooting wary glances at Jack and Sebastian but hardly seemed to notice her.

The two guards dragged him to a chair, fastened his handcuffs to the arm, and stepped back. He looked up, defiance flashing in his eyes. "Why am I here?"

Jack rose to his feet and stalked toward him. He stood, staring down, and the man's insolent glare faltered. "What's a vampire doing here?" he asked.

Jack ignored the comment. "You remember a job you did eight years ago?" he said.

The man frowned. "I've done lots of jobs."

"This one should be quite memorable. You were employed to kill a thirteen-year-old girl."

"So?"

Jack's fist moved faster than Tasha's eyes could follow and blood oozed crimson from the man's nose. "Do you remember?"

"Yes." His reply was sullen yet still defiant.

"What happened at the hit?" Jack asked.

The man's eyes flashed around the room. For the first time, he appeared nervous. "I killed her," he said.

"Is that all?" Jack asked, and he nodded. Jack turned to her. "Tasha?"

She stood up and shuffled forward to stare down at the thing that had haunted her dreams for so long. He stared back, something stirring to life behind his eyes.

"Who's she?" he asked but Tasha could hear the recognition in his voice.

"Well, I'm certainly not a ghost." She thought for a moment. "Why did you attack me?"

When he didn't respond, she reached out with her mind and plucked the answer with ease. "He did it for the money," she told the others. "He was paid to kill me."

She turned back to him. "So why didn't I die? Why did you leave me alive?"

"What are you?" he asked. His glance shifted to Sebastian, and this time, real fear showed in his face. Tasha ignored his question and searched deeper.

"He was paid by somebody else," she said. "They knew about the telepathy, and they wanted me, but they also wanted a live werewolf. They found a way to get both. He attacked me and sold me to the Facility."

Sebastian hissed, and she glanced at him. "We have few rules," he said. "But the most sacred is we never give information to humans. We do not sell out our own kind. It's the only reason we've remained secret for so long."

"Does he know the name of his contact at the Facility?" Jack asked.

"Yes, it's Dr. Latham. You met him. He was in charge of my case."

"What about the man who paid him to kill you?"

"I don't know." She concentrated on Oswald and saw a picture inside his head—a man handing over money. She tried to deny what she was seeing, but it was impossible. "Why?" she whispered.

"Tasha?"

She glanced up to find Jack staring at her with understanding in his eyes.

"You knew," she said bleakly.

"I suspected."

"My father paid to have me attacked?"

"No, he paid to have you killed."

"But why? And how did you know?"

"We don't know why yet, but we found his name in certain records."

"That's why you made me question him, isn't it? It wasn't because he wouldn't answer. You just knew I wouldn't believe unless I saw it for myself."

Her world was falling apart around her. She stood alone and abandoned in the ruins, searching for some sort of explanation. Her father would never have harmed her. But the truth sank in, and she dropped into a chair, her legs refusing to hold her any longer.

She couldn't go home. Even if there was an explanation, she couldn't go home until she knew what it was.

"What do we do with him?" Jack said to Sebastian.

Oswald looked up, fear in his eyes.

"You know what you've done is punishable by death." Sebastian shook his head in disgust. "Take him away. Do what you like with him."

Seth grinned and dragged the man from the room.

A shiver fluttered down Tasha's spine. "What will they do to him?"

Jack looked at her thoughtfully, and then shrugged. "I like my blood given freely. Seth prefers to take his."

She shivered again, suddenly cold, and she wrapped her arms around herself. "So what's next?"

Jack came over and crouched down in front of her. "You could forget about all this. Forget about your family. Let others deal with it."

"I can't. You don't understand—my father is all I have."

Sebastian moved to stand besides Jack. "You have the pack now. They are your family. You're one of us."

She jumped up. "But I'm not! For years, everyone has told me I'm a werewolf, but I've never turned. Why? If I'm one of you, why don't I turn?"

Jack went over to the side table and poured himself a drink. He swallowed it in one gulp and poured himself another.

"Can't you just tell me?" she asked.

Jack glanced over at Sebastian, who shrugged.

"Sex," Sebastian said.

"What?"

"You're a virgin. When you have sex, you will turn."

She stared at the werewolf, unsure whether to believe him.

"Normally, it happens soon after the attack," Sebastian continued. "We don't, as a rule, change children, and once our blood is in your veins, your own blood flows hot."

"Mine didn't," she said. She could have added that at least it hadn't until she met Jack.

"Probably your age and incarceration affected you. That will change."

She had a sudden flashback to the image of Sebastian's lean, taut body poised above her own. Her muscles clenched. She closed her eyes for a brief moment before striding over to where Jack stood.

She took the glass from his hand and swallowed the drink down. "Right," she said. "So, am I correct in thinking if I never have sex, then I'll never turn. Never become a proper werewolf. I can live a normal life?"

"In theory," Sebastian replied. "But it won't work out like that. You'll give in."

"Oh, I think I can manage to hold back."

Sebastian shook his head. "You'll feel the pull of the full moon. Besides Tasha, it's a gift, not a curse."

"Yeah, I met your doctor friend—he really sees it as a gift."

"Connor is an exception and there are reasons. But only a small number of those attacked, survive. You were lucky."

"I'll try to remember that," she said, not even attempting to keep the sarcasm from her voice. Then she had a thought. "The sex, does it have to be with another werewolf?" She avoided looking at Jack as she asked this but saw Sebastian's gaze turn sharply to the vampire.

"No," he said. "Any sex will do. Now, I must go speak to the pack, explain why I gave one of our own to the vampires. They won't be happy."

He left the room and Tasha forced herself to turn and face Jack. "Is that why you wouldn't have sex with me in the Facility?"

He nodded. "I knew you had no wish to perform for your captors."

"Why didn't you tell me?"

"I told you why. Do you think you would have liked the consequences if your jailors had discovered that little piece of information?"

An image of Johnson's clammy hands flashed through her mind and Tasha shuddered in revulsion.

"Besides," Jack continued. "It wasn't my place. Pack law needs to be taught by the pack. We do not interfere with others' laws. That's why Oswald had to die. He sold pack secrets to outsiders."

"You're not an outsider."

"I'm not pack. Sebastian and I work together, often for a common cause, but we are different. Tasha, if you accept pack law, you have a place here, a family. They will protect you."

"Better than my first one did?" she asked, unable to hide the bitterness in her voice. "I can't believe my father wanted me dead. Why, Jack? What's wrong with me?"

Jack reached out and pulled her into his arms, holding her close to the long length of his body.

Every inch of him imprinted onto her skin, and for few seconds, she allowed herself to relax.

"Nothing," he said. His hands slid down her arms and glided up over her body, tangling in her long red hair. He tilted her head back and looked down into her eyes. "Absolutely nothing," he whispered the words into her mouth, kissing her cheek, slanting her head back further to lick at the soft flesh of her neck. The scrape of his fangs sent a shiver of pleasure through her.

"Do you know how much I wanted to take you?" he asked. "How hard I was each time I fed?"

He backed her up until the edge of the table was pressing at the small of her back. His large hands came up to cup her face and he kissed her again, this time on the mouth. He nipped at her lower lip until she opened to him, and his tongue pushed into her, hot and wet, as his hips thrust his rock-hard erection against her.

A scalding heat flooded her body, and she gasped into his mouth. She'd wanted this for so long. The kiss hardened, a sharp nick, and the copper taste of fresh blood filled her mouth. Jack groaned and ground his hips harder into her. He slid one hand down over the sweep of her hipbone and between their bodies. His palm cupped her through the denim, and liquid heat flowed from her. He pressed upwards. She moaned and rubbed herself against his hand.

Jack lifted her onto the edge of the table, still kissing her mouth. He spread her legs, pressing his hardness where his hand had been, rocking against the very core of her. The zipper of her jeans slid down, and his hand pushed inside. One finger slid into her slick, slippery wetness. Tasha's head fell back as pleasure flooded her body. A whimper escaped her lips, and she was drowning in exquisite pleasure. She never wanted it to stop—she needed more.

"Not on the table, Jack," a voice said from behind them.

Jack went still above her.

"You know," Sebastian continued, "I really would have expected a little more finesse from somebody with your experience."

Jack withdrew his mouth from hers, licking a last drop of blood from her lips. He looked down at her, his eyes a little rueful as he removed his hand from between her legs. She bit back a whimper of loss and closed her eyes.

When she opened them, Sebastian was leaning in the open doorway, a watchful expression on his face. "Perhaps," he said, with a sharpness in his voice that she didn't quite understand. "You should tell her we don't feed vamps, at least not voluntarily. Ditto for fucking them."

Jack took a step away, and Tasha had to fight the urge to reach out and hold on to him. "That's pack lore," he said to Sebastian. "Not vampire lore."

"Great, just great," Tasha said, pulling up the zip on her jeans. "So this is my new family, huh? What is he, my father?"

Jack smiled. "I doubt that's the position he has in mind." He sighed. "It's probably for the best. You need to think about what you want. In the meantime, I'll find out what I can about your father."

As the door closed behind him, Tasha had a desperate urge to call him back, but he was right. She needed to come to terms with all she'd learned before making any decisions. Sex was off-limits until she decided whether she wanted to join the pack for real or try for a normal life. She couldn't believe she'd let Jack go so far when minutes earlier she'd stated she was quite capable of saying no, if that's what it took to remain human. Still, she couldn't help gazing longingly at the closed door.

"It really isn't done, you know," Sebastian said almost gently.

She glanced at him. "What isn't?" she asked, her thoughts still on Jack.

"Sex with a vampire." Sebastian poured them both a drink. "It's not drugged," he said when she hesitated. "We have accepted you as one of us now. But Tasha, it would be much easier for you if you truly became one of us. Sleep with me tonight and run with the pack afterward." He ran his hand down her arm, and her skin tingled under the touch.

"I promise you you'll enjoy both experiences."

Gazing up at him, she realized he was as beautiful as Jack, in his own way. She could do what he asked and let him deal with everything. But she knew she wouldn't. Her body still throbbed from Jack's touch.

It was Jack she wanted.

But first, she had to confront her father and find out what had happened. There must be some explanation for what he'd done, some way she could still go home.

"I can't," she said. "At least, not yet."

He sighed and let go of her arm. "Then sit with me for a while. You must have questions."

She sank into the chair behind her and took the drink from his outstretched hand. She waited until he was sitting comfortably.

"So," she asked. "Do vampires really sleep in coffins?"

Sebastian shook his head in disgust. "You're obsessed," he said. "Obsessed with a bloodsucking leech."

Tasha smiled. She hadn't expected an answer but hadn't been able to resist the temptation to wind him up. Obviously, the habit hadn't died with Johnson. Sebastian's eyes narrowed on her smile.

"So," she said quickly. "Tell me all about werewolves."

Chapter Seven

Acres of thick woodland surrounded the house, enclosed by a six-foot wall circling the entire perimeter. Tasha had spent the day meandering through pathways not made by human feet, breathing in the scent of growing things. It felt so good to be outside, to be free.

She knew there were wolves around her; she could sense their presence, smell their feral odor. But the thought didn't frighten her. Even without the full moon, Tasha felt the pull of the night and a part of her longed to break free. She knew she had to make a decision—had to decide whether she wanted to be a real werewolf. She'd been thinking over the things Sebastian had told her the night before. He'd made the whole werewolf thing sound breathtaking, wild and exhilarating, and deep down, Tasha knew what her decision would be. Still, she needed to face her father first, find out what had happened all those years ago.

She stayed in the forest long after night had fallen only returning to the house as the sickle moon rose above the trees. Jack lounged on the veranda, one shoulder against the wall, arms folded across his chest. He studied her closely as she climbed the steps toward him. "Have you decided?"

She nodded. "I have to see my father."

"I thought you would. We're meeting him tonight."

She bit her lip. "Does he know I'm alive?"

"He knows nothing. We approached him through official channels. He believes he's coming to a budget meeting."

The door behind them slammed, and she looked across to see Sebastian. "I'm coming with you," he said.

Jack raised an eyebrow.

"We protect our own," Sebastian said.

Jack's eyes narrowed. "She's not yours yet," he growled.

Sebastian smiled. "Did you come out without any supper tonight?" He turned to Tasha. "Vampires tend to get a little bad tempered on an empty stomach."

"I've fed," Jack snarled.

Tasha glared at him. Who had he fed on? She bit back the question.

"Good," Sebastian replied. "I wouldn't want you distracted."

Sebastian drove them into the city. Jack sat beside him in the front with Tasha in the back. No one spoke, and she was glad of the silence to try and make sense of her thoughts. She was going to see her father after so many years. She should have been happy, excited. Instead, she couldn't dislodge the cold hard dread that had settled in her stomach.

The streets of London flashed past almost unnoticed and eventually they arrived in the underground parking garage of a huge office block. She followed Jack and Sebastian through the silent building. Once out of the elevator, Jack turned to her. "Are you sure you want to go through with this?"

She peered up into his face, but his expression was blank. "I don't think I have an option," she replied.

"Of course you have an option," Sebastian said. "You can let us deal with it for you."

"What exactly does 'deal with it' involve?"

"We kill the bastard," Sebastian growled. "Hell, do you want him to live after what he did to you?"

"We don't actually know what he did or why," Tasha said.

"Tasha," Sebastian said. "The evidence is overwhelming. This can't turn out well for you. Let us sort it all out."

But she blocked the words out. There had to be a reason—she wouldn't allow herself to consider the alternative.

After a minute, Jack sighed. "Okay, come on." He led her through the dark corridors.

"What is this place?" Tasha asked.

"Just an office building. My company owns it."

"Your company?"

He smiled. "Vampires need to work too, you know."

Beside him, Sebastian snorted. "Don't you believe it; they're all lazy bastards, sleeping all day."

A light shone from the open doorway of an office. Tasha's heart slowed as they approached. Jack squeezed her arm and then pushed open the door, and Tasha found herself in a huge, ultra-modern office, all black leather and stainless steel. Three men stood by the desk. Jack nodded, and two of the men left the room, leaving the third standing alone.

Tasha took a step forward, but Jack put a warning hand on her arm. She stared at her father.

He'd hardly changed in eight years and a wave of longing washed over her. This was the father she remembered from her childhood. She shook off Jack's hand but could feel him and Sebastian taking up positions on either side of her. She didn't need to be telepathic to sense the menace radiating from them.

Her father was staring back at her now, a slight frown of recognition on his face.

"Dad," she said.

The frown disappeared. It was replaced fleetingly by alarm, which he quickly covered, leaving his expression blank. "Natasha?" He stepped toward them, his movements jerky as though he was in shock, and Jack and Sebastian shifted a little closer. "My God, Natasha, is that you? I thought you were dead." The words were forced, but Tasha could sense the truth in them. "What happened?" he asked.

"That's what we're here to find out," Sebastian said from behind her.

Her father's eyes shifted past her to rest fleetingly on each of her two bodyguards. "Who are you?" he asked. "I was told I was meeting the finance team about budget changes to my program."

"Instead," Sebastian said. "You're meeting with us about why you paid a werewolf to murder your own daughter."

"A werewolf? What are you talking about?"

"We have his confession. You'd be dead already, but your daughter seems to want to give you the benefit of the doubt. We don't. You have five minutes to explain before you die."

Her father turned toward her. "Natasha, please I would never..."

Tasha closed her eyes and reached out with her mind. And met with a complete blank. He was shielded. She opened her eyes and looked into his, and all of a sudden, she knew there wasn't going to be a happy ending. "Why, Dad?"

"Natasha, I don't know what these people are talking about. I'm overwhelmed you're here, that you're not dead."

"He's lying, Tasha," Sebastian growled in her ear. "Read him, and let's get this over with."

"I can't," she said.

"What do you mean, 'can't'?"

"He's shielded, like the guards at the Facility."

"Then perhaps we need to use a more conventional means of persuasion." Sebastian took a step toward the other man. "Do you know what we are?"

"You look like mercs."

"Mercs?" Tasha asked.

"He means mercenaries, paid killers," Jack said. "Don't you, Dr. Grant?" He smiled, but it didn't reach his eyes, which remained as cold as polar ice. "Oh, we're killers all right, and sometimes for money, but you can be very sure, that right at this moment, I would happily kill you—just for fun." He flashed the tip of one fang, and Tasha's father took a step back. "You know what I am," Jack continued. "But then my companion here is something else entirely."

Sebastian reached out one arm, and Tasha watched in fascination as the fingers turned into claws. She gasped. She had lived with this talk of werewolves for so long she'd stopped thinking about what it actually meant. Would she be able to change like that?

"With a little practice," Sebastian drawled in her ear. "Sleep with me tonight, and you'll see for yourself." She glanced at his face in surprise, and he laughed. "I don't need to be a mind reader to know what you were thinking," he said.

She turned to her father. He was backed up against the wall, fear and revulsion on his face.

"I don't understand, Natasha. How did you come to be with these..." He hesitated. "...people? I thought you were dead."

"It seems your paid assassin got greedy," Jack said. "Saw a chance at some extra cash and sold her."

"I don't know what you're talking about."

"I saw you, Dad. I read the man you paid."

"You can do that? You have that much control?" He rubbed at the spot behind his left ear.

Sebastian's eyes narrowed at the movement. "Jack, you've been studying the implant you got from the guard. Can you remove it?"

"Not here," Jack replied. "At least not without killing him."

"Well," Sebastian said. "Killing him would be my choice, but I doubt it would improve our chances of getting information. What about using some of your persuasive vampire skills?"

Jack shrugged. "Might work. On the other hand, with the implant it's just as likely to blow his brain. We don't know enough about them yet. Tasha, do you want to try first?"

"Why, Dad?" Tasha asked again. "How could you do that to your own daughter?"

He glanced away for a moment. When he looked back, his eyes were cold. "I could do it," he said. "Because you're not my daughter."

"What do you mean? Who am I?"

"You're a laboratory experiment, in vitro fertilization, DNA modification. You were grown in a test tube."

"But why?"

"We were researching telepathy. We wanted to increase strength. Your genetic parents were mild telepaths. We had managed to identify the gene that gave them their talent, and then we modified it. Once you were born, it was decided you would be grown in a home environment as near normal as possible."

Tasha's head was about to explode. She was finding it difficult to take in. "What about my mother? Did she know all this?"

"Of course she did. And she wasn't your mother. But she loved you. She knew nothing about the—" he paused and glanced from Jack to Sebastian "—other."

"You mean about you paying a werewolf to kill me."

"I didn't know he was a werewolf. And, no, your mother loved you. She was devastated when you disappeared. Heartbroken."

"So why did you do it?"

"I was under orders. There'd been problems with the others."

"Others?"

"You were one of a batch."

"I have sisters and brothers?"

An expression of distaste crossed his features. "If you can call them that. Anyway, most of those brought up on the outside have been eliminated."

"On the outside?"

"In home environments like yourself."

"But why were they killed?"

"They became telepathic. We were told to look for certain signs."

"But I don't understand. Isn't that what you were trying for?"

"Yes, but at the time, we hadn't developed the shielding technology. What we were doing was confidential, and the handlers thought it was best not to be exposed. We had plenty of samples still in the labs. It was either eliminate you, or lock you up for life."

"So you were doing them a kindness," Sebastian said. "How sweet."

Tasha rubbed the spot between her eyes. "So you bred telepaths and then killed them so they couldn't read your minds?" She shook her head in disgust.

"The orders came from the very top. I argued, but Frank insisted."

"Frank?" Tasha asked.

"Frank Latham, my boss at the unit. Anyway, Frank said some of the others hadn't been able to cope, had gone crazy—we couldn't risk leaving you on the outside. He put me in touch with a man called Oswald. I didn't know he was a werewolf. Back then, we weren't even sure they existed. It was supposed to be quick. You weren't supposed to suffer. And you have to understand, I'd always known it was a possibility."

"Did you ever love me? At all?"

"I never allowed myself to love you."

Tasha closed her eyes to shut him out. She couldn't bear to look at him anymore. Her whole life had been a lie. She'd spent eight years yearning to return to a family, which had never been hers to begin with. A father who had never loved her, who had arranged to have her murdered. She shivered, and Jack's hands slid over her shoulders, pulled her back to rest against him. She realized how hard she'd been holding on to the hope that somehow it was all a mistake, that there was some explanation for what she'd seen in Oswald's head. As she started to shake, Jack's hold on her tightened.

"So, can we kill him now?" Sebastian murmured, his eyes cold and steady.

Her father was staring at them. "I'm a scientist. I just did my job. I followed orders. Natasha, you have to listen to me." He took a deep breath. "Natasha, please, let me talk to you alone."

She shook her head, pressed herself back into Jack.

"For your mother's sake. She loved us both—she wouldn't want this."

Tasha needed time to let it all sink in. She didn't know if she was ready to stand by and see her father die. Even if he wasn't actually her father.

"Let him go," she said, and saw the tension drain from him.

"He tried to have you killed," Sebastian said.

"Please, I don't think I can stand much more of this. Just let him go."

Sebastian shook his head in disgust, but then nodded in resignation. "Don't presume this is over," he said to her father before taking him by the arm. "I'll see this piece of shit off the premises. Then I need to get back to the house."

He paused in front of Jack and Tasha, and then leaned down and kissed her on the forehead. "Remember, you have a family now. You can forget this scum. Look after her," he said to Jack.

"Natasha," her father said. "I need to talk to you. There are things you need to know. Here..." He reached into his pocket and handed her a card as Sebastian dragged him past. "Call me, please."

The door closed behind them. To Tasha, it was like saying goodbye, not only to her old life, but also to all her dreams. Yet, she had no choice—her old life had been a lie. She had to look forward. She had a chance at a new life now, with the pack.

She pulled herself out of Jack's embrace and turned to face him. He smiled, shrugged out of his jacket, and tossed it on the back of the black leather couch. Next, he unbuckled the shoulder holster, laid it on top of the jacket, and then crossed the room to a cabinet and poured them both a drink.

He took a seat on the couch. His long legs stretched out in front of him and stared at her through half-closed eyes. A ripple of excitement shot through her. He patted the seat next to him. "Come and sit for a moment."

She sat down and took the drink he offered but put it on the table untouched. "What is this place?" she asked. "Do you work here?"

"I own the building. We use it as headquarters."

"Headquarters of what?"

"We're a small group who believe our time of living in secrecy is coming to an end. We keep an eye on the interactions between our kind and humans. We also do contract work, often for the government."

"What sort of contract work?"

"It wasn't an accident or a coincidence that I was at the Facility. We'd been watching them for a while. One of my men had gotten too close and been taken. He died. He was young, not strong, and he couldn't withstand the hunger. Or maybe they killed him just to see if they could." He shrugged. "So I went in."

"Weren't you in danger?"

"No, I'm older, stronger."

"How old?"

"A few hundred years. Old enough, anyway."

Tasha closed her eyes and tried to imagine living so long. No wonder he thought of her as a child. When she opened her eyes, Jack was regarding her intently.

"How do you feel?" he asked.

"Numb," she said. "All the way here, no, even before that, ever since the meeting with Oswald, I've been trying to fool myself into believing there's an explanation, that my father didn't actually pay someone to kill me. Okay, so he's not my father, as it turns out, and I can't decide whether that makes it better or worse. It's as if my whole existence is a lie. You know, through the last eight years, all I could think about was getting back to my family. Now it doesn't even exist."

She reached over, picked up her drink, and took a sip. "Ugh! What is this?"

"Fifty-year-old scotch," Jack said wryly.

She put it down.

"Sebastian was right, you know," Jack said. "You have a family now. You belong with the pack. And there's a job for you here, if and when you want it."

"A job? Doing what?"

"We could always find use for a telepath, and we already have a number of wolves on the team."

She thought about it. "My father was shielded. That must mean they're still working with telepaths. There may be others like me out there."

"We'll look into it. You can help if you decide to work with us."

She sat back, closing her eyes. There was a place for her, a job. She wasn't alone; she had friends. She would join the pack truly become one of them. She opened her eyes and glanced at Jack, her heart beating stronger at the thought.

"You know, you should have let Sebastian kill him," Jack said. "I don't trust him not to come after you again. You need to be able to protect yourself better. Once you make the transition, you'll be stronger, faster, you'll heal even quicker. You'll be almost impossible to kill."

"I know. I'd already decided to join the pack."

"You had?"

She nodded. "So there's something I need to do."

Chapter Eight

Tasha nibbled on her lower lip. She didn't know what she would do if Jack rejected her now, but she had to take the risk. "Jack, will you make love to me?"

He smiled. "I'd already decided to do that, but you needed to make the decision yourself. But let's be clear here, you'll be different. It won't be easy to overcome the stigma that goes with having a vampire lover."

"I don't care. I'll always be different anyway."

"Good."

They were silent for a moment. Tasha glanced sideways at Jack. She'd wanted this for so long, but now she was scared. "I don't know what to do."

"I do," Jack said. "Get up."

She frowned but rose to her feet and stared down at him. He appeared relaxed, almost indolent as he sprawled on the sofa, his head back against the cushions, long legs stretched out in front of him. His eyes gleamed emerald through the thick curtain of his lashes, never leaving her.

"Take off your clothes," he ordered, and her skin quivered with anticipation.

"Ooh, I love it when you go all masterful on me."

Jack shook his head. "Just take off your clothes, Natasha."

Her mouth went dry, and she licked her lips. She unbuttoned her shirt, her fingers clumsy, her body trembling with expectation. She slipped out of the shirt then unfastened her jeans and slid them down her legs. She kicked off her shoes and stood for a moment in her underwear. Jack said nothing. He continued to watch her as she removed the rest, until finally, she stood before him naked.

"Come here," he said.

She forced her legs to move and went to stand in front of him. His eyes glittered as they moved over her bare flesh, making her skin tingle. The feeling intensified on the tips of her breasts, between her legs, cramping the muscles of her stomach, and she swayed toward him.

He reached out and caressed the soft skin of her belly, down over her hip, slipping between her legs to stroke her inner thigh where the blood thundered so close to the surface. She was melting from the inside out, but she had to ask one thing before they went any further.

"Jack?"

"Yes?"

"You're not just doing this because you feel sorry for me, are you?"

He laughed softly.

"What's funny?" she asked.

"Stop thinking so hard."

She wished she could. She really did. "Make me," she challenged.

He stared at her, allowing the mask to drop so she glimpsed the fierce predatory beauty beneath, and something close to fear unfurled deep within her. Reaching out, he pulled her to him, so she fell across his legs. He leaned down and kissed her savagely. His lips were brutal; his tongue thrusting hot and wet, into her mouth, his whole body hard against her own. It was minutes before she came up for air, panting. "Jack?"

He sighed. "Yes?"

"I feel strange. This whole wolf thing, it's not going to happen right now, is it?"

"No, not quite yet."

"Good, because I'd hate to try to eat you."

He laughed again. "Feel free," he murmured, leaning down and licking slowly across her breast, biting gently on the swollen tip. "Because I definitely plan to eat you."

Lifting her effortlessly, he turned her so she lay on her back beneath him. "Do you know how long I've wanted this?" he asked, pressing his body into hers. "What you did to me in that cell, rubbing your sweet little body against mine? Teasing me. Begging me to take you."

He stood up then and stripped off his shirt, swiftly followed by the rest of his clothes, and Tasha stared. "Wow," she said, mesmerized by the sheer size and beauty of him, the evidence that he really did want her.

He grasped her knees and parted her legs, coming down to kneel between them. "This isn't going to be slow or gentle," he warned as he reached down and touched her between her thighs. He parted her drenched flesh, opening her to him, his nostrils flaring. One long finger pushed inside, and her inner muscles clenched around him. He withdrew his finger slowly, spreading the moisture over the tight little nub, already engorged with need. He rubbed over it repeatedly with the pad of his thumb until she was writhing against him. When her hips bucked uncontrollably, he withdrew.

He sat back and regarded her for what seemed an age, then slowly clasped his hand around his erection. Tasha followed the movement and stared at him in awe. His erection was long and hard, the skin silky pale, stretched, the head darker, swollen with the same need she was drowning in. He leaned toward her, positioning himself, and she closed her eyes as he nudged at the opening to her body. He paused, and then thrust into her, sheathing himself in one skillful move. Tasha cried out in shock; he was huge, scorching hot, filling her completely. She lay still for a moment, as her body grew accustomed to his. His large hands slid beneath her to cup the backs of her thighs and pull her closer to him. Her head fell back, and he came down over her, his mouth at her throat.

She flinched at the sharp, quick stab as his fangs pierced her skin. Then gasped, but he gave her no time to think as he started to move inside her, almost leisurely at first, withdrawing, and then pushing into her with a slow grinding sweetness. She bucked under him, needing more, and he increased the tempo until all she could do was wrap her legs around him, dig her nails into the satin skin of his shoulders, and hold on as he drove them both higher and higher. She writhed and twisted, wanting more, but unsure as to what it was she needed.

He went still, eased his fangs from her throat, and rose above her. Her blood stained his lips, his black hair was loose around his shoulders, his green eyes fierce as he stared down into her face. And suddenly, she knew what it was she wanted. She wanted all of him, his body *and* his mind. She reached out with her inner sense and crashed straight into the wall of his mental defenses.

"Please, Jack," she whispered. "I love you. Let me in."

Something flickered behind his eyes, then the wall melted, and she was deep in his mind. He started to move again, his eyes never leaving hers, and, through the link joining them, she shared his exquisite pleasure. It echoed her own, with each thrust of his hard body. And beneath the pleasure, she could sense the love he felt for her, and how close he was to complete surrender. She sank into the sensations, rising up to meet each stroke, the feeling building within them until finally, when she thought they could take no more, he went rigid above her, pressed once more, and they both exploded into a million pieces.

"Double wow," she said and heard his soft laughter as she faded into blackness.

"Tasha, wake up."

She ignored the words and snuggled closer, loving the feel of his hard body against her own. He nipped her earlobe between his teeth.

"Ouch," she said. "What was that for?"

"We need to get you back. The pack is waiting for you."

She sat up reluctantly. "You know, I'd sort of forgotten the whole werewolf thing. Is it really going to happen?"

"Yes, and Sebastian said the sooner the better."

"You talked to Sebastian about this?"

"I wanted to be prepared."

She sighed. "Just one kiss then?"

When he didn't move, she leaned across and kissed the pale skin of his chest, licking her tongue across one hard nipple as she trailed her fingers over the ridged muscles of his belly, wrapped them around the hard, silken length of him. She leaned across him, breathed softly over the swollen head, and he jerked beneath her fingers.

He groaned, reached down, and pulled her up until they were face to face. "Just one kiss…" he replied.

Sometime later, she stirred uneasily.

"Jack?"

"Hmm?"

"I feel strange. I mean—really strange."

He glanced into her face. "Shit." He sat up and grabbed her hand. "Come on, we're out of here."

They were silent on the drive back to Sebastian's. Tasha sat tense beside him, fighting the trepidation building up within her.

"Relax," Jack said.

"I can't."

Prickles were running up and down her skin, and she rubbed her arms trying to ease the sensation. She could sense something alien stirring inside her, peering out from her eyes. Opening the window, she let the cool air soothe her.

The drive seemed to go on forever, but at last, Jack pulled up in front of the house. He came around and opened her door. "I can't come with you," he said as she got out. "But I'll see you tomorrow night. Good luck."

"Will I need it?"

He smiled. "No."

He pulled her to him, and gave her a lingering kiss on the lips, his tongue sliding over hers.

"Tomorrow night," he murmured.

The car disappeared down the drive. All around her, the night pulsated with expectation. Tasha couldn't see anyone, but she could sense them waiting for her. Close by, a wolf howled, and she followed the sound, walking slowly around the back of the house and into the dark woods. In a clearing, she found the pack, and at the center, Sebastian stood, still in human form. She walked forward, and the crowd parted for her, forming a circle around her and Sebastian.

He looked down at her and shook his head. "Been feeding the leech again?" Then he smiled and held out his hand. Tasha took it, and he drew her into the center of the circle. He released her hand and began to unbutton his shirt. "You don't need to undress, but the clothes vanish when we change. We find it easier to take them off."

She nodded and slowly removed her clothes.

Sebastian watched her, his eyes gleaming with appreciation, but she couldn't concentrate. A change was happening inside, making her body tremble.

"Relax," Sebastian murmured, "It only hurts if you fight it. Let it flow through you."

Her skin was too tight, stretched over her bones. The feeling was building and building until she raised her head to the sky and screamed. She fell to her knees, her fingers clawing at the wet earth, the wolf within her rising to the surface, demanding to be released.

Sebastian fell to his knees beside her. Then he was gone, and a huge silver wolf stood in his place.

She stopped fighting and felt herself shift—felt her wolf's leap for freedom—and a moment later, she stood on all fours, panting. She shook herself, turned her head to stare at the dark russet fur of her back, lifted one paw and sniffed the air. The night was rich with smells; the tang of the wet earth, the musky fragrance of the other wolves, and far away the scent of prey—the intoxicating odor of hot blood and warm flesh. Filled with a wild elation, she raised her head to the starlit sky and howled. All around her, the others joined her song.

The silver wolf was before her, pouncing playfully, swatting her nose. He nipped at her shoulder then turned and ran. And she followed, racing after him through the dark forest.

She woke the following morning in her own bed, naked. After a brief knock on the door, Sebastian entered. He was dressed in faded jeans and a dark blue shirt, which exactly matched his eyes. He sat down on the bed, his gaze searching her face. "How do you feel?"

"Fantastic. It was the best night of my life."

"Good. So, how was it with the leech?"

Tasha frowned. "Stop calling him that."

He grinned. "Are you defending him? God, it must be love. So how did it go?"

"How did what go?"

"You know..." Sebastian waggled his eyebrows in a suggestive manner.

"Mind your own business."

"Hey, you can't blame me for being interested," he said. "Vampires are such secretive bastards."

"Well, I don't think he sleeps in a coffin if that helps."

He shook his head. "Just be careful. Don't let him overwhelm you." He ran his fingers almost absently over his throat. "I know what it's like."

"You? I thought you said you didn't feed vamps."

"Actually, what I said was, we don't voluntarily feed vamps." He shrugged. "When Jack first approached the pack, we fought. We fought. I lost. He fed. It was just the once, a dominance thing more than anything else. I'm only telling you because I know how good it can feel."

Tasha's eyes widened. "Did you and he—?"

"Have sex?" Sebastian finished the sentence for her. "Mind your own business. Anyway, it was a long time ago."

"How long?"

"Fifty years, give or take a few."

Tasha ran her eyes over him. He looked pretty good for someone who had to be at least seventy.

"So, are werewolves immortal?" she asked.

"No, but we are very long-lived. The truth is we tend to come to some sort of gruesome end long before we reach a natural death." He shrugged again. "Vampires tend to destroy themselves. We destroy each other. It's the nature of the beast."

"And humans, like my 'father,' what about them?"

"Oh, they destroy everything." He smiled. "Anyway, I just wanted to make sure you were fine after last night. You did great by the way. Welcome to the family."

She lay in bed for a long time after he left. She'd told Sebastian the truth; it had been the most amazing night of her life, and she didn't want anything to spoil it. But she knew she had to talk to her father. She needed to know what he could tell her if she was to have any chance of moving on with her life.

Picking up the phone from beside the bed, she dialed the number.

Chapter Nine

"She's gone," Sebastian said.

Shock hit Jack in the gut. Had something happened, something gone wrong when she'd shifted? "Gone? Gone where?"

"Don't worry—I've got people following her as you asked—she won't come to any harm."

"She'd better not." He should have expected this, should have never let her out of his sight, but he'd had no choice last night. She'd needed the other wolves when she shifted for the first time and they wouldn't have tolerated his presence.

"You have to let her do this," Sebastian said. "She'll never be free of him until she accepts what a bastard he is."

Jack knew Sebastian was right, but everything screamed at him to protect her from harm and her "father" was a double-crossing bastard. What sort of man could bring up a child, and then casually have her murdered? And Jack still wasn't convinced Tasha's mother's death had been an accident.

He'd keep that from her if he could.

Last night had been amazing, he'd felt her deep in his head, and he hadn't minded. Hell, he'd liked it. He couldn't hide anything from her, but the opposite was also true. She loved him.

"I'm going after her."

"I never expected anything else." Sebastian tossed him a cell phone. "My men are on speed dial."

Her father had promised to come alone.

Tasha watched from the shadows as he spoke to the two men who had accompanied him to the meeting place. A moment later, they disappeared into the darkness of the alley behind him.

It was a trap. She should have felt worse, but deep down, she'd expected nothing else. Still, it didn't prove everything he'd told her that morning was lies. Was she a danger to those she loved? Unless she found out, she could never be with Jack as she longed to be.

Something moved behind her. Every muscle tensed, and then relaxed as a hand stroked the hair from her neck, and a soft, slow kiss brushed against the flesh of her throat. At the slight scrape of fangs, her body quivered, heat pooling at her core. She pressed herself back against the hard length of him. After a moment, she stepped away and turned to face him.

"Jack," she said, "what are you doing here?"

"You were followed from the house. You were never alone. We guard our own."

"Am I yours?"

He leaned forward and kissed her again, this time on the lips. "Forever," he said. "Now, let's go. I'll deal with your father."

"No, Jack. I have to do this. I talked to him on the phone this morning. He said I was dangerous."

He raised an eyebrow. "Sweetheart, you're a telepath and a werewolf. People don't get much more dangerous than that." He smiled. "Except for vampires, of course."

She shook her head. "You don't understand. He said the others like me had gone crazy, been unable to control their powers. They'd killed innocent people, and I could do the same. I'm a danger to anyone I get close to."

"And you believe him?"

"No. Maybe." She sighed. "The truth is I'm not sure. But don't you see, unless I find out for certain, I can't be with you. I can't be with anyone. Besides, he also said he had information about my family—my real family. I have to know."

Jack looked down at her for a long moment, and then nodded. "Okay but give me five minutes before you go out there."

He glided through the shadows, slipping into the alley behind her father.

She waited, peering into the darkness where Jack had disappeared. After a few minutes, she stepped forward. "Dad."

He jumped and then turned around to face her, a frown forming on his face.

"Dad," she urged when he remained silent. "Where's the information you promised?"

Her father glanced around to search behind him.

"I think he might be waiting for his friends," Jack said, stepping out of the shadows. "But I'm afraid they won't be joining you after all." He stared into the other man's eyes and raw power radiated from him. "Ask him, Tasha, he has to answer."

Her eyes darted to Jack's face. "Last night you said it was dangerous to use your powers on someone with an implant. That it could kill them."

Jack shrugged. "Does it matter?"

She looked at the man who had been her father, searching for some vestige of the love she'd once felt. "No, it doesn't matter. Am I dangerous?" she asked.

"No." The word was dragged from him.

"Then why did you lie?"

"I needed to get you away on your own—kill you."

A sense of relief washed through her at his words. It was over. At last, she could let him go. She just needed to know one more thing. "You said there were others like me. Was that a lie?"

"No. There are more."

"Where are they?"

"I don't know. Only Frank knew."

Tasha turned away in frustration.

"Have you heard enough?" Jack asked.

She nodded, and Jack released the man from his gaze.

For a second, he slumped against the wall. When he straightened, he held a gun pointed at Jack, but he was glaring at Tasha. "You should have died when you were supposed to."

Tasha focused on the gun, and the power grew within her. A soft growl trickled from her throat. Jack turned toward her, green eyes piercing the darkness between them.

"Tasha?" he warned.

But it was too late. The change was flowing through her, natural, perfect. One moment she stood before them—the next, she was leaping on all fours. Disbelief flashed in her father's eyes, followed by horror as she knocked the gun from his hand and tore into his throat in one fluid move. There was a moment of exhilaration as bone and cartilage crushed between her jaws, and the warm metallic taste of fresh blood filled her mouth. Life left him as she crouched above his body, and a faint cry of regret reverberated through her mind.

"Tasha, come."

She heard Jack's voice as though from a distance and peered up at the tall figure looming over her. She snarled softly.

"Tasha," he said again, and held out a hand. She sniffed at the outstretched fingers, and a wonderful feeling flooded her. *Jack.* The name whispered through her brain.

He looked at the body beneath her and smiled wryly. "And you wondered if you were dangerous," he mused before turning away.

Tasha glanced down once at the body of the man who had been her father, then leapt lightly off and trotted after the dark figure. She nudged his leg with her nose until he reached down and stroked her head.

"Come on," he said, his long fingers ruffling the soft fur on her neck. "Let's go home."

BOUND TO MOONLIGHT

Sisters of the Moon
Book 2

by

NINA CROFT

Chapter One

Anya's finger tightened on the trigger.

The chill of the metal penetrated her skin, sending icy tendrils curling through her body. She waited for the cold to seep into her mind, to take her to that peaceful place. The place she always went when she had a job to do.

Tonight, peace remained elusive, and she shifted restlessly.

Dusk fell, and the last daylight faded into darkness. Anya lay on her belly, stretched out on the soft detritus of the forest floor, her sniper rifle resting on a rotting tree limb in front of her. Her nostrils filled with the reek of decay mingled with the musky aroma of wild garlic crushed beneath her. Above her head, the breeze rustled the leaves in the tree canopy. Aside from that, the woods were silent. She reached out with her mind but found no one within listening distance.

She was alone.

For a moment, she savored the feeling. Closing her eyes, she pressed her forehead to the rough bark of the tree limb. And in the solitude of her mind, she finally acknowledged the truth that had been plaguing her for so long. She didn't want to do this anymore.

The *click* of a door opening snapped her from her thoughts. She raised her head, her movements slow and careful, and sighted down the length of the rifle. The scents and sounds of the forest faded around her as all her senses focused on the figure that emerged from the open door.

She recognized him immediately. Sebastian Quinn. Her target.

The man they'd told her was responsible for the death of her sister. The sister she had never known. Would now *never* know.

The shot would be easy from here. She'd expected him to be wary; after all, she'd captured three of his people over the past week. Instead, he appeared relaxed, standing on the steps in front of the house as though he were posing for her.

She studied him through the scope. While she'd seen photographs, they hadn't done him justice. Pale blond hair fell over his forehead, framing the face of a dissipated angel. His long, lean body was dressed in faded jeans and a dark blue shirt that perfectly matched his wicked blue eyes.

He raised his head and sniffed the air. His eyes narrowed, and he swung around, his gaze seeming to penetrate her hiding place.

He knew she was here.

Without conscious thought, she reached out to his mind and instantly froze. She probed again but slammed into an impenetrable barrier. He was shielded. Why hadn't the Agency told her? Did they even know?

For a brief moment, she considered taking the shot but pushed the idea aside. The mission had been compromised. Besides, she would give away her location, and she'd bet he had people watching from the house.

Anya peered down the scope one last time. Across the distance, his gaze captured hers, and she blinked to break the contact.

Wriggling backwards on her stomach, she stayed low until she reached the cover of the dense trees. As she came up on her knees, she glanced back over her shoulder, and knew that he had sensed her movement. He stared straight at the spot she'd been hidden, a fierce grin spreading across his face.

He spoke briefly into a cell phone then started to strip off his clothes.

What the hell was he doing?

She knelt transfixed as he tore off his shirt and tossed it to the ground. His skin was golden, sleek muscle over bone, broad shoulders, and a lean almost concave belly. His hand went to the belt at his waist, and Anya scrambled to her feet and ran.

She raced through the forest, weaving between the huge gnarled oak trees, her boots making no sound on the soft ground. Branches snatched at her clothes, scratching the exposed skin of her face, and still she ran.

In the distance, an owl hooted, and a wolf howled. The eerie sound shattered her concentration, and she stumbled over an exposed root. She righted herself as a second wolf answered. Flinging herself behind a tree, she leaned against the rough bark. Panic flared, and she shoved it down, then forced her breath to slow, concentrating her mind.

There were no wolves in England, not outside of a zoo anyway. Likely they were using hounds to track her, but they still sounded far away. She had time. If she could make it to the wall surrounding the property, she'd be free.

She opened her mind. She could sense no one close, and some of the tension drained from her. Stepping forward, she peered into the thick darkness between the trees, trying to orientate herself. She still clutched the rifle in her hand, and she hefted it across one shoulder and crept through the forest.

Five minutes later, she stood beside the tall wall that ran around the entire perimeter of the compound. She reached out to touch the uneven stone, a sigh escaping her lungs. Now she was safe, she could admit how rattled she'd felt. The night hadn't gone well, and her handlers would not be pleased. But there would no doubt be another chance.

Something moved on the edge of her vision, and she whirled around. Too late. A huge, grey object slammed into her. She lost her grip on the rifle as she crashed to the ground. Rolling, her hand went instinctively to the pistol at her waist. She came straight back on her feet, the pistol grasped in her hand, adrenaline surging through her veins.

And she froze.

For a moment, her mind refused to accept what she saw. Wolves surrounded her. Her fingers clenched around the gun, searching for a target, but there were too many. Her eyes darted everywhere, hunting for an escape. She had a full clip in her gun, there was still a chance she could get out of here.

A silver wolf stepped forward from the pack and padded toward her, tail held low, muzzle peeled back in a snarl that revealed razor sharp canines.

Raising her pistol, Anya stared into its face. In that instant, she recognized the flash of humanity in the wolf's dark blue eyes. Shock ripped through her, and she hesitated. She could have shot a man with ease, but not this wild, beautiful creature. Releasing her breath, she accepted defeat and lowered the pistol.

Something struck her from the side. She stumbled back, falling to the ground, her head cracking against the stone wall. And darkness swallowed her.

Chapter Two

His wolves milled, restless and hungry. Sebastian growled low in his throat, and they backed away, melting into the forest. He shifted back into human form and crouched beside the fallen sniper. The body lay face down, lifeless, and Sebastian swore under his breath. He hoped to hell the man wasn't dead. They needed to find out who had sent him and whether their missing pack members were still alive.

He pressed his fingers against the sniper's throat. The skin felt warm and the pulse strong—still alive. He rolled the body over and swore again.

His sniper was a woman.

Not that it made much difference, but if it came down to using conventional methods to get them to talk, he'd have preferred dealing with a man. Something about torturing a woman didn't sit well with him, but he'd do what he had to do. Someone was targeting his pack, and he needed to know who and why, and then he needed to stop them.

She was tall for a woman, dressed in dark pants and a dark shirt, her blond hair pulled into a plait down her back. It was easy to see how he had mistaken her for a man. From a distance.

Up close, she'd be impossible to mistake for anything other than a woman. A beautiful woman with prominent cheekbones and a wide sensual mouth. His gaze dropped to her chest and the swell of small breasts beneath her shirt.

Her hand still clasped the pistol, and he wondered for a moment why she hadn't taken the shot. He shrugged, then loosened her fingers and tossed the gun to the ground next to the sniper rifle that lay close by. The rifle wasn't a model he recognized; he guessed it must be some sort of prototype. Could she be military?

She groaned low in her throat, and his gaze flew back to her face.

Dark brown eyes flecked with gold stared up at him. They widened then looked around wildly. She started to push herself up, and he drew back his fist and clipped her lightly across the chin. She collapsed back to the forest floor, and Sebastian rose to his feet.

He picked her up with ease, slung her over his shoulder, and headed, naked and barefoot, back to the house.

Riley, his second, was already back and dressed. Opening the door, he led the way down the narrow stairs into the basement, unlocking the silver cage that stood in the center of the room.

Sebastian dropped his burden onto the small cot and stood for a moment staring down at her. Still unconscious, her dark lashes formed shadows on the pale, flawless skin of her cheeks. Her wide, lush mouth parted with each shallow breath, and watching the slight movement, an unexpected fire stirred to life low in his belly. A trickle of unease ran up his spine. This woman was nothing more than a means to an end. The only reason they had taken her alive was to make her talk.

He glanced at Riley. "Go get my clothes. I left them on the steps."

"No problem."

Sebastian turned back to his prisoner. Who was she? More importantly, who was she working for?

This had to be connected to the search for Tasha's sisters.

Tasha was the newest member of his pack. She was also a powerful telepath and until six months ago, she'd been a prisoner at the Facility, an organization carrying out illegal research into the paranormal. His group had freed Tasha, and destroyed the building, but it had soon become clear that The Facility was merely one arm of a monster with tentacles wrapped around every powerful organization in the world.

Tasha and her husband, Jack, were now following a lead in Russia, while Sebastian had promised Tasha that he would keep up the hunt for her family here. The sisters who'd been created at the same time as Tasha, from the same DNA.

They'd had a lead. Frank Latham had run the government laboratory where Tasha was born. He'd also turned up at The Facility where she'd been a prisoner since her attack by a werewolf assassin, eight years ago. They were getting close to finding him. Maybe too close, because now somebody had come after them. Three of Sebastian's people had gone missing in the last week.

Riley returned and threw a bundle of clothes to him. Sebastian pulled on his jeans but tossed the shirt over the single upright chair before turning back to the woman. He needed to search her for anything that might give a clue to her identity, and that would be easier while she was unconscious. Crossing the room to the small cot, he hunkered next to her. He unlaced one black combat boot and tugged it off. The second followed, and he dropped them on the floor.

As he reached to unbuckle the weapons belt at her waist, he glanced back over his shoulder to where Riley loitered in the open doorway. "Get out."

Riley raised an eyebrow but turned and left.

Sebastian unfastened the snap and tugged her pants down over her slim hips. Her legs were long, slender, her skin pale.

The pants had no labels, nothing that could give any indication of where she had come from. She was obviously a professional. Leaning across, he flicked open the buttons on her shirt. She didn't awaken, and he slipped his hands under her shoulder, heaved her up, and stripped the shirt from her. Like the pants, it had no labels; he hadn't expected any.

She lay on her back on the grey blanket, now wearing only a black cotton bra and black panties, stark against the whiteness of her skin. His gaze ran over her. She was almost too thin. But while each rib was clearly visible, and her abdomen was a hollow dip, the long lines of her muscles were clearly defined. She appeared at that peak of physical fitness only achieved by hard training.

He had to finish this. He slipped his hands beneath her and flicked open the clasp of her bra, tugged the straps down over her arms, and tossed it on to the pile of clothes.

He told himself he was just doing a necessary job, but he couldn't prevent his eyes from lingering on the smooth skin. Her breasts were small but perfectly formed with pale pink nipples. He had a sudden urge to run his palm across them, see if they would stiffen to his touch. His body tightened at the thought, and he frowned. He was no sex-starved monster. There were a number of unattached females in the pack, and as alpha, he had his pick and never looked outside for lovers. Yet here he was going hot and hard at the thought of touching an unconscious woman. She wasn't even his type—too thin, too unfeminine. He tried to ignore his reaction while he looked at her for any clue.

A red mark marred the skin beneath her right breast. It appeared as though something had pressed against her skin. He sat on the cot beside her and stroked one finger along the line. Her skin was silky soft, but she flinched at his touch, then rolled onto her side and curled into a ball. He leaned down picked up her bra and ran his hand along the lower seam. Something snagged against his fingers. Turning the bra over in his hands, he found a small pocket attached to the cotton and, tucked inside, a foil packet containing three pills. They could be suicide pills, but why would she need three? More likely, they were some sort of performance enhancing drugs. He pushed them into his pocket. He'd get the lab to analyze them. It might give a clue to who or what they were up against.

She lay facing the wall, and he stroked a hand over the smooth curve of her spine down to where the black cotton panties covered her bottom. His finger flirted with the edge then he hooked the finger in the band and slid them down over the endless length of her legs. He held the scrap of cotton up in his hand, but they hid nothing, no labels, no little nametag conveniently sewn in to reveal her identity. He'd known there wouldn't be. He could at least be honest with himself. He'd wanted to see her naked and now his eyes were drawn to the pale blond curls peeking out from between her thighs.

At the sight, the fire in his belly flared hotter, his balls ached, and inside him, his wolf stirred.

Sebastian stood up quickly, shoving the panties into his pocket. He'd never considered himself a pervert and lusting after unconscious women was definitely perverted in his books. He had to get out of there. He could do nothing more until she awoke, and for some reason, she presented far too much of a temptation.

A temptation he didn't need and didn't want. He couldn't afford to see her as a woman, only as an enemy who had come here tonight to kill him. Furthermore, an enemy who very likely possessed the information he needed to find his missing pack members.

Long ago, he had sworn an oath to protect the pack, which meant he would get that information by whatever means possible. His squeamish feelings could not be allowed to get in the way. He had no illusions it would be easy. She was obviously well trained and tough.

He turned to go, but at the last moment, he returned to the bed, tugged the blanket from under her, and covered her naked body.

Chapter Three

A nya shot bolt upright on the small bed.

Where was she?

Her head pounded. She ran a trembling hand over her scalp. There was no blood, but a lump the size of an egg accounted for the pain. Then she remembered. She'd crashed into the stone wall. Just before...

She screwed her eyes up tight, but behind her closed lids, she still saw those blue eyes staring at her out of a wolf's face. Could she have been hallucinating? She hadn't been due a pill for hours yet, but maybe her health had deteriorated. Dr. Latham had told her they had it under control, but maybe he didn't want to scare her. Though to be honest, that didn't sound like something Dr.

Latham would concern himself about. But maybe he thought it might limit her effectiveness in the field.

The room was almost dark, but even in the dim light, she could make out her surroundings. She was in a cage, and for a moment, she had to fight the familiar panic that flared to life inside her.

She swallowed and looked around, searching for anything that might help her escape. The cage held the narrow cot she was lying on, a table, and a single upright chair. The floor was bare concrete, and a surveillance camera in one corner of the ceiling stared down at her. Were they watching her even now?

Silver bars enclosed all four sides, and the cage stood in the center of a square windowless room, with a single steel door opposite where she lay.

Her fingers tightened on the scratchy grey blanket clutched in one hand. Beneath it, she was naked. They must have stripped her, but they wouldn't have found anything to lead back to the Agency.

She'd been active for five years now, but this was the first time she'd been captured. She tried to stay calm and go over the training, but fear clawed at her insides at the thought of what they might do. Through the training sessions, she'd pretended to be so tough—she'd never broken—but afterwards she'd always thrown up, and the memory still had the power to make her stomach heave.

Her handlers had told her this was a ruthless, well-organized group involved in everything from gunrunning to drug dealing. No way would they let her go. So this was the end. A wave of regret washed through her; she didn't want to die before she'd had the chance to live.

Her clothes lay in a pile on the floor. She reached to pick them up, just as the outer door opened. As light flooded the room, her hand fell back to her side and she blinked.

Sebastian Quinn stood framed in the doorway. She reached out with her mind but crashed into the same wall she'd hit earlier. He was shielded; she couldn't read him. Where would he have obtained the technology?

He strode into the room followed by a second man. Her glance darted to him, then back to Sebastian.

Unlocking the cage door, he stepped inside, then handed the key to the other man who locked it from the outside and left the room. The cell suddenly seemed much smaller. She knew he was six-foot-one, but in the confined space, he appeared larger. Of course, she'd seen his file, but nothing could have prepared her to face him in the flesh. A shiver ran through her. She'd trained with men, fought them, even killed them, but none had ever had this effect on her. It was odd that she should feel her first hint of real desire from a man destined to kill her.

"Get up," he ordered, his tone icy cold.

For a moment, she considered ignoring the command. But what good would it do? Better to find out what fate had in store for her. She swung her legs around and stood, dragging the blanket with her. Pain skewered her brain as though her head would split, and she swayed then stiffened her spine. She looked across at her clothes and back at the man standing before her. "Can I get dressed?"

He seemed to consider the question, but finally lifted one shoulder in a careless gesture. "Go ahead."

Relief flooded her. Nakedness was a tool many used in interrogations, women especially felt vulnerable. She'd been trained to cope, but she didn't want to be naked in front of this man. Still, she suspected it would be pointless asking him to turn around, so she dropped her blanket and reached for her clothes.

Her panties were missing. She glanced at him, and he pulled the scrap of black cotton from his pocket and tossed them to her. Then he sank onto the single seat and watched as she pulled on her clothes.

She picked up her bra. Her pills were gone, and her heart stalled. Did he have them? Anya pushed her panic aside. After all, if they killed her—as she was sure they would—she would hardly need her medication.

One problem at a time.

She finished dressing—her heart rate slowing once she was covered—and sat down on the bed to pull on her boots.

"You don't need the boots," he said, and she dropped them but stayed seated on the bed.

For a minute, she stared down at the concrete floor and considered what approach to take. When she looked up, she forced an expression of puzzlement into her eyes.

"Why am I a prisoner?" she asked.

He ignored the question and asked one of his own. "So, what were you doing here tonight?"

Anya shrugged. "Taking a walk in the forest."

"Hmm, taking your top of the range, prototype sniper rifle out for a walk, were you?" He stretched his long legs out in front of him and regarded her thoughtfully. "Why don't we save some time, cut the crap, and you tell me what you were really doing?"

"I told you—"

He held up his hand, and she stopped.

"Perhaps," said, his voice devoid of expression, "we could start with why you came here to kill me."

"I don't know what you're talking about."

"Then, how about—where are my people?"

"I don't know—"

He leapt up from his chair, gripped his fist in her shirt, and pulled her to her feet. Dragging her across the room, he slammed her into the bars of the cage behind her. The breath left her lungs in a *whoosh*. Then he was pressing her into the bars with his hard body. He leaned in close to her ear, and his warm breath whispered against her neck. "I *will* make you talk," he murmured, and she shivered at the dark promise in his voice.

He released his grip on her shirt and stepped back, shoved his hands in his pockets and regarded her closely. "It goes against my better nature to hurt a woman, but I have three people missing and to get them back I am willing to put aside my better nature. And if I do find myself too squeamish to do whatever's necessary, there are a few of my people who actually enjoy that sort of thing. An hour with them, and you'll be begging to tell me everything you know."

She drew herself up tall. "There's nothing you can do to make me talk."

His smile didn't reach his cold blue eyes. "You say that, but you don't believe it. You're tough"—he drew in a deep breath, and his nostrils flared—"but I can smell your fear."

It was true. The intoxicating scent of her fear filled the room, and inside him, wolf awoke and howled to be free.

Something about this woman called to him and his wolf. He could still feel her body imprinted against his, and his balls ached for relief. He didn't trust himself around her. Maybe he *should* hand her over to his men, but the thought of anyone else touching her, roughing her up, marring that flawless skin, made him grit his teeth in denial.

He'd studied many people in his time. Just because she was afraid did not mean she would break under torture. Many of the toughest people experienced fear but did not give in to it. Some possessed a certain type of stubbornness that refused to break.

She moved suddenly, pushing off from the bars and high kicked him in the chest. He shuddered beneath the force of the blow but stood his ground. Any ordinary man would have been down. Unfortunately for her, he was far from ordinary. Her eyes widened, but she whirled around in the confined space and kicked out again. He grabbed her ankle and dragged her off balance, so she crashed to the floor, her skull slamming into the hard concrete with a dull *crack*.

She put a hand to her head then stared up, her brow furrowing as she studied him. "What are you?"

"You don't know?"

She blinked and shook her head, but he could see the acceptance dawning in her eyes. She'd seen them in the forest. No doubt up until this point she'd been attempting to delude herself that what she'd witnessed wasn't real.

Maybe this was the way to make her talk.

Sebastian fell to his knees beside her. He put a hand on either side of her head and lowered his face to hers. Wolf rose up inside him, peered out of his eyes, and a growl trickled from his throat. Wolf wanted to smell her, and Sebastian buried his nose against her neck. She smelled divine, and he gave in to the urge and tasted her, licking his tongue along the warm flesh of her throat, hovering over the pulse point where her blood thundered through her veins. She flinched beneath him then held herself immobile as he crouched over her. He could feel his hunger mounting. Forcing it down, he rose to stand beside her.

She lay at his feet, her eyes huge. "It was you in the forest. I thought I'd dreamed you."

He didn't answer, just watched as she pushed herself up, first onto her elbows. She winced but gritted her teeth and struggled to her feet, gripping the bars for support. He didn't think she was faking her weakness. She'd hit her head hard out in the forest earlier and again just now.

"Turn around," he said.

She frowned. "What?"

"I want to have a look at that scalp wound. The last thing I need is for you to collapse and die on me before I can make you talk."

He put his hands on her shoulders, and she flinched under his touch. Tightening his grip, he turned her around. Her hair had come loose, and he ran his fingers through the silky strands. A red, angry swelling marred the smooth line of her skull, but the skin hadn't broken. He turned her back to face him, and slipped a finger beneath her chin, tilted her head so he could look down into her face. Her eyes were an amazing color, bitter chocolate flecked with gold. The pupils weren't dilated, and he was pretty sure she wasn't concussed.

Her lips were slightly parted. Without thinking, his hand moved from her chin to her face, and he stroked the pad of his thumb over her full lower lip, swollen where she had worried it with her teeth.

Her eyes widened and her body stiffened, but she didn't move away. Sebastian slipped his thumb between her lips and felt the warm, wet velvet caress of her tongue. His reaction was instant, his cock stiffening in his pants.

A deep longing filled him, to pick her up, carry her to the cot, and lose himself in her body. Instead, he pulled away and stepped back, shoving his hands in his pockets to stop himself touching her. She stared at him, a bemused almost hurt expression on her face, and he had to bite back the need to tell her everything would be all right.

Which would very likely be a lie.

Jesus, what was it about this woman? He was in trouble. He had to get out of there. He crossed to door and banged on the bars.

"Riley," he called. "Let me out of here." He turned back to her. "What's your name?"

She shrugged. "Anya."

"Well, Anya, I don't want to hurt you, but my loyalty is to my people. I will do anything needed to get them back... or avenge their deaths." He shook his head. Why was he explaining?

Riley entered the outer room and unlocked the cage. Sebastian stepped out and glanced back at Anya; she hadn't moved.

"I'm going to leave you alone for a while," he said. "I want you to think about it, and when I come back, you will tell me what happened to my people." He waited while Riley locked the door and then he turned to leave.

"Sebastian."

He glanced back over his shoulder. She gripped the bars and stared back at him. "What?" he asked.

"I'll never talk."

A pain clenched his heart. "Then I think we will both live to regret it."

Chapter Four

Anya reached up with a trembling hand and touched her lips.

What had just happened?

For a minute back there, she'd thought he was going to kiss her.

Who was this man, who threatened her with torture one moment then touched her with a gentleness she'd never experienced before? At the memory of that touch, her eyes stung, and she blinked, feeling the unexpected dampness on her lashes. She never cried. What would be the point?

She backed up and sank down on the cot, rolled onto her side, and curled into a tight ball as though she could shut out the world. But he would be back soon, and she needed to decide what to tell him. If anything.

The Agency was all she knew. All she had ever known. They had created her, brought her up. She owed her very life to them and without the medicine they provided for her daily, she would die.

All that was true. But recently, she had come to hate her very existence. She had spent all her life at the Agency, but sometimes, out on a mission, she would watch people go about their lives, and the craving to be part of the world had grown inside her until it was a constant companion.

But she wasn't a person. She was a thing the Agency had made in a test tube and trained as a weapon. She belonged to them. But she didn't want to kill for the Agency anymore. She'd found it hard even when she had believed she fought on the right side. Now she no longer believed.

She wished she could read Sebastian's mind. The Agency had told her he headed up a group of mercenaries. A group who would do any job for the right price. Somehow, that didn't ring true anymore. Why would a mercenary be shielded? It must mean he knew of the work the Agency had been doing with telepaths.

She'd long suspected that the Agency was carrying out other research. From time to time, she'd catch flashes of strange minds imprisoned in the cells beneath the building. She hadn't understood who or what they were; only that they were something other than human, and she'd tried to close her mind to their pain and suffering. Was that when her doubts about the Agency had begun?

Her mind flinched away from thinking about what she had seen in the forest. Now she forced herself to confront the truth.

Sebastian Quinn was a wolf. A werewolf.

Of course, that didn't mean he couldn't also be a mercenary, or that he hadn't been responsible for the death of her sister—hadn't blown up the Facility where her sister had lived. But what if it had all been lies?

She rolled onto her back and rubbed a hand across her temple trying to ease the throbbing in her head. It should be getting better, but she suspected that more than the bang on the head was affecting her. The muscles of her arms and legs ached and each breath caught in her lungs. Worry nagged at her mind; she had no notion how long she had before the symptoms overwhelmed her. She needed her medication.

Closing her eyes, she tried to come up with a plan. Sebastian wanted his people back, but she didn't even know if they still lived. And besides, she wouldn't give him the Agency's location, not until she was sure who the bad guys were.

He needed the information, and Anya had no doubt he would follow through with his threats. The dull ache in her head flared into pain. To Sebastian Quinn, she was nothing more than a means to an end. A way of finding his people. Why did that thought have the power to hurt her?

Maybe the best she could hope for was to die from her illness before he got round to torturing her.

The ringing of the phone brought Sebastian out of his light sleep. It rang again and he picked it up.

"It's Tasha," the woman on the other side said. "What's happened to Jonas?"

Sebastian recognized the distress in her voice, and he pressed his fingertips against his eyes, trying to clear his mind. "How do you know about Jonas?"

"He's dead, isn't he?"

Shock tore through him. "Dead?"

"You didn't know?"

He remained silent for a minute, thinking it through. Tasha was telepathic, and through her ties with the pack, she could feel the other pack members, sense their emotions, if they were stressed, afraid—dead.

"Are you sure?" he asked.

"I felt him last night—such pain—then nothing. What's going on, Sebastian?"

"They took him a week ago. He was the first, then Travis and Maria."

"I haven't sensed them. I think they must be alive. Who took them?"

"We don't know, but we captured a sniper in the woods last night. We're hoping she can tell us something."

"You want me back?"

He thought about it. If his little sniper came from where he suspected, likely she'd be shielded, and Tasha would be able to tell them nothing. On the other hand, if she wasn't shielded, Tasha could extract the information with ease and without the need to hurt Anya.

"Come back," he said.

"Okay, we'll be with you by tomorrow night."

Sebastian wanted them back as soon as possible, but Jack was a vampire; it would be dangerous for him to travel during the day. "Don't take any risks," he said.

"We won't."

"Let me know if you feel anything from Travis or Maria."

He put the phone down and stared into the darkness. He hoped tomorrow night would be soon enough, but if more of his people died because he was too squeamish to torture an assassin, he would never forgive himself.

Again, he considered handing her over to someone who would be more than willing to do what was necessary to make her talk, but he couldn't do it. His whole being rejected the idea of anyone harming her. Hell, the idea of anyone even touching her.

Anyone but him.

She was his.

The thought brought him up short.

Over fifty years ago, he'd killed the old alpha and taken on the role of leader, and in all that time, he'd never put an outsider before his pack. He couldn't believe he was even thinking about it now. Why did she affect him so strongly?

He glanced up as Riley entered the room. He came to stand in front of Sebastian.

"The prisoner—she's ill—there's something wrong with her."

Sebastian frowned. "What?"

"How the hell should I know? You told me not to go in there."

"So how do you know she's ill?"

"Looks like she's got a fever. The room's cool, but she's sweating, and she seems to be unconscious."

"Could she be faking it?"

"I don't know. I'm not a doctor."

Riley's tone was terse, and Sebastian's eyes narrowed on him. "Do you want to tell me what's got you all pissed off?"

"Yeah, I do. That woman tried to kill you last night and she may know the whereabouts of Maria and the others. Why the hell aren't we making her talk?" He ran a hand through his short hair. "Look, I understand. She's a woman, and you don't want to do it. Hell, I don't want to do it, but I will if you can't. The pack has to come first."

"Jonas is dead."

Riley closed his eyes, and Sebastian gave him a moment to compose himself. Riley and Jonas had been close. When he opened his eyes, they were dark with pain. "Are you sure?"

Sebastian nodded. "Tasha felt it."

"What about the others?"

"Still alive—she thinks."

"For now." Riley's expression hardened. "We need to make that woman talk."

Sebastian knew it, but he wouldn't give a job to anyone else that he wouldn't do himself. His gut clenched, but Riley was right. "I'll go see her now."

He let himself into the room. Through the bars of the cage, he could see her where she lay on her back on the small cot, unmoving, her eyes closed, her pale face glowing with a fine sheen of sweat. Every few seconds, a tremor ran through her body.

He hurried to unlock the cage door. She didn't open her eyes as he crossed the cell to sit on the mattress beside her. He stroked a finger down the softness of her cheek and found the skin burning hot. As he laid a palm on her forehead, she rolled onto her side, curling against him as shivers racked her body.

She burrowed her head into his thigh. He sat for a minute. What the hell did he do now? He was sure she wasn't faking it, and he didn't think it could be anything to do with the bang to the head. Which left the pills. Was she ill?

He tapped her on the cheek. "Anya, wake up."

She didn't respond, and he shook her slightly. Her eyes blinked open, dazed and unfocused.

"I'm so cold," she mumbled.

Wrapping the blanket around her, he gathered her in his arms, picked her up, and held her cradled against his chest. He kicked open the cage door and strode out.

As he passed Riley on the staircase, the other man raised an eyebrow.

"She can't tell us anything if she's dead," Sebastian snapped.

"Hey, I didn't say a word."

Sebastian ignored the comment. "She needs a doctor. Get Connor on the phone. Tell him it's an emergency."

Not waiting for an answer, he strode past the other man. He carried his burden to his own room and laid her gently in the center of the bed. Then crossed the room to the cupboard and pulled out two blankets and laid them over her.

He stood looking down. She was unconscious again. In the bright sunlight, her skin appeared even paler, tinged with the pallor of death. He swore. Pouring a glass of water from the jug on the bedside table, he sank down next to her. He pulled her up, so she was leaning against the wall, and took the foil packet of pills from his pocket.

He tore one free. The tablet was small, white and bore no markings to identify what it could be. Sebastian had no clue what they were, and if they did turn out to be suicide pills, he'd be killing her. But he sensed she was running out of time, and he suspected the pills were the only thing that might save her life. He shrugged aside his doubts and put his hand to her lips. They were dry now, and he slipped a finger inside and pried open her mouth.

As she started to struggle, he put his arm around her shoulders and held her tight against him. She bit down on his finger. He swore and pulled free. Her eyes were open now, dark with pain, and she twisted so she could look into his face.

"Are you torturing me?"

"Not yet."

"I hurt. Am I dying?"

"Not if I can help it."

She smiled then, a slight curve of her lips that didn't banish the fear from her eyes. "I don't think you can."

"Sweetheart, I can do anything I want to."

"I'm not your sweetheart. I'm not anyone's sweetheart." Her tone was sad and defeated. "I'm scared," she whispered.

He had an urge to take her in his arms, hold her, tell her everything would be all right. But how could he? He'd never been any good at lying. Instead, he said, "Open your mouth."

"What?"

"Open your mouth."

This time she did as she was told, and Sebastian placed the pill on her tongue. He picked up the glass of water, put it to her lips, and she swallowed convulsively.

For a minute, he held her close, her cheek resting on his chest. Then he slipped his arm from her shoulder and laid her back on the bed, tucking the blankets around her.

Her eyes opened and captured him with her dark gaze. "Why are you being nice to me?"

"I'm not. I'm saving your life so you can tell me what you've done with my people."

"Your people—are they wolves, like you?"

He nodded.

"What's it like to be a wolf?"

Sebastian was silent for a minute as he thought about the question. He'd not become a werewolf from choice, and for many years he'd bitterly regretted what had been done to him. That was far in the past now, and he'd long ago accepted, and come to love what he was. He leaned back against the wall and tried to put his feelings into words. He talked of how it felt to be wolf, of the magic that bound the pack together, of racing through the forest under a full moon. Finally, he fell silent and glanced down. Anya was sleeping.

He rose to his feet and stared down at her. What the hell was he doing? He'd never felt like this in his life before. All his instincts screamed at him to protect her.

Unable to leave, he dragged a chair close to the bed and settled down to watch her sleep.

A light tap sounded at the door. Sebastian glanced up, sensing the restless energy of the man waiting outside the room—it looked like the doctor had arrived.

"Come in."

Connor hovered in the doorway. Six-foot-four of pent-up alpha werewolf in denial.

Five years ago, Sebastian had saved the doctor's life after an injured werewolf he'd been treating had shifted and savaged him. Connor had never seemed particularly grateful.

Now, he came when his alpha called, and he shifted at full moon when he had no choice, but otherwise he did his best to ignore the fact that he was a werewolf.

Sebastian had been there himself, and he knew Connor was fighting a losing battle. His wolf was too strong, one of the strongest Sebastian had ever encountered.

"I heard you captured an assassin," Connor said.

Sebastian nodded at the unconscious woman and Connor's eyes widened. He crossed the room, placed his bag on the floor, and sat on the bed beside her. He studied her for a moment before turning to face Sebastian.

"You want her to live?" he asked, his expression blank. "Or just well enough to talk?"

"Both," Sebastian replied. He took a deep breath. "Can you do it?"

"I have no clue what's wrong with her. If you just want her to talk, I could give her a stimulant. It would get her lucid enough to make sense."

"Will it work?"

Connor shrugged. "I can also give you something to increase her sensitivity to pain. That way, you might get her to talk before the stimulant kills her. Or you might not."

It sounded as though that option gave no guarantee they would get the information they needed, and relief flooded Sebastian. "And the alternative?"

"We try and work out what's wrong with her."

Sebastian handed him the two remaining pills. "She had these on her when we captured her. I've given her one and she seems to be resting easier."

"Maybe we should wait and see then. In the meantime, I'll get these analyzed. If I can work out what the cure is, I can take a guess at the illness." He tore off one pill and handed the other to Sebastian. "I'll check her over and take a blood sample as well, but the tests will probably take too long, so these are our best bet. If it looks like it's working, give her another when she wakes up."

Chapter Five

She wasn't dead.

That much she knew, but no more. Not where she was or how she had come to be there. Anya shifted slightly, and a sharp pain ripped through her head. So she lay still, eyes closed, until the pain faded. Her brain was fuzzy, her thoughts sticking like glue, but she had a faint memory of falling asleep with Sebastian's deep, rich voice caressing her ears.

Her back was blissfully warm, her front freezing where she'd kicked off the blankets. She rolled over, seeking the source of the warmth, and her nostrils filled with a musky, wild scent she didn't recognize. Soft, silky fur brushed against her skin, and she remembered.

Wolves.

She shifted away and half opened her eyes. A huge, silver wolf lay on the bed beside her. Head resting on its paws, eyes open; it watched her closely. Some part of her mind told her she should panic, run. Instead, as the dark blue gaze captured hers, her fear receded.

A shiver racked through her body. The wolf raised its head and inched closer on its belly, slowly, as though she was a wild creature it might startle into flight.

She was so cold and tired, and she could feel the heat emanating from the wolf. Reaching out, her fingers sank into the thick pelt. The wolf moved closer, until it lay against the length of her body, and she closed her eyes. As consciousness faded, she snuggled deeper into the warmth.

When she woke the second time, she knew she was on the mend, though she still didn't want to move. The pillow was soft under her head, and as she breathed in, her nostrils filled with a warm, masculine scent. Not what she usually woke up to. Her eyes flew open.

The dim light revealed that she was out of her cage. The room was large, with high ceilings and pale walls. The meager light shone in through two tall windows, and beyond the glass she could see the moon, just past full.

No longer cold—she was burning up.

But the fire wasn't inside her. She lay still and analyzed her immediate surroundings. A bed. A comfortable bed. Wrapped tight in blankets and spooned against something hard and scalding hot.

She'd never woken next to another person before. Then she had a faint flashback to waking earlier, and not alone, but her brain shied away from examining that memory.

She lay tucked into the curve of a large, masculine body, the whole length of him imprinted along her back. She was still fully dressed, though her own clothes were gone. In their place, she wore grey sweats and a white T-shirt.

The man was naked.

His arm curled around her, his hand splayed against her belly. Without looking, she knew it was Sebastian Quinn, wrapped around her as if he didn't want to let her go.

For long minutes, she lay unmoving. The pain in her body had dulled to a throbbing ache and her head felt clearer.

Finally, she shifted slightly, and the hand on her stomach tightened, then slid up her body to rest on the curve of her breast. She held herself immobile as his palm rubbed across her tightening nipple, and a shiver of reaction ran through her. Shock...pleasure. The thought made her pull away. He didn't attempt to hold her, and she twisted around to face him, wincing as pain shot through her skull.

His head lay on the white pillow, but his eyes were half-open, sleepy, gleaming dark blue through a thick veil of lashes. Wolf's eyes. She swallowed and forced the question out.

"Were you the wolf?" she asked.

He nodded. "You were cold. It was the easiest way to warm you up."

"I'm not cold now."

"No. But I was tired." He came up on one elbow and stared down at her, a lazy smile on his face. "And you are in my bed."

"I am?"

He nodded. "How do you feel?"

"Better. You gave me the pills?"

"One. You can have another now."

He sat up, the sheet and blankets falling to his waist. She didn't want to stare but couldn't help herself. His chest was smooth and golden, his shoulders broad, his arms sleek with muscle. He handed her a pill, and she looked down at it.

"I'll get you some water," he said.

He slipped out of the bed, seemingly unconcerned that he was naked. She wished she could be so nonchalant. Watching him walk away, the powerful muscles rippling under his skin, her breath caught in her throat. As he disappeared into the bathroom, the door swinging shut behind him, she breathed again.

She had to hold on to the thought that this man had been responsible for the death of her sister.

Maybe.

She hated the doubts that plagued her constantly. Before, things had been so easy. She'd not liked what she did, but at least she'd believed she was doing some good. Righting some wrong. Now, she could no longer deny the suspicions that clouded her mind.

What could she do? She was trapped. Without the medicine the Agency gave her, she would be dead within days.

Maybe that would be better.

But she wanted to live, to experience everything life had to offer. Her eyes flicked to the bathroom door. She desperately wanted to know what it felt like to have a man hold you in his arms, whisper words of love, tell you he—

She cut off the thought. She'd always been a dreamer, but she'd come to realize there was no place for dreams in this world.

The bathroom door opened, and the muscles clenched in her belly. If she'd thought the back view magnificent, the front was breathtaking. Her eyes slid down over the long length of his body. Golden skin, broad chest, lean abdomen. She glanced lower, and her eyes widened.

He was aroused, huge, and hard. As she stared, his cock twitched, and her gaze shot to his face.

He raised one eyebrow, glanced down and grinned. "Don't worry about it. It's a natural reaction to my waking up with a beautiful woman."

Coming to a halt beside the bed, he handed her the water. Anya reached for the glass. Their hands touched, and she jumped as a shock ran through her fingertips. She kept her eyes glued to his face as she placed the pill on her tongue and swallowed it down.

He thought her beautiful. Nobody had ever told her she was beautiful before.

She watched as he picked up a pair of jeans from the floor and pulled them on. He sank into the chair next to the bed, long legs stretched out in front of him, and regarded her, his face expressionless. She looked away and studied the room instead. His room, he'd told her. Why had he brought her here? Why hadn't he let her die?

"You're being nice," she said.

He gave her a wolfish smile. "Just until you're better."

She bit her lip. "Then what?"

"Then you tell me who you're working for and what you've done with my people."

"Are you going to make me?"

She searched his face, saw the smile slide away and his eyes turn to ice. She shivered.

"I'll do whatever I need to get my people back," he said.

The words filled her with a wild longing to be one of his people, to belong somewhere, be part of something she could believe in.

"Why not now?" She forced herself to ask.

He raised one shoulder in a casual shrug. "The doctor said it could kill you. We need you alive. You know, you could save us both a lot of bother and just tell me."

She wished she could, but while she had begun to doubt the Agency, she couldn't yet bring herself to betray the only people she had ever known. First, she needed to find proof.

"I can't," she whispered.

His eyes turned colder, his expression hardened with resolve, and a prickle of unease crawled down her spine. She turned her face from him, slid down in the bed, and curled into a ball.

He sighed audibly, but she heard him rise to his feet and cross the room. The door opened and, finally, the key clicked in the lock.

The moment he was gone, the urge to call him back hovered on her tongue. She bit down hard on her lower lip and swallowed the words. She couldn't allow herself to weaken.

She had to find a way out of here.

Chapter Six

Despite the imminent threat of torture, Anya slept again.

She woke to bright daylight. Blinking a couple of times, she realized she felt almost back to normal. She slipped out of bed. Her legs were steady as she crossed the room and tried the door. Locked.

She went to the window and peered out. Below her, a man stood on the gravel driveway, a rifle held loosely in his hands, a pistol holstered at his hip.

Anya reached out with her mind. This one wasn't shielded, and although his brain had a strange flavor, she could read his thoughts with ease. He was worried about someone called Maria. He wished he could be out searching for her instead of guarding some woman who should be locked in the cage.

She turned away and did a quick search for anything she might use as a weapon. The room was sparsely furnished—a man's room, the colors neutral, no unnecessary ornaments, but a heavy looking jug stood on the table by the bed that might come in useful.

She headed into the bathroom, drank a glass of cold water, and splashed some over her face. The shower looked tempting, but she didn't want to waste the time. She was sure she could take out the guard before he could get a shot off, and she needed to get out of there. Once they realized she was better, they were sure to return her to a more secure place, and she'd find it much harder to break out of the cage.

She went back into the bedroom and came to an abrupt halt.

Sebastian leant against the wall beside the door, still dressed only in jeans, arms folded across his chest, a grim expression on his face. A ripple of fear ran through her. She swallowed and forced herself to step further into the room.

"Feeling better?" he asked.

She swallowed, then nodded.

"Want to talk?"

"No."

"One of my men is dead."

She shook her head. What could she say?

His expression darkened. "I have to take you back to the cage." He pushed himself off from the wall and stepped toward her."

In the bright light of day, she appeared fragile, her skin pale, but she no longer looked sick, and Sebastian knew he couldn't put off questioning her any longer.

Tasha had called. She and Jack expected to get back that night, but she'd said she was getting feelings from Maria. She was in pain and weakening. Sebastian had to find out what Anya knew or lose another member of his pack.

He gritted his teeth and pulled the cuffs from his back pocket. "Turn around."

She looked at him warily but didn't move.

"Goddamn it, turn around." He grabbed her shoulder and spun her around, and she gasped. He took her right wrist and slipped on the cuff, then her left. He pushed her to her knees, and she didn't fight him. Part of him wished she would.

She knelt on the wood floor, her head bowed, her blond hair loose around her shoulders. He pressed his fingers to his skull and took a deep breath. "Don't make me do this, Anya."

At the use of her name, her gaze lifted, and she blinked up at him. "You must do what you have to do."

"Is that why you do what you do? Because you have to? Do they have something on you?"

She shook her head, her teeth worrying at her lower lip. "It doesn't matter."

Frustration tore at him. Why couldn't she give in?

"You know," he said, "everyone breaks in the end. Why make this hard on yourself?"

She studied him out of those golden eyes. "Would you break?" she asked, and her tone held genuine curiosity.

He opened his mouth, but found he couldn't lie to her, and closed it again. He shoved his hands in his pockets and turned from her to stare out of the window. "No."

When he turned back, she shrugged helplessly, and his anger mounted, tinged with a sense of helplessness he had never experienced.

She called to something deep inside him; something he hadn't even known existed. Holding her in his arms through the long night had felt so right. How was he supposed to take her downstairs and hurt her? Cause her pain and keep on causing her pain until she talked. Everything screamed at him that it was wrong.

He had to find some other way to get through to her. He sank down onto the bed behind him and ran his hands through his hair. Maybe he needed to remind himself of what was at stake here. And maybe make her see his people as real and not just targets she had been ordered to acquire.

"Jonas was the youngest of us—he was only twenty-two."

"Jonas?"

"He's the first of my people you took." He pictured the boy in his mind, Tall and lanky, with overlong dark blond hair that fell into his eyes. Always so eager. "Four years ago, he was turned against his will by a lone wolf. He was almost out of control when we found him, but he was a sweet kid, and he's worked hard to fit in. And now he's dead. He didn't deserve that."

"I'm sorry."

"Are you?" He sighed. "Maria is older—she's the second of my people you took—almost as old as me. She changed voluntarily because she fell in love with a werewolf. He was killed in a turf war. and she moved here to get away from the memories. She's strong and powerful and she won't break easily. In fact she'll die before she breaks."

Anya looked away and he jumped up, then hunkered down beside her, he took her chin in a fierce grip and forced her to face him.

"It's too late for Jonas. But not for Maria and Travis. There's still a chance to save them. Only you can help me do that."

"I can't help you." She blinked, her eyes bright with unshed tears, and his heart twisted.

"You cry for them, but you won't tell me where they are?"

"I can't."

He dropped his hold of her chin and straightened. He had to get out of there. And somehow, he needed to find the strength to make her talk. At the door he glanced back. She hadn't moved and appeared so vulnerable with her hands bound behind her. Without giving himself time to think, he crossed back, crouched behind her, and unlocked the cuffs.

Then he stalked out and slammed the door behind him.

Chapter Seven

Sebastian let himself into his office and flung himself into the leather chair behind his desk. Opening the drawer he pulled out the bottle of whiskey he kept there. He took a long pull from the bottle and sank back and stared at the ceiling.

Someone cleared their throat and he glanced through the open door. Connor stood in the doorway.

"Is she awake? he asked.

"Yes."

"Has she talked yet?"

"No."

Connor raised an eyebrow, then shrugged. "I've got the drug I mentioned. It will increase her sensitivity to pain. Might make her talk if you haven't managed yet."

"Will it do any permanent damage?"

"On its own, it shouldn't. You just inject straight into the muscle." He reached into his pocket and pulled out a small case. Flicking open the lid, he showed Sebastian the contents. Three syringes filled with a pale green liquid. He placed the case on the desk in front of him. "I'll be off then."

He turned and left the room. Sebastian stared at the case. Acid burned at the back of his throat and he closed his eyes and forced up an image of Maria. Rising to his feet, he picked up the case, and headed back up the stairs.

He hesitated at the door and the unlocked it and pushed it open.

She was sitting on the floor, where he'd left her, arms wrapped around her knees. But she pushed herself to her feet as he entered. Her eyes were dry now and wary, darting to the case he held in his hand.

He placed it on the dressing table and just resisted the urge to wipe his hands down his jeans. Christ, he didn't want to do this.

For a minute, he stood staring at her, his eyes narrowing at the flicker of awareness that flashed across her face.

He stalked towards her. She backed away but came up against the edge of the bed, and he reached out and clasped her upper arms. His fingers tightened to give her a brief feel of the inhuman strength in his grip.

"You can't fight me."

"I won't. Do what you have to do."

She licked her lips with her small pink tongue, and the heat that coiled in his belly was like a physical pain.

Without conscious thought, he leaned down and pressed his lips to hers. She didn't fight him, and he gave in to the urge he'd been battling since the first moment he saw her. He kissed her savagely. His tongue thrust inside her mouth and found her hot and wet and sweet. For a minute, he lost himself in the taste of her. Then her tongue fluttered tentatively against his, and the heat inside him burst into flames.

Her body moved against him now, her hands gripping his shoulders, her hips pushing into his. She wanted him, and the knowledge sent a wave of relief washing through him.

Perhaps this was how to reach her. His grip tightened on her arms, and he picked her up and tossed her on the bed. He stood, looking down. Her pale skin was flushed now, her lips parted, swollen from his kisses and trembling. He needed to taste her again, and he dropped to the bed beside her, came down over her, his arms braced on either side of her shoulders. He lowered himself, until his face was close to hers, and her breath shivered across his skin.

"Tell me to stop," he muttered against her mouth.

She went still beneath him, and he pulled away so he could look down into her eyes. They were wide, bewildered. "I should," she said. "But I can't."

"Then tell me what I need to know, and *I'll* stop."

He knew it was a lie. Only she had the power to bring this to a halt now, but she made no move to stop him. Instead, she reached up and curled her fingers in the hair at the back of his neck, pulling him down to her.

Oh, God, what was he doing?

This woman was his enemy, his pack's enemy, but he couldn't resist her as her mouth opened under his. He kissed her for long minutes. His tongue pushed into the moist heat of her mouth, and he tasted again the sweetness of her. Her tongue stroked against his like warm wet velvet fueling the fire inside him. His balls ached viciously, and his cock was already rock hard inside the confines of his jeans.

Sebastian tore his mouth from hers and raised himself up on his elbows, staring down into her wide-open eyes. He lowered his body until his hips pressed into her stomach then ground his erection into the softness of her. She went still beneath him.

Anya drowned in the dark sensual promise of his eyes, in the hard erotic promise of his body.

He wanted her.

This wasn't some trick to make her talk. This was genuine desire, and the realization flooded her mind and body with heat.

She'd had lovers before. Guards at the Agency, but she'd never been sure that they weren't acting under orders. They had all been shielded, and she was unable to read their thoughts. She'd taken them anyway, because she needed something to stave off the loneliness. But she had never wanted any of them like this, had never suffered when they had left her, as they always did.

Now, here was another man, also shielded, but his thoughts weren't hidden from her. They were plain on his face. Hunger and need. Guilt and desperation.

She recognized the emotions because they reflected her own. She wanted this so much it was a pain clawing at her insides.

How could she?

But even as the questions raced through her mind, her body melted beneath him.

He slipped a knee between her legs, separating them, so he could sink into the V between her thighs. He rotated his narrow hips against her core, and heat pooled at the center of her body. A low moan escaped her lips.

"Tell me to stop," he said again. She shook her head mutely.

At the back of her mind, a small voice whispered that this was her chance to get him off guard, make her move. Escape. And she would. Soon.

First, she needed to know what his skin felt like, what he tasted of.

She looked up into his sensual face as he pressed into her, sending a wave of pleasure crashing through her body. Pushing back against him, she rubbed her hips against his shaft, trying to get some relief from the pressure building inside her.

His eyes closed as he groaned.

The realization that she could bring him pleasure heated her skin. She didn't want to lay here, quiescent. She wanted to be the one in control.

She moved suddenly, shoving him onto his back and rolling on top of him in one fluid move. His eyes shot open. For a moment, she though he meant to fight her, then he relaxed back and watched her through narrowed eyes.

Anya straddled his lean hips then lowered herself onto him, a knee on either side. She stared into his face.

"Let me touch you?" she said.

Heat flushed his sharp cheekbones. He nodded.

Her hand reached out and splayed across the hard wall of his chest. His skin was smooth and hot, and she ran her fingers over the swell of muscle, laid her palm flat against him and felt the thud of his heart.

A sense of urgency filled her, to feel his skin against hers.

She pulled the T-shirt over her head and tossed it to the floor. Her bra followed. He watched her through half closed eyes as she leaned over and rubbed her bare nipples across his chest. They tightened into hard little buds, so sensitive that each brush across his skin sent ripples of pleasure shooting through her. Still she needed more. She raised herself up, so her nipples grazed his face. His lips parted, and he licked a long slow swipe across her breast, before drawing one taut peak into the warmth of his mouth, suckling her.

A pulse throbbed between her thighs; her sex swollen and wet, as her insides turned molten and threatened to slide from her body.

She pulled back before she lost all control, sat on her heels and looked down at him. The hard line of his erection pressed against the material of his jeans, and she traced it with one finger.

He groaned as she opened the button and lowered the zipper, so he sprang free, thick and full. The skin was taut like satin, pale and silky, the head rosy and flushed with blood. It pulsed and twitched with a life of its own.

She shifted down the bed, so she could reach him with her mouth. Leaning close to him, she paused and flicked a quick glance up the long line of his body, to his face. The skin was stretched tight across his cheekbones, and his dark eyes gleamed from behind his thick lashes. As she stared, he shifted beneath her, and she pressed a palm to his chest and pushed him down.

She blew gently over his swollen shaft, then kissed him lightly on the tip. Her tongue flicked out. He tasted salty, and she rolled her tongue around the rim, reveling in the warm musky scent that filled her nostrils.

She was drowning in the taste of him, hovering on the brink of losing all control. First, she needed to make *him* lose control. Drawing the engorged tip into her mouth, she sucked gently and heard the indrawn hiss of his breath. His hips rose beneath her, thrusting more of him into her mouth until he filled her. She sucked harder, loving the tension that filled his body, the knowledge that she held him on the edge.

Her hands moved down to cup his balls. She squeezed, and he exploded. He gripped the back of her head, holding her against him while his hips jerked, spilling his seed into her, and she swallowed convulsively.

Finally, his body lay still, and his tight grip loosened. His warm hand smoothed down over her neck as a lazy, rueful smile curved his mouth.

"I didn't mean for that to happen," he said.

She licked her lips. "I did."

"Just give me a minute to recover."

"A minute?"

"Maybe two. In the meantime…"

His hands clasped her waist, and he lifted and turned her, so he straddled her hips and she lay beneath him once more.

"My turn," he murmured.

He leaned down and kissed her lips then trailed light kisses across her cheek. His warm breath tickled her neck as the tip of his tongue traced patterns on her ears, down the line of her throat. He kissed her collarbone, moved lower, and her nipples tightened beneath his heated gaze, sending darts of pleasure shooting to her belly and lower. A slow smile curled his lips. Reaching out, he trailed one long finger over her breasts. He plucked at her nipples with his finger and thumb, then bent his head, took one tight little bud into his mouth and bit down.

The sensation blew her mind.

He kissed her stomach, his tongue dipping into her navel, swirling patterns on her skin, and she was almost overwhelmed by the exquisite pleasure. He pushed down the waistband on her pants, and his mouth moved lower.

She had to act now, before she lost it completely. Before she decided never to go back, to stay here with this man for whatever time she had left. Her thoughts warred with the feel of his mouth moving over her skin, moving closer to the core of her desire.

But even from the short time she had known him, she'd perceived that Sebastian was a man who would honor his responsibilities. Soon, he would come to his senses, remember his missing people.

And she couldn't hold that against him.

But it meant she had to go now, before she was completely undone, before she gave in and told him anything he wanted to hear.

Anya took a deep, calming breath. Staring over his shoulder, she focused her powers on the heavy stone jug that stood on the bedside table. The jug lifted easily, flew through the air, and crashed down on the back of Sebastian's skull.

His eyes widened, filled with confusion. A shudder ran through his body, and he collapsed on top of her.

Anya lay beneath him, unmoving. Her face was wet, and she realized she was crying silently into his shoulder. After a minute, she swallowed her tears and pushed her hands against his chest. She dragged herself from under him and stumbled to her feet.

With trembling fingers, she picked up her bra and T-shirt and pulled them on.

She rubbed her hand across her face and turned to go. At the door, she paused and looked back. She tiptoed to the bed and sank down beside him, picking up the pieces of the broken jug scattered around his head.

She stroked the silky hair back from his cheek. It occurred to her, fleetingly, that she could quite easily complete her mission now. He was helpless. All she needed to do was open the vein in his throat, and his life would drain away. She traced her nail down along the faint blue line. Beneath her fingertip, she could feel the throb of his life force. So fragile.

She stood up abruptly. This time she didn't stop at the door.

Chapter Eight

The walls were closing in on her.

Since she'd got back to the Agency, Anya hadn't been able to shake the feeling of being trapped. A sense of evil hung about this place. She'd done her best to ignore it in the past, but now the doubts that had plagued her so long crystallized into hard, cold certainty.

Everything inside her screamed that Sebastian was not the immoral mercenary the Agency made him out to be. She might not have been able to read his mind, but she'd sensed his innate strength and goodness. He was like the moonlight his people loved, a bright light in the darkness of night. Whatever else she did with her life, she knew she had to right the wrongs she had done to him and his pack.

She'd told her handlers that Sebastian was dead.

The lie wouldn't hold up for long, but she hadn't wanted to reveal that she had left him alive. If she'd admitted to the failure of her latest mission, she was unsure how the Agency would react, and she needed her freedom—however limited it was.

Unfortunately, that freedom did not include access to the lower levels of the building where prisoners were kept.

As darkness fell, she sat in her room on the ground floor, staring through the bars of her window. She sensed the people as they left the building, forced herself to wait until only the nighttime guards remained. She knew where they were stationed and chose her route to avoid them, gliding through the corridors.

Halting around the corner from the elevator, she opened the top two buttons of her shirt, and took a deep breath.

The guard looked up as she approached, every muscle alert, but he relaxed as he recognized Anya. "Hi," he said. "What are you doing up so late?"

She shrugged. "I couldn't sleep. Still hyped up from the job. I needed someone to..." she paused and curved her lips into a smile. "...talk to."

His eyes flickered over her, lingering on the swell of her breasts and the expanse of cleavage revealed by the open shirt.

"Well, you can *talk* to me anytime, babe."

She stepped up close and reached out a hand, pressing her palm against his chest, and felt the thud of his heart accelerate beneath her fingers. Sliding her hand up over his shoulder, she curled her fingers around his throat, found the pressure point, and squeezed.

Grabbing him as he fell, she lowered his unconscious body to the ground. She frisked him quickly, took his gun and shoved it down the back of her pants, then used his own cuffs to secure his hands in front of him. He wore a keycard round his neck, and she broke the chain and sent a silent prayer that the card would give her access to the cells below.

Her skin prickled as the elevator descended deep beneath the ground, and she swallowed the nausea that rose in her throat. She'd spent five years of her life down here, imprisoned in one of the cells beneath the Agency.

Up until the age of eleven, her life hadn't been so bad. She'd had people who looked after her, taught her, and a certain amount of freedom. Then her powers had emerged. At that point, the Agency hadn't yet developed the shielding technology, and they obviously hadn't wanted her reading their minds. They'd locked her down here, her only contact with guards who knew nothing. Even so, the brief glimpses into their minds had terrified her. Their thoughts made her stomach churn with fear and revulsion, and she'd soon learned to block them from her mind.

She hadn't seen the sun again until she was sixteen, and by that time, she would have done anything to survive, to stay out of that cell. So she'd done what she was told, become what they wanted her to be.

It had taken her seven long years to realize that however much she wanted to live, sometimes the price was too high.

The elevator came to a halt, and she shook her head, dispersing the memories.

Down here, the walls were bare concrete with bright strip lighting. The miasma of evil was stronger; the scent of despair and death saturating the air and clinging to the walls. Anya stood for a moment, unsure which way to go, when a low moan echoed down the empty corridor. She followed the sound, coming to a halt in front of a steel door. A small glass window in the front allowed her to peer inside. A woman huddled beneath a blanket on the small cot, motionless. Maria?

Anya moved on to the next cell where a man sat hunched on the bed, hands dangling between his knees.

The stolen keycard slid easily into the slot, and the lock clicked open.

The man glanced up as she pushed open the door, but he didn't rise. His dark eyes were dulled by pain and fatigue. Reaching into his mind, she found him unshielded, and she could sense the wolf lurking deep inside. His thoughts were slow, sluggish. He believed her another come to torment him, force him to shift. He hoped he could hold out. He wished they would torture him rather than make him listen while they tortured Maria.

"Sebastian sent me," Anya said quickly.

A light flickered in his eyes. "Sebastian's here?"

She shook her head. "No, but you're getting out. Follow me."

She turned and left the cell without waiting for an answer, then opened the next door along and stepped inside. The air was thick with the acrid scent of blood. She crossed to the small cot and crouched down beside it, brushing the woman's long dark hair from her face. She moaned and curled into a ball, hugging the thin grey blanket around her naked form, but Anya caught a glimpse of the scars that crisscrossed her body, many still seeping blood.

"She's alive?" A voice asked from the doorway.

Anya nodded. "You need to wake her."

He crossed the room and sank onto the mattress, resting a hand on the woman's shoulder. "I could hear her screaming. They told me they would stop if I shifted."

Anya straightened and stepped away to give him more room. "Did you?"

He shook his head. "It's one of our most sacred laws. We never change in front of humans. We never give up our secrets."

"Will she be okay?"

He nodded. "We heal pretty fast, and she can shift once we're out of the building."

"Will that help?"

"It heals most things." He squeezed the woman's shoulder. "Maria, wake up. We're getting out of here."

Her eyes remained closed. Her face was a mass of bruises, her lower lip swollen where she had bitten through. He shook her gently, and at last, her eyes flickered open.

She licked her lip, wincing. "Travis," she said. "What's happening?" She looked around her, her eyes settling on Anya. "Who are you?"

"It doesn't matter," Anya replied. "Can you walk?"

Maria wrapped the blanket around herself and struggled to her feet. She swayed and put a hand out to balance herself against the wall. Anya watched as the other woman gathered her strength and nodded grimly.

"What about Jonas?" Travis asked. "The other man. He was taken before me."

"He's dead."

"I thought he must be, but I hoped…" Travis rubbed his hand over his eyes. "Why? What is this place? What do they want with us?"

"They kept asking me about Natasha," Maria said. "Where was she? Was she alive?"

"Did you tell them?" he asked.

"Of course not." Her voice was full of scorn.

Anya had gone still at the name. "Natasha?"

Maria looked at her, suspicion flaring in her eyes. "Who *are* you?" she asked again.

"Sebastian sent her," Travis answered.

Maria frowned. "How do we know she's telling the truth? It could be some trick to get us to talk."

Anya didn't answer the accusation. Instead, she reached into Maria's mind and saw the image of a woman, tiny with long red hair and golden eyes. "Natasha—she's not dead?"

She plucked the answer from Maria's mind. *No.*

"Where is she?"

She read the answers with ease. Natasha was in Russia with her husband, and she was one of them—a werewolf. Anya saw an image of a red wolf running through the forest, and a sense of wonder filled her. Natasha was beautiful, and she was free.

The last of her doubts vanished, and she turned away to hide the tears that threatened to spill over. "Follow me," she said. "We have to get you out of here."

Why had the Agency lied to her? Why had they told her Natasha was dead? Was it merely to send her against Sebastian? But she suspected it had to be more than that. They must have known she had doubts, had probably guessed that she dreamed of leaving this place, of finding her family.

By telling her she had a sister and that the sister was dead, murdered, they had isolated her, taken away one of the main reasons for her wanting to leave.

The thoughts whirled in her head as she led the two werewolves down the dark corridors. Maria seemed to gain strength with each step she took and soon she was walking unaided.

Anya stopped by a small ground floor window at the back of the building, and she turned to face Travis.

"The alarm will go off when I break the window. You'll have about two minutes to reach the perimeter." She pulled the gun from out of her pants and held it out to him. "Here, take this."

He shook his head. "Keep it. We'll shift as soon as we're out of here."

"Wait until you're over the wall," Anya said. "There are cameras inside the grounds."

He looked at her closely. "You're not coming with us?"

"I can't. I have something I need to finish here."

"Okay and thank you. We owe you a debt." He turned back to the window.

"Wait," Anya said.

Travis and Maria both turned to look at her.

Anya bit her lip. "Tell Natasha that I would have liked to meet her."

"Who are you?" Maria asked again.

This time Anya answered. "I'm Natasha's sister."

Without waiting for a reply, she raised the pistol and smashed the glass, knocking out the jagged edges. Immediately, the shrill ring of the alarms filled her ears. "Go!"

Maria scrambled through the window, dropping to the soft grass below. Travis followed. He glanced up once, then they were both away. Racing across the lawn. It was only a hundred yards to the wall and within seconds they were over and had vanished into the night. Anya stood for a moment until she heard the howl of a wolf then she turned and hurried away.

Natasha was alive, and Anya wanted to live so badly it burned a fiery pit in her chest. She had only one chance—to find a supply of the medicine they gave her. If she found the pills, it would buy her some time; without them, she would be dead within days. She remembered Sebastian saying he had given one to a doctor for analysis. Maybe they would find something. Maybe they would help her. But how likely was that? She might have saved two of his people tonight, but she had also caused the death of one of them. Jonas had died because of her. Sebastian would never forgive her for that.

She made her way back to the medical center. In the distance, she could hear the thud of booted feet. They'd go first to the window where the breach had been, but she didn't have long.

She forced down the panic and looked around her. Where would they keep them? She started on the overhead cabinets, methodically taking out tubes and bottles, tossing them on the floor behind her when they proved useless. By the time she'd finished the cabinets, her panic was rising again. She emptied whole drawers onto the floor, crouched down and pawed through the contents, but found nothing. They had to be here somewhere.

The door clicked open.

Anya whirled around, reaching for the pistol.

Too late. She stared into the barrel of a gun and watched as the finger tightened on the trigger.

Chapter Nine

"She's still alive," Tasha said.

At her words, Sebastian paused his pacing of the office and turned to face her. "Sorry?"

"Maria. She's still alive. I can sense her."

He should have felt relief, but nothing could ease the black guilt that saturated his mind. Maria might be alive now, but for how long? They were no closer to finding where she had been taken, and he'd allowed the one person who might have had that information to escape.

Tasha perched on the edge of the sofa, nibbling on her lower lip. "It's not your fault."

"Yes, it is."

She opened her mouth to argue, but Jack spoke first. "He's right—it is his fault." He shook his head, his green eyes mocking. "How the hell did this woman manage to knock you out?"

Sebastian had no clue. He'd swear the jug had been nowhere near her hand, but then his mind had been on other things. He had a flashback to the feel of her hot wet mouth engulfing his cock. The sweet taste of her on his tongue.

Even now, he couldn't get her out of his mind. He shifted uncomfortably.

"Ahh," Jack said. "That's how."

"Am I missing something?" Tasha asked.

"At a guess, your esteemed alpha allowed his dick to overrule his brain." Jack studied Sebastian, one eyebrow raised. "I'd like to meet this woman."

Sebastian scowled. "Well, it doesn't look as though that's going to happen any time soon."

The front door slammed. A moment later, Riley hurried into the room, closely followed by Travis and Maria, both dressed in grey sweatpants and matching T-shirts. Clothes left in the foyer for any returning wolves.

Sebastian leapt to his feet, the tight band around his chest easing. Maria looked a mess, her whole body drooping with exhaustion, but she was alive. She was also staring at Natasha, a curious look in her eyes.

"Sit down," Sebastian ordered.

The two sank side by side onto the sofa, and Riley handed them both a drink.

"Now tell me what happened," Sebastian said.

Travis swallowed his beer in one gulp then looked at Sebastian. He appeared surprised at the question. "Weren't you expecting us?"

"Why would I be expecting you?"

"You sent the woman to get us out of there."

"I didn't send anyone. We didn't even know where you were being held."

Travis frowned. "She told me you'd sent her. Why would she lie about that?"

"So we would go with her," Maria answered the question.

"What did she look like?" Sebastian asked.

"Tall, slender, long blond hair."

Sebastian's whole body stiffened as a wave of hope washed through him. "Anya." It had to be Anya, but nothing made sense. Why would she knock him out, then go back and rescue his people?

"Who's Anya?" Tasha asked.

Maria looked at her strangely. "She said she was your sister."

Tasha jumped to her feet. "What?" She spun around to face Sebastian. "Did you know?"

"Not the sister bit. Anya is the assassin who tried to kill me." Sebastian ran a hand through his hair. It was beginning to make sense. Not good sense, but sense. "We've been following leads to find your family," he said, getting the thoughts straight as he spoke. "We'd traced them to an organization called the Agency that we've been investigating for years. They're a private company, but big, with connections everywhere, including the military and the government. My guess is we got too close, and they picked up that they were being investigated. They sent someone to take out pack members. Then two nights ago they sent an assassin to kill me."

"Well, they obviously didn't succeed," Jack drawled.

"We were ready for them and managed to capture the shooter. It was a woman. Her name was Anya."

"And you let her seduce you, knock you on the head, and escape." Jack's tone held disbelief.

Sebastian stared at him through narrowed eyes. "It wasn't quite like that."

"So how was it?"

Sebastian sat in silence for a moment. Tasha came to stand beside him; she put a hand on his arm, and he stared up into those golden eyes. Eyes filled with hope. "Tell me about her," she said.

He took a deep breath. "She was ill. I don't know what was wrong with her, but I took her out of the cage..."

"Why?" Jack asked.

"I thought she was dying. Nobody should die in a cage. Connor didn't know what was wrong with her, but she had some pills. I gave them to her, and she seemed to get better. She wouldn't talk though. Wouldn't tell me where they were keeping the pack members they'd taken." He crossed the room and poured himself a drink, came back to stand before Tasha. "Then you told me Jonas was dead. I was going to make her talk. Do whatever I had to."

Jack smirked. "So you thought you'd fuck her, and she'd be so impressed that she'd tell you everything. Instead, she whacked you over the head and got away. How the hell did you let that happen?"

Sebastian frowned. He thought back to that last memory of her. His head between her thighs, the taste of her on his tongue, her hands curled into his hair, gripping his skull. Both hands. It didn't make sense. How could she have hit him? "I don't know," he said slowly. "I'd swear she couldn't have hit me, but something did. A jug actually, a stone jug, but it was on a table across the room. How… " He broke off and shook his head.

"Telekinesis," Natasha said.

"What?"

"When I was a prisoner at the Facility, they did tests on me. Tried to make me move things with my mind. I could never do it. But maybe my sister can."

"Christ," Sebastian muttered.

"So is she working with them?" Jack asked.

"She must be," Sebastian replied. "She was good, and she'd been well trained. If we hadn't been expecting her, she would have taken me out."

"If she works for the Agency, why did she free Maria and Travis? And if she changed her mind, wanted out, why didn't she come with them?"

"She said she had something she needed to finish," Travis said.

"What?"

Sebastian could hear the frustration in Tasha's voice.

Travis shrugged. "She also said to tell you that she would have liked to know you. It didn't sound as though she was expecting to see you anytime soon. If at all."

Sebastian heard the words, and fear trickled down his spine.

The Agency had to know she'd helped his wolves escape. And from what he had learned of them, they were a ruthless organization and would not take her betrayal lightly. Was she already dead? His whole mind rejected the idea.

Tasha had dropped into the chair behind her. "Oh, God. Why didn't she come back? Why did she have to stay behind?"

Her question echoed Sebastian's thoughts. Had she stayed because she was afraid of Sebastian? That he would want revenge for her escape?

Jack went to his wife, picked her up and sat with her in his lap. He stroked the long red hair from her face and murmured to her. "We'll find her. We'll get her back."

"How?"

"We know where she is," Sebastian said.

"Yes," Jack replied. "But unfortunately, they know we know. We're going to have to move fast, or we'll get there and find them gone."

"There's another scenario. They know who and where we are. They've come after me once. These guys have an army at their disposal. What's to stop them coming after us first?"

"Would they risk the exposure?"

Sebastian shrugged. "They know what we are, that we won't involve the authorities in this. I think they'll come after us here." He stood thinking for a moment. "Riley, I want you to get everybody out. Take Maria, but we'll need Travis to lead us back there. Leave somebody out in the woods to watch this place. I want to know if anything happens."

"Where do you want us to go?"

"You can go to my place in the city," Jack said. "It will be safe. Tasha will go with you."

"No, I won't."

Jack looked at her, something passed between the two of them, and he nodded.

"Okay, let's get out of here."

Sebastian's cell phone rang. He listened for a moment then shoved it in his pants pocket. "I think we're too late. There's a breach on the perimeter wall. It looks like they're already here."

Then the world exploded in a ball of light.

Chapter Ten

Anya lay on her back on the table, the steel icy cold against her spine. She wasn't restrained in any way, but she couldn't move. They'd given her some sort of drug, and she'd lost all track of time. Now, her mind was alert, but her body refused to obey. She could turn her head slightly, but beyond that... nothing. Clamping her eyes tight closed, she tried to control the panic that clawed at her insides.

All around, she could hear movement. They were tearing the Agency down, moving out. Of course, they would presume their location must now be known.

Soft footsteps crossed the tiled floor. They stopped beside her. "I know you're awake, Anya."

She opened her eyes. Dr. Latham stood looking down at her. She'd always thought he had the coldest eyes she had ever seen, pale blue like ice.

"You can speak. Why did you do it? Why did you let them go?"

She tried to shake her head, but still couldn't move. She swallowed. "You lied to me. You told me my sister had been murdered."

"So your sister is alive? We weren't sure."

The question gave her hope. They'd been asking Maria about Natasha, so it was obvious they didn't know where her sister was.

He studied her for a moment. "We did it for your own good. You were obsessed with finding her. In hindsight, it was a mistake to tell you about her existence."

"Why did you?"

"You were becoming depressed. We believed it would give you something to live for. We hoped to regain your loyalty. You were a valuable asset. We didn't want to lose you."

An asset. Anya winced at the word. That was all she had ever been to the Agency. This man had known her from the moment she was born, but he still didn't see her as a person.

"So what else have you lied about?" Latham asked. "Is Sebastian Quinn really dead?"

She didn't answer, and he shrugged.

"It doesn't matter anyway. We sent a team to take them out. I just got a message that the house has been destroyed."

A wave of anguish swept through her. Sebastian couldn't be dead. He'd been more alive than anyone she had ever known. She took a deep breath and forced her grief aside—she couldn't afford it right now. Because maybe her sister was still alive—Maria had believed Natasha was in Russia. Surely far enough away to be out of the Agency's reach. Maybe there was still a chance Anya could escape? Find her sister and finally, find somewhere to belong.

"Where are you taking me?" she asked.

"I'm not taking you anywhere."

Latham reached out a hand and stroked a finger down her face. She flinched.

"It's a pity," he said. "You hold a certain sentimental value for me. You were the first of my creations. It's why I kept you alive for so long. Now I'm afraid you've outlived your usefulness, and we can no longer trust you." He smiled then, but his eyes remained cold. "Well, almost outlived your usefulness. I'm sure we can learn some interesting facts from studying your brain."

She looked beyond him. A medical cooler box stood on the table beside him. Suddenly she realized what he meant to do. She struggled to move, but the drug held her bound.

"Don't worry, you won't feel a thing." He was right. She felt nothing as he slipped the needle into the vein at her wrist.

She watched, despair flooding her mind as he depressed the plunger.

As the light faded, gunshots sounded in the corridor outside. Something moved in the open doorway. Anya rolled her eyes to look, and hope filled her mind, as the darkness took her.

Sebastian leapt across the room. He knocked Latham to the floor and stared down at the woman on the steel table. Her eyes were closed. He could see no sign of life. He laid his hand on her throat and felt not the slightest flicker, though her skin was still warm.

"You're too late—she's dead," the man spoke from the floor.

Sebastian growled low in his throat. "What have you done to her?" A red haze of rage covered his vision, fury surged through his body, and his wolf rose within him. He dropped to his knees and grabbed the man around the throat, shaking him. "What have you done?"

"Sebastian, leave him."

Jack's voice cut through the fog of rage.

"Sebastian! Connor is here. He'll help her, but we might need Latham alive."

He looked up to see Connor leaning over Anya's body. Forcing down his fury, he loosened his grip on Latham's throat and rose to his feet.

"Can you do anything?"

Connor picked up a bottle from the table beside them and read the label. He nodded. "I think so." He turned to Jack. "Pass me my bag."

He rummaged through the contents and came out with a syringe. "Open her shirt," he said to Sebastian. "Quickly. This has to go direct to the heart."

Sebastian tore open the buttons and spread the shirt. He didn't breathe as Connor rubbed one finger down her chest, over the gentle swell of her breast, feeling for the gap between the ribs. He held up the syringe and stabbed it into her heart, depressing the plunger in one swift move.

For a moment, nothing happened. Sebastian swallowed the fear rising inside him. But as he reached out to shake her, her whole body convulsed. Her spine arched, and she came up off the table, then collapsed back and her eyes opened. She stared around; her gaze caught Sebastian and held him.

"You're alive," she whispered.

Relief washed through him. "So are you." He grinned. "Was I supposed to be dead?"

"Latham said…" She paused. "It doesn't matter." Her gaze left him and fixed on someone behind him. Her eyes widened in wonder.

He turned to see Tasha standing beside him. She reached out a hand and touched Anya's cheek. "I'm Tasha."

Something passed between the two women. Anya managed a faint curve of her lips. "I'm Anya."

She closed her eyes. Sebastian stroked her cheek and glanced across at Connor. "Is she going to be all right?"

"She should be. Maybe a little weak for a while, but once the drugs clear her system, she'll be fine."

Anya's eyes blinked open and for a moment horror flared in the golden depths. "He was taking my brain." A tear trickled down her cheek. "He was going to dissect my brain."

"Shh," Sebastian murmured. He wiped the tear with the pad of his thumb. "He can't do anything anymore."

She relaxed then, the tension draining from her body as she faded into unconsciousness once more. Fear clamped his heart in a vice-like grip, and he turned to Connor.

"Don't panic. She's just asleep," Connor said.

Sebastian exhaled and nodded. "Get back to the house," he said. "They might need you."

He watched as Connor left the room then turned to look at Latham who lay on the floor, Jack standing guard over him. Sebastian's fists clenched as a black wave of hatred rose inside him. He crossed the room and kicked Latham savagely in the side. "That's for Anya," he said. He kicked him again, feeling the crunch of ribs. "And that's for my goddamn house."

"Sebastian."

At Jack's softly spoken word, he hesitated, then turned to stare at the vampire. "Jonas is dead, and we still don't know how bad it is back at the house, and this man is responsible."

They'd managed to take out the unit sent after them, but not before the house had been destroyed. Tasha was sure none of his people were dead, but there were still some trapped in the rubble.

"I know, but we should get out of here."

Sebastian cast another look of loathing at Latham, who lay moaning, clutching at his ribs. "Kill him," he growled.

Jack pursed his lips. "He might be able to tell us something. Tasha still might have family out there."

Sebastian wanted the man to die. Now. He'd been going to take Anya's brain. If they'd been even minutes later...

He forced himself to think straight, put aside his personal feelings. "Tasha, it's your choice."

Tasha turned from where she still hovered over Anya. She peered at Latham, and Sebastian could see his own hatred reflected in her eyes. She bit her lip. "I want to see him die so badly, that I can taste it. But you're right—he might be able to tell us something. I suppose we should take him with us."

Sebastian's gaze searched the room for something to tie him with, but before he could move, Latham pulled a gun from inside his coat.

Sebastian went still, every muscle tensing. The gun wasn't aimed at him or Jack, but at Tasha where she stood hovering over her sister. Beside him, he heard a low growl rumble from Jack's throat.

"I'll shoot her," Latham said. "Back off, let me go, and she'll live."

Sebastian held himself rigid. He glanced sideways at Jack and saw the darkness rise up in the vampire's eyes. Jack nodded, an almost invisible movement of his head, and moved in a blur of speed.

At the same time, Sebastian leapt towards Tasha, grabbing her and hurling her to the floor. A gun roared, and a sharp pain sliced through his side. He turned. Jack no longer appeared human, his eyes burning with green fire, his lips drawn back revealing razor sharp fangs. He had Latham in a death grip, arms around his chest, pulling him back against his body. The gun clattered to the floor, but it was too late to save Latham now. Jack wrenched back his head and lunged, ripping out his jugular, spraying crimson blood across the white-tiled walls, filling the room with the heavy, coppery scent of blood.

Jack spat and released the body. It crumpled to the floor at his feet.

Sebastian stared for a long moment, but Latham was clearly dead; his throat ripped out, his eyes staring. He turned his gaze to Jack. "Right then, we'll question him later, shall we?"

Jack stared back, the darkness still glowing behind his eyes, and Sebastian tensed his muscles ready for the attack. Then a shiver ran through the vampire, the muscles of his face relaxed, and he looked away.

Releasing his breath, Sebastian pressed a hand to his side; his palm came away stained crimson.

Jack crossed to where Tasha lay on the floor and crouched down beside her. "Are you okay?"

She nodded. "I don't think Sebastian is though."

They both turned to look at him.

"It's nothing. I think." He stripped off his shirt. The bullet had entered through his back, close to his waist and exited through his front. He wiped the blood away with his shirt. The wound was bleeding copiously, but he didn't think anything important had been hit. "I'll be fine once I shift."

He moved to the table where Anya lay, still unconscious.

"I'll take her," Jack said.

"No, I will."

He scooped her up, ignoring the twinge in his side, and held her close against his chest. "Let's get the fuck out of here."

Chapter Eleven

She wasn't dead.

It was becoming a recurring thought on waking. Anya lay completely still. Afraid to try to move in case she couldn't. Afraid to open her eyes in case she saw something she really didn't want to see.

What had happened? Latham was going to take her brain. Cut her up. Her eyes flew open, and she stared at the ceiling.

"Anya?"

She recognized the voice, and her heart rate kicked up. Sebastian Quinn. Rolling her head to the side, she stared into his eyes. He looked back, searching her face.

"You're awake," he said. "How do you feel?"

She thought about it for a moment. "I feel okay. What happened? I thought..." she trailed off. She'd thought Latham had killed her. She'd felt the prick of that last injection.

"We got there in time. You were dead, but we gave you an adrenaline shot. It brought you round."

"Why?" she asked.

He frowned. "Why what?"

"Why did you bring me round? Why did you save me?" She paused for a moment, but she wanted no more lies. "I took your people. One of them died."

"You saved the other two."

"I was sent to kill you. I would have shot you that night."

He shook his head slowly. "I don't think so. I don't think you wanted to kill me."

Fury and guilt battled inside her. "Do you think that mattered? No, I didn't want to kill you. I never wanted to kill anybody."

"So why did you?"

She took a deep breath and faced the truth. "Because I wanted to live."

He sat back in his chair and sighed, running a hand through his already rumpled hair. "We've all done things we'd rather not do, in order to survive."

She looked at him, curious. "Have you killed?"

"I've killed to protect myself and to protect my pack. It's really no different."

Anya searched his face, found compassion and pity. She didn't want his pity. She wasn't sure what she wanted, but pity came nowhere close. He was so beautiful, even the exhaustion stamped clear on his features couldn't detract from that beauty. She remembered that first sight of him; how it had pulled at something deep inside her.

She dragged herself up, so she leaned against the headboard. Weakness still lingered in her body, but that would be from the drugs Latham had given her. Her head felt fine, her mind clear, no dull, throbbing ache that would show she needed her medication. How much time did she have?

"How long have I been here?" she asked.

"Around four hours."

She had a while yet. Maybe they had taken Latham. Maybe he would tell them how to make the drug. "The doctor who was there when you found me—what happened to him?"

"Latham? He was killed."

She closed her eyes, clutched the sheet in her fingers, and fought the despair that threatened to overwhelm her.

"What is it, Anya?"

She felt the mattress depress as Sebastian sank down beside her. At the touch of his hand on her cheek, her eyes flew open. He was close, so close she could breathe in the musky scent of him. He cupped her cheek with his large hand, tilted her head so she had no choice but to look at him. "Anya, tell me."

She swallowed. "I need medication. I have some sort of genetic disease. If I don't get the medication every day, I die."

"We know about the pills. Our doctor is working on it now. But he also took a sample of your blood. And Anya, he's pretty sure you don't have any genetic disease."

"What?"

"He found traces of poison. Some sort of strychnine derivative he couldn't identify. He thinks you were poisoned deliberately."

"Why?"

"Probably as a deterrent to stop you from running, and a way to solve the problem if you did, or if you were captured. As long as you got the antidote each day you were fine."

Anya turned away to hide the pain she knew must show in her eyes. They'd done this to her with cold deliberation. No doubt, they'd planned to let her die when her usefulness was over. The pain washed away on a tidal wave of black hatred. She wished Latham was still alive, so she could kill him herself.

But maybe if it was poison, they could reproduce the antidote. She forced herself to ask the question. "Does your doctor have a cure?"

"Not yet, but we won't stop until we find one."

She wanted to believe him, but she doubted it would be so simple. The Agency had spent years and billions of dollars doing all kinds of research; if they'd wanted her to die, they wouldn't have given her anything easily cured. Her doubts must have shown on her face.

Sebastian leaned forward and kissed her on the lips. "We *will* find it," he said. "We've spent too much time searching for you to let you go now."

"You've been looking for me? Why?"

"Tasha found out you existed about six months ago, and we've been looking ever since. For you and your sisters."

"I have other sisters?"

"At least two more, we think. We believe that's why you were sent to kill me. We'd gotten too close. Now, as much as I would like nothing more than to crawl into that bed and forget about the rest of the world for a very long time, there's someone who's been waiting to see you."

He stood up, and for the first time she noticed a blood stain on his shirt. "You were hurt?"

"It's nothing. It will heal once I shift."

"So why haven't you shifted."

He shrugged. "I've been waiting for you to wake up."

"Why?"

He came back and stood looking down at her, studying her. "The answer is—" Head down, he was silent for a moment, "—I just don't know." She thought he meant to tell her no more, then he sighed. "The truth is, from the moment I saw you, you called to something inside me. It's strange, many in the pack form bonds, they mate for life, but while I've had women, I've never mated, always been alone, and I've been happy that way. Now, for the first time, I don't want to be alone anymore."

"Oh."

"So now you know. Think about it." He whirled around and left the room.

Anya sat staring after him, warmth stealing over her as she considered his words. A moment later, the door opened, and a woman entered. Anya knew who she was. She remembered her briefly from the Agency, and she had seen her inside Maria's head.

Natasha, her sister.

She was small, much smaller than Anya, with long red hair pulled back in a plait, revealing a pointed face and huge golden eyes. Those eyes stared into hers, and Anya was flooded with a mindful of information. More sensation than actual thoughts, she caught brief flashes of a life, running through the forest, a black-haired man with green eyes...

Natasha held her gaze, eyes wide and Anya realized her sister must be having the same experience. She shook her head, glanced away and the contact was lost.

"Sorry," Tasha said. "I didn't know that would happen." She studied her, head cocked to one side. "We don't look much alike." Then she grinned. "Nothing alike in fact. I'm Tasha."

"I remember."

"I've been waiting for you to wake up. Sebastian wouldn't let anyone else sit with you. Which was interesting."

It was, and Anya filed the fact away to think about later. Now she wanted to know about her sister. "Sebastian said you were looking for me. Thank you."

Tasha shrugged. "I always wanted a sister."

"Me too."

Suddenly, Anya couldn't keep the tears from falling. They welled up in her eyes, rolled down her cheek. That someone she had never met should care enough to come after her. The thought wiped away the bitterness of all the betrayals in her life.

Tasha hurried the last few steps to the bed. "Hey, I'm not that bad."

Anya smiled through the tears. "They're good tears not bad."

Tasha's face turned solemn for a moment. "I know." She gestured to the bed. "Can I join you?"

Anya nodded, and Tasha climbed into the big bed and settled herself back on the pillows. She reached out and took Anya's hand. "I predict we're going to be lifelong friends."

Anya bit her lip. Just how long was her life going to be? She pushed the thought away. No matter how long she had left, she could enjoy this moment. "Tell me," she said.

Tasha's lips curved into a grin. "Tell you what?"

"Everything. Tell me everything."

Hours later, she drifted off into sleep, her hand still clasped in Tasha's.

When she woke, the room was in darkness. She raised her head, and a small moan escaped her. Behind her eyes, she could feel a dull throbbing ache.

Time had almost run out.

Chapter Twelve

Sebastian stared at the doctor. "There has to be something you can do."

Connor shook his head. "There's nothing. I've never seen anything like this poison. Given long enough we could break it down, find out what's in there, but we don't have long enough."

Sebastian took a deep breath. "How much time do we have?"

"Twenty-four hours, more or less."

Wild frustration roared inside him. He turned away and punched his fist into the wall. The pain broke through the fog of rage, and he managed to force it down. He had to think clearly. There had to be a way.

"What about putting her into a coma?" he asked. "Give you time to find the antidote?"

"Won't do any good. The poison will keep working. I'm sorry, Sebastian. Of course we'll keep looking, but there's just no way. Here, I've brought some painkillers." He handed a packet to Sebastian. "They'll help at the start. She'll probably need something stronger at..." He trailed off.

"At the end," Sebastian concluded bitterly.

He rubbed his eyes. He couldn't believe this was happening. To find her again, only to lose her. He'd been back to the building where they had found Anya and torn the place apart but found nothing that could help. He didn't know what to do next, and the feeling was new and painful.

"You know there's only one thing that could save her now." Connor interrupted his thoughts.

Sebastian glanced into the other man's face. He knew what the doctor was referring to, but his whole being rejected the idea. "Not yet—it's too risky. Not until there's no hope."

"There is no—"

The door opened and Connor cut off his words. Sebastian turned. Anya stood framed in the doorway, dressed in a pair of his sweats and a black T-shirt. She'd showered, and her hair was still damp. Her face was pale, her eyes huge, but she smiled when she saw him.

"Hi. Tasha showed me where to find you." Anya looked from him to Connor. "Are you working?"

Sebastian forced a smile. "No. Come on in. This is the doctor I was telling you about."

He shot Connor a warning look. He didn't want Anya to know what the doctor had just told him. Not yet anyway. Connor gave a brief nod of his head.

Anya stepped into the room and looked from him to Connor, and back to him. "Has he found anything?"

Her tone was almost blank, but she couldn't quite hide the hope, and it broke Sebastian's heart. He kept his smile in place. "Not yet, they're still working on it. Connor dropped in with some pills that will help for the time being."

"Help?"

"With the pain," Connor answered. "Does your head hurt at all?"

"A little."

She was staring at the doctor, a strange expression of concentration on her face. Suddenly Sebastian knew what she was doing.

"Connor, get the hell out of here."

Connor looked quickly into his face, and then hurried from the room. Sebastian turned to Anya.

"You were too late," she said. "I'd already read him."

Pain splintered his heart as a wave of helplessness washed over him. "I'm sorry."

She shook her head. "Don't be. It's not your fault. I'm just glad I had this time."

"We haven't given up. They're still looking."

She raised an eyebrow in disbelief, then shrugged. "Could I have those painkillers?"

"I'll get you a glass of water." He watched as she took two of the pills. "Is the pain bad?"

"Not bad, no. But if I'm going to die, I plan to enjoy my last few hours." She sipped at the water and watched him over the rim of the glass. "I was thinking about what you said earlier, about not wanting to be alone."

"You were?"

She nodded. "I don't want to be alone, either."

Sebastian took the glass and wrapped his arms around her. He held her tight, as though he could absorb her into his skin, and breathed in the sweet scent of her hair. After a few minutes, she pulled out of his arms and stepped back.

"I can't promise you forever," she said. "But whatever time I have left, is yours."

Her words tore at something inside him, and Sebastian threw back his head and howled. He knew he had to pull himself together, but his wolf was clawing to be free. Wolf recognized his mate and wanted to make her his. Sebastian ruthlessly forced him down. He wasn't ready to make that decision. He would not take that route. Not yet. Not until all else was lost.

Anya stared at him, her eyes wide, and he knew his own must have changed. She reached out and rested a hand on his arm. "Please, Sebastian, stay with me."

He took a deep breath and nodded. "What would you like to do?"

Her eyes wandered over him, hot and hungry, and a fire stirred to life low in his belly. "I want to make love with you," she said. "Here. Now."

Sebastian glanced around the office and raised an eyebrow, but her words made the flames burn hotter. The need to stake his claim, mark her forever as his, consumed him, as though he could keep her in this life by force of will. A lie, but it hid his despair.

"I think that could be arranged."

And he pulled her back into his arms.

Anya could feel the leashed power in the arms wrapped tight around her, the strength held in check, and even through the shield, she sensed his concern, the care he was taking not to let go. She'd seen the wolf in his eyes, but she wasn't afraid of his wolf, and she didn't want him to be careful. She didn't want him to treat her as though she was fragile, as though she might shatter if he kissed her as hard as she wanted to be kissed.

"I'm not going to break," she said.

"I don't want to hurt you."

"You won't." She reached up and framed his beautiful face with her fingers, stared into his eyes, human once more. "Make love to me, Sebastian. Make love as though it's the only time we'll ever have."

Pain flared in his eyes, and she watched as he fought for control. He was too strong willed; she needed him to lose himself in her. She craved him, as she'd never wanted anything before, a deep burning need that threatened to overwhelm her. He *had* to feel the same.

Stepping back, she pulled her T-shirt over her head, and tossed it on the floor between them. Her hands moved to her waist, and she pushed the sweats down over her hips and dragged them off to stand before him naked.

He looked at her for long moments then turned away to cross the room and kick the door closed. He stripped as he came back to her, moving with the lithe grace of an animal. As each item of clothing dropped, her pulse picked up a notch. By the time he stood before her naked, the blood was thundering in her veins. He was already huge and swollen, hard and ready for her. She reached out and trailed her fingers down his chest, dragging her nails across his nipples then laid her palm flat where she could feel the rapid beat of his heart.

"You are the most beautiful thing I have ever seen."

His lips curved into a smile. "And I'm all yours."

He stood, perfectly still while she explored his body with her eyes and her hands, ran them over the smooth swell of muscles, then traced the line of pale hair down over his ridged abdomen. Only when she wrapped her hand around the silky steel of his erection did he move, his head falling back, exposing the taut line of his throat.

She leaned into him and kissed his chest, his throat. Small biting kisses, tasting the saltiness of his skin as though she could devour him, make him part of her. It wasn't enough, and she clutched his shoulders and dragged his head down to hers so she could kiss him full on the mouth.

At the touch of her lips, he came alive. His hands curved around her neck, and he held her steady. The kiss was fierce, his mouth wide open over hers and his tongue thrusting inside, filling her. She thrust back, pushing into his mouth, running her tongue along the hard edge of his teeth.

His arms came around her, sliding down the length of her back to settle on the globes of her bottom. He massaged them roughly then lifted her, so she felt his inhuman strength. Wrapping her legs around his hips, she writhed in his arms to get closer, until the burning heat of his erection nudged at her stomach.

He carried her a few steps until the cool, smoothness of the wall pressed against her back. She leaned back against it while his hand moved between their bodies, holding her breath as his skillful fingers parted the already drenched folds of her sex.

His eyes glittered with desire. They held her gaze as one long finger pushed inside her. At the same time, his thumb found the tight little bud between her thighs, and pleasure shot through her, moist heat flooding her sex. The sensation was exquisite, and she throbbed beneath his touch. He rubbed lazy circles around her clit, and she bit her lip as she waited for him to touch her there again, so sensitive now that she knew she would implode. Finally, the pad of his thumb grazed lightly over her, and she went still. She held her breath as he stroked her, massaging the swollen bud until the pleasure intensified past bearing, and she exploded.

When she came back to herself, he was staring down at her, his eyes hooded. He leaned in close, his breath feathering against her hot skin. He kissed her softly on the lips and whispered in her ear.

"Tell me what you want."

"I want you. Inside me. Please, Sebastian."

He shifted her in his arms, lifted her higher. The tip of his cock scorched her. Finally, he slowly pushed himself inside, and the feeling was so indescribably good that she groaned. He paused when he was in as far as he could go, his eyes closed for a moment, and he sighed.

"God, but that is the best feeling in the world," he muttered.

His eyes opened, and he started moving inside her, shoving in and out of her slick heat, his hands holding her firmly in place, his lips playing over her breasts, her face.

The speed increased until it was wilder than she could have ever imagined, and Anya gave herself up to the emotions flooding her, focused only on the point where his big body ground itself into hers. The pressure was building again, she never wanted it to stop, but she desperately needed release. He thrust into her, grinding his hips against her core. Her lips parted in a scream as she tumbled headlong over the edge. She fought for a moment, but then gave in to the waves and waves of pleasure that washed over her.

He came with her, and even through the pleasure, she felt him pulse as his seed spilled inside her. His head went back, and he howled.

Sebastian carried her through the silent building, back to her room, where he lowered her onto the bed.

He lay down beside her; he was already hard again, and she pressed against him. Framing her face with his hands, he stared down into her eyes.

"I love you," he said.

His words melted something deep inside her, wiping away the betrayals of the past. Anya wanted so much to respond, and she could see the expectation in his eyes. But how could she say the words when she knew she was going to leave him. It seemed like the ultimate betrayal, and her words of love lodged in her throat. She bit her lip then forced her mouth into the curve of a smile.

"I'm glad I didn't shoot you," she murmured.

Disappointment flickered in his eyes, followed by understanding. "So am I."

He kissed her then, and slowly pushed inside her, filling her completely. This time, they made love with a slow, delicious eroticism that left her shaking against him.

Wrapping her in his arms, he pulled her close and together they drifted into sleep.

Sebastian didn't know how long he had slept, and he cursed. He didn't want to waste any of their precious time together. Rolling onto his side, he reached for Anya.

She lay at the edge of the bed, far away from him. He shook her lightly, but she didn't wake. Her skin was scorching to the touch, and a sheen of sweat coated her pale face. Panic flared to life. He shook her, harder this time. She moaned but her eyes remained closed.

Sebastian threw back his head and screamed into the night. "No!"

Chapter Thirteen

He'd run through the dark city streets, careless of who might see him. Run until his wolf was exhausted, then he'd slunk back, the need to be close to Anya driving him on.

He knew what he had to do—the only thing he could do to save her—but fear tore at his insides.

He shifted in the alley at the rear of the building, picked up his clothes from where he'd dropped them, and let himself in. He found Tasha waiting for him in the foyer. Sebastian made to walk past her, but she stopped him with a hand on his arm.

"You know it's the only way," Tasha said.

He shook off her hand. "Why don't *you* do it, then?" he snarled.

"You're the strongest of us. You'll give her the best chance. Please, Sebastian."

He paced the foyer, fighting down the nausea that churned in his gut.

"Why are you so scared?" Tasha asked.

He realized he was still naked and pulled his pants on, more to give himself a moment to think than from any sense of modesty. Dropping the rest of his clothes on the floor, he came to stand in front of her. "Do you know how many humans survive the bite?"

She nodded. "Not many, but there's more to it than that. I know there is. Anya is dying—this might be her one chance." She studied him for a moment, and Sebastian winced at the compassion in her eyes. "The other wolves told me you've never turned anybody," she said. "Why? What happened, Sebastian?"

Sebastian sighed. He knew he was going to attempt it. He couldn't stand by, watch Anya die, however much he feared the consequences. But Tasha deserved to know the risks.

"I was twenty-eight when I was bitten, and I'd been married less than a year." He paused, remembering back; it was over fifty years ago now. "We were in love. I wanted her with me in every way. So I bit her."

"She died?"

"No, she didn't die. She went insane." He forced himself to go on. "I hadn't asked her if she wanted it, I thought—" He broke off. What had he thought? That she loved him enough to take any risk? He shook his head. "In her lucid moments, she cursed me, said I'd turned her into a monster. She was pregnant, I didn't know, but when she lost the baby, it tipped her over the edge. She became uncontrollable, dangerous."

"What happened?"

"I killed her. I put her down like a rabid dog, and I swore I would never do that to anyone again."

"I'm sorry."

"Don't be. It was a long time ago."

"But Anya isn't your wife. I survived, and genetically we're the same. She'll come through it. I know she will."

"Let's hope so." He turned away and headed up the stairs.

Tasha followed him into the room and hurried to the bedside. Anya lay where he had left her, still unconscious, but tremors ran through her body.

Guilt rose bitter and dark. "I should have asked her while I still had the chance."

He shook his head. He knew why he hadn't asked her. He'd feared she would say no. That deep down, she saw him as some sort of monster just as his wife had done. And what difference would it have made? It would have come to this anyway. He could not have stood by and let her leave him without trying this last resort.

He had to do it now, before the last of her strength drained away. It might already be too late, only the strongest survived.

He turned to Tasha. "You need to leave."

She nodded mutely then leaned down and kissed Anya's pale cheek. "Be strong," she whispered.

When the door closed behind her, Sebastian sank down on the edge of the bed. He cupped Anya's cheek and pulled her into his arms. The fever had left her, and shivers racked her slender frame. For a moment, she snuggled against him, seeking his warmth, and a flicker of hope rose inside him. But she didn't awaken, and Sebastian laid her gently back on the mattress.

He took a deep breath. He knew the statistics. The highest chance of success was if the wound had the potential to be fatal. If he was going to do this, he had to do it right. However much he hated the idea of hurting her.

Rising to his feet, he stepped back, stripped off his pants, and called to his wolf. Wolf had been waiting, and the change came over him swiftly, the power and strength flowing through him. He stood for a moment scenting the air, sensing the wrongness.

Then he padded to the bed and leapt lightly up, sinking down on his belly beside the unconscious woman. Wolf wasn't conflicted. He knew what he wanted. What she needed.

He licked her face, then nuzzled her neck, the tender spot where her throat met her collarbone. His lips drew back, and he sank his fangs into the soft flesh.

The warm, coppery taste of blood filled him, but for once his hunger didn't rise. Her body jerked, her back arching, but she didn't regain consciousness. He forced himself to worry at the wound until he felt the hardness of bone beneath his teeth. Biting down hard, he heard the *crunch* as the bone gave way beneath the force of his powerful jaws.

Releasing his hold, he backed away. Then forced the change to come over him.

Back in human form, he stared down for a moment, reaching out to feel the pulse still fluttering in her throat, stroking the back of his hand along her skin. She didn't wake. He hurried to the bathroom, splashed his face and gulped down water, then got the medical kit from the cabinet. It was best not to close the wound, but he could clean it.

Blood soaked the pillows and sheets, but he didn't want to risk disturbing her by changing them. She was better off unconscious.

Usually it could take days before they would know the outcome. But she was so close to death, that the next few hours would tell whether she would live or die. He pulled on his jeans and sank down into the chair by the bed, took her hand in his, and waited.

She woke to a world of pain. She was on fire, burning from the inside out. She tried to sit up, but her body wouldn't obey, and she collapsed back down, squeezing her eyes tight shut.

"Anya?"

She recognized the voice. A hand slid into hers and held her tight, and a sense of peace washed through her, pushing back the pain.

"Don't fight it, Anya." A gentle kiss on the forehead. "I love you."

At the words, she relaxed, and the darkness took her once more.

When she woke again, she knew she was going to live. She was still in pain, but it was localized now, not her entire being. And her head was blissfully clear. She tried to peer down at her shoulder, but darts of intense agony shot through her. Instead, she blinked open her eyes and stared into Sebastian's beautiful face. He was smiling. So she was definitely going to live. She licked her lips.

"How long?" she asked.

"Twenty-four hours." He touched her lightly on the forehead. "How do you feel?"

"I hurt."

"It will pass. Here, open up." She did as ordered, and he placed two pills on her tongue. "Swallow."

She swallowed. "What happened?"

He glanced away and she would swear it was guilt she saw in his eyes. He jumped to his feet and turned, paced the length of the room a couple of times, before returning to stand over her, his shoulders tense. What had he done? She was alive and she'd been dying. How bad could it be?

"I bit you," he said.

"What?"

"I turned you into a werewolf. It was the only way I could stop you dying."

Her mind was blank for a moment. Then she gritted her teeth against the pain and pushed herself up, so she was sitting facing him. "I'm a werewolf?"

He ran a hand through his already messy hair. "There was nothing else we could do. I'm sorry."

"Why are you sorry? Is it such a bad thing?"

"It was dangerous. Not everyone survives."

She frowned. "I was dying anyway."

"Many people think of us as monsters."

"You're not a monster."

"And I should have asked your permission, but I left it too late, and I couldn't let you die. Not without trying."

She peered inside herself but could feel nothing different. "I don't feel like a werewolf."

He smiled. "Give it time."

It was starting to sink in—she would have time. "Am I alright? The poison...?"

"It's still there, but you're stronger now, you're able to fight off the effects. And once you shift for the first time, you'll clear the poison from your system."

"And I'll be cured?"

"You'll be perfect."

She closed her eyes and let it sink in. She'd believed it was over. Those last hours with Sebastian had been the best of her life. But now she had a whole long life stretching in front of her, with Sebastian at her side. He loved her. She was filled with a bubbling sense of anticipation. Blinking open her eyes, she grinned. "When?" she asked. "When can I change?"

He returned her grin, the tenseness draining from his body. Sinking down onto the mattress beside her, he took her hand, stroking his thumb across her palm so her skin tingled. "Sex. You won't shift until you've had sex."

Her eyes widened. "With you?"

"Well, with anyone actually. But that's obviously not an option, so of course with me."

The painkillers were kicking in, and the pain had faded to a dull ache. She rolled her shoulders and tried not to wince. "Now?"

"Maybe when you feel a little better."

"I feel fine. Honest." It was a lie, but she didn't want to wait. "Why don't you try kissing me, and we'll see how we go?" He shook his head, but she tightened her grip on his hand and tugged him closer. "Just a kiss."

But as his lips touched hers, she knew a kiss would never be enough.

Epilogue

They left the pack far behind, her pads making no sound as she raced through the shadowy forest under a fat yellow moon. Effortlessly, she weaved through the ghostly pines, reveling in the stretch of muscle and sinew.

All the fears and betrayals of the past fell from her as she ran, replaced by a wild exhilaration, until she was aware of nothing but the wind flowing past, and the huge silver wolf that kept pace by her side.

It was her first time, and she knew he watched her, worried about her.

Anya woke, back in her own body, wolf only a lingering memory. She felt vitally alive and knew that the poisons of the past had been expunged from her mind as well as her body. Dawn hovered to the east, tinting the sky orange and crimson. She lay on a bed of leaves on the soft forest floor, curled around Sebastian's naked body. She didn't want to move. She could stay here forever, in this moment.

Sebastian stirred, his eyes opening. He rolled onto his back and stretched his long body. Her breath lodged in her throat at the sight of him as it always did. He caught her staring and smiled sleepily, his eyes darkening with passion. Reaching out, he stroked her cheek, and she turned her head to kiss his fingertips.

"Are you all right?" he asked.

She nodded. More than all right and there was something she needed to tell him. It was safe to say the words now. "I love you."

"I know." And he dragged her into his arms and kissed her.

BOUND TO SECRETS

Sisters of the Moon
Book 3

by

NINA CROFT

Chapter One

It was a bloody good place to die.

The thought flickered through Dr. Connor McNair's mind as he stared out across the bleak landscape of Rannoch Moor. Ironic really, considering the main purpose of this trip had been to take Connor's mind off his troubles.

"You're half Scottish, aren't you?" Sebastian had said. "You should feel right at home. Get the hell over there and find out whether there's any truth in the rumors. It's probably nothing, but if there is a tie-in to the Agency, we want to know."

It hadn't been a request, but an order. For a brief moment, Connor had considered ignoring it, bringing this farce to a head. The problem was he no longer knew what Sebastian's reaction would be. Once he would have been certain; Sebastian didn't allow any dissent from his people and would strike down anyone who disobeyed.

Now, Connor wasn't so sure. He hated to admit it, but Sebastian was a good leader. He'd seen that Connor teetered on the edge and he'd sent him here to distract him. But Jesus, this place was enough to turn anyone suicidal.

Mist wreathed a flat heather strewn landscape, dotted with grey lakes and bisected by the distant line of the railway.

He shivered as the damp air brushed his skin, and even this early in the year, a swarm of midges hovered around his face. Swatting them away with one hand, he scanned the horizon. Apart from the flies, nothing moved. He was pretty sure anything capable of moving would have packed up and left this godforsaken place long ago.

On the other hand, it suited his grim mood.

He could have gone straight to the hotel. Instead, he'd left Rannoch station, slung his rucksack over his shoulder, and set off across the moor. He wasn't expecting to find anything right away. Hell, he wasn't actually expecting to find anything ever—this was a waste of time—but after being in the crowded train, so close to so many people, he'd needed fresh air. These days, people made him uncomfortable, put him on edge, made him...hungry.

For a second, the mist burned off, the sun shone down and the whole world changed. Light sparkled off the water and the fresh green grass waved in the gentle breeze.

He caught a movement out of the corner of his eye and turned, searching the flat expanse. Nothing. But as he turned away, something shifted again at the edge of his vision.

Far in the distance, a shapeless black mass streaked across the moor. Connor squinted, trying to make out what it could be.

A wolf?

The creature paused in its headlong dash and reared up on its hind legs. A pony, with a small figure clinging to its back. A pale face peered at him, but they were too far away for him to see clearly. And then they were off again.

"Hey, wait," Connor called out with little expectation of being heard.

He swore loudly, shrugged off his rucksack, and dropped it to the grass. Then he took chase. It was wonderful to be moving. The strength flowed through his muscles. He felt alive, and for a brief time the heaviness of spirit dropped away as he leaped over tussocks of heather, and the scent of crushed herbs rose from under his feet.

Running with inhuman speed, he was catching up quickly. The rider turned to look. A girl, and Connor could make out the horror on her features when she realized he was so close.

The black pony stopped abruptly, and they whirled around to face him. The girl held up a hand, palm facing him, and shook her head fiercely.

Connor came to a halt ten feet away.

"No," she whispered, her voice hoarse as though from lack of use. "I can't...you must go. Please."

"I don't want to hurt you." Connor kept his tone soothing as he took a step closer.

"Not me. You."

For a moment, he had no idea what she meant. Then pain flooded his mind. He tried to focus but a red hot poker drilled into his head, molten metal seeping into his brain. His control slipped away and he fell to his knees. He tried to fight, but the pain was unbearable as though his brain boiled in his skull. He collapsed to all fours, his back spasmed, his head lifted, and he howled.

Beneath her, Dubh screamed in terror. The pony reared up, tossing Keira from his back. The animal sped away as she landed hard, rolled, and came up on her knees, still trying to control the outflow from her mind. But the power held her in a vice-like grip.

She dragged herself through the damp bracken, knowing that only distance could save him now.

How had he gotten so close?

This was her fault. She'd spied him across the moor and the ever present loneliness had welled up inside her. Without thinking, she'd nudged Dubh nearer, but she'd never meant to get close enough to harm him.

Just to look.

She was pathetic.

But he'd been so beautiful, and as she had gotten closer, she had sensed the waves of anger and pain crashing off him. She'd wanted to help him. Fool—she couldn't help anyone, only cause more pain.

She'd kept to a safe distance. Even so, she should have left before he'd spotted her. But how could she have known he'd give chase, and that he'd be faster than anything she'd ever seen?

The howls cut off abruptly, and the grip on her mind relaxed its fierce hold. She was on her feet and running in seconds. But something stopped her. A tingling in the air, like she'd never sensed before. She came to a halt as though some invisible force called to her. Turning slowly, she swallowed her fear. He couldn't be dead. Not this fast.

A gasp escaped her throat.

He crouched on his hands and knees, his spine arched, head thrown back. As she watched, a change came over him and his form shimmered and shifted in the clear afternoon light. A moment later, he vanished and a huge black wolf stood in his place. For long seconds, the animal stood, neck drooping toward the ground, his sides heaving.

He raised his head and dark eyes, flecked with gold, gazed at her. He blinked a couple of times as though to clear his mind and stared at her some more. Then he took a step forward.

Keira lost the ability to move. She stood, her feet fixed to the ground while the wolf padded across the distance between them. This couldn't be real. That was why she wasn't running.

But he was the most beautiful creature she had ever seen, and he held her in thrall. His head came as high as her shoulder, much taller than a true wolf—further proof he couldn't be real. Maybe her sad, pathetic mind had finally broken completely.

She probed his brain, sensing the man still there beneath the much simpler animal brainwaves. But he felt hazy, cut off from her.

Werewolf.

The word flashed into her brain and she saw it for truth.

He stopped only inches from her and studied her, head cocked to one side, eyes wary. She could see the understanding and caution in them. But no pain.

Whatever he was, he was immune to her mind, and her lips curled upward in a brief smile. She reached out a trembling hand and laid it on his head. His fur was silky soft beneath her palm.

The wolf showed no fear. He took a final step toward her and nuzzled her with his cold nose, poking her in the belly, sniffing her fingers. A warm velvety tongue came out and licked her palm.

And Keira sank down onto the coarse grass and burst into tears.

She never cried. Well, almost never. The last time had been when she'd finally accepted that her "mother" was never coming back, even though she'd known it was going to happen. That had been nearly six months ago.

The wolf nudged her. As Keira peered up through tear-drenched eyes, he lowered himself to the ground. Then she wrapped her arms around the huge warm body and cried some more. Finally, exhausted by the release of emotions she'd kept locked in tight, she closed her eyes and gave in to the sleep she usually found so elusive.

Rain on her face woke her. The clouds had closed in and it had started to drizzle. It took Keira a moment to realize she was snuggled up against the most enormous dog she had ever seen. She breathed in the warm musky scent of wild animal.

Werewolf.

A sense of wonder filled her, but no fear. Maybe because she no longer feared death. Perhaps some part of her even craved the release.

But if he'd been planning to eat her, she was sure he would have done so by now. He'd had plenty of opportunity. No, she felt safe and that was something she hadn't felt in a long time.

She reached out with the lightest of telepathic touches. His dark eyes narrowed as though he sensed her intrusion, and she backed off not wanting to risk causing him pain.

He was different from the other animals she'd encountered on the moor. They had been her only companions for years, ever since her powers had grown too strong to contain, and she'd almost broken her mother's mind. From that point on, she had lived alone. Her mother had regularly brought her food and clothing and they had watched each other from afar, never daring to come too close. All the same, Keira still worried that she had somehow contributed to her mother's early death.

She occasionally saw walkers from a distance but she'd perfected the art of disappearing. Until this man. She remembered the way he had sniffed the air. And the incredible speed. He had raced across the moors much faster than even Dubh could ever go. As fast as a...wolf.

She sat up, pulled away, and studied the great beast. He lay on all fours, his huge head resting on his front paws, watching her out of cautious eyes. Keira scrambled to her feet uncertain what her next move should be.

The wolf watched for a moment longer and then rose gracefully to stand beside her. She marveled again at the sheer size of him. A shiver thrummed through the air around her and her skin prickled with that same sensation she'd felt earlier—seconds before he changed, and it came to her what he was about to do. He was changing back. He couldn't. This close she would blow his mind.

She took an instinctive step away and shook her head, panic building inside her.

"No, you mustn't. Don't change back. I'll hurt you. Kill you. I can't help it. I can't control it." She didn't know if he understood her, but he blinked once and dropped his head as though to agree to her demands.

The tension in the air vanished and relief flooded her mind. She stared at her feet. She had to leave. She knew that, but regret filled her as she contemplated the return to loneliness. Maybe it would be better if he did kill her. He could rip out her throat with one bite of those razor sharp teeth. But even now, she realized she didn't really want to die, she just wanted an end to this strange half-life she lived. "You must wait until I'm gone," she said. "Do you understand? Wait until I'm..."

She studied the surroundings and pointed at a clump of bushes about a hundred feet away from where they stood. "Wait until I reach those bushes, then you can change. You understand?"

He nodded once.

She turned to go, but swung around and hugged the animal once more, burrowing her nose in the thick, silky fur at his throat. "Thank you for keeping me warm," she murmured and forced herself to release him. "Goodbye."

This time when she turned, she kept walking, but after only a few steps, she glanced back over her shoulder. The wolf was right behind her padding along on silent paws.

Maybe she could have a little longer.

"You won't change back into a man?"

He inclined his massive head.

This was wrong. She knew it. She didn't know who or even what he really was. How could she trust him? Nearly ten years had passed since her mother had helped her flee from the Agency laboratory where she had lived all her life. The Agency had wanted to terminate her back then, and as far as she knew, nothing had changed. They still wanted her dead and her only hope was to hide; bury her secrets out here in the wilds of the moors with only the animals for company.

Could he be from the Agency? But she didn't believe that. She had seen briefly into his mind and sensed no taint of evil. Just a wildness at the very core of him. That would be the wolf. And a self-hatred she recognized as close to her own.

She made a decision. "Come back with me. For a little while."

She turned toward the keep but then changed her mind. When she'd first seen him, he'd carried a rucksack. He must have dropped it when he chased her. She started walking back the way they had come. The wolf stalked after her.

Eventually, she found the bag resting among the heather. Picking it up, she hefted it over her shoulder and headed toward home.

The wolf kept pace behind her, his huge paws making no sound on the thickly grassed ground. Even though she couldn't hear him or see him, each breath she took saturated her nostrils with his warm, feral scent. Not quite wild animal. Wolf tinged with human and a hint of something she had never encountered before. Magic maybe. She peered over her shoulder and found him watching her, intelligence in his wolf's eyes.

Finally, she halted beside the old keep. The tower loomed dark gray above her, the base surrounded by huge rocks fallen from the walls. From the outside, the place appeared ruined, but she led him around the walls, held back the branches of a rowan bush, and gestured for him to enter. He gave her a narrow eyed glance, and then sniffed cautiously at the opening before he disappeared inside. Keira followed, letting the bush fall back behind her, hiding the entrance. Stepping past him, she led the way through a half-tumbled arch into the room that had been her only home for the last ten years.

Connor woke in the night. Moonlight spilled into the room from a window high up in the wall and deep inside him, his wolf stretched sleepily. His head pounded and he had a huge erection. Neither of which was a common occurrence for him these days.

Werewolves didn't get sick, although they did get erections. Except him. He'd been too pissed off with life lately to even think about sex.

Now he lay on his back on a makeshift bed on the floor of a ruined castle with a woman's warm, sleeping body draped over him, her arms wrapped around his middle, her head on his bare chest. He stayed very still as he remembered what had happened.

The girl on the pony. Excruciating pain. The shift.

She'd told him not to change back because she couldn't control whatever it was she had done to him. Shit, it had hurt—like his brain was melting from the inside. But obviously, she was no danger when she slept, because apart from the headache, he felt fine. Good really. And he realized that for the first time in years, he hadn't awoken engulfed in the black hatred, which had colored his life so much since the attack.

He always shifted back to human form when he slept. Sebastian had told him that would change once he had more control, which he'd get if he gave in and shifted more often. He'd replied he didn't want to shift more and he didn't want more control. What he did want was an end to the nightmare his life had become. Obviously, that wasn't going to happen.

But yesterday was the first time he'd shifted when it hadn't been forced on him by the full moon. And she'd done it to him.

Without moving, he peered down to where her head rested against him. A long tangle of dark hair framed a face with pale skin drawn too tightly over cheekbones and deep shadows beneath her eyes. He recognized the signs of exhaustion. Now, she slept like the dead.

He wished he'd paid more attention when Sebastian had told him why he was here—some weird story about a huge black monster that sucked people's brains from their heads. But they'd been chasing every rumor that might be connected to Anya's sisters and the Agency, and up until now, they had all proved to be nothing. He'd presumed this would be the same. Consequently, he'd been going through the motions. He'd supposed all he needed to do was turn up, prove the rumors were the usual load of crap, and then he could get back to being miserable in more congenial surroundings.

Instead, he suspected what he was going to have to do was phone up Sebastian and tell him he'd actually found one of Anya's sisters.

Except his cell phone had been in his pants pocket when he shifted and presumably had vanished along with his pants. Luckily, he had a spare pair of those if not a spare phone. He'd have to head into town and pick up a new one. But in the morning.

Because he was tired. And for the first time in an age, he could contemplate the idea of falling asleep *and* waking up. He slipped his arm around the woman's slender waist, closed his eyes, and drifted off into a deep, dreamless sleep.

When he woke the second time, he was alone.

At least he hadn't ripped her to pieces.

Chapter Two

*W*ho are you?

Connor scribbled the words on a piece of paper from the notepad by the bed. Looking around the large room, he wondered how long she had been here. Years, he would guess. Despite the dereliction, the place had a lived-in feel. The only furniture was a single chair and the narrow mattress—so she obviously lived alone. But colored rugs covered the rock floor and paintings, mainly of animals and the moors, brightened the stone walls. And there were books everywhere; everything from cookery to torrid romances.

His rucksack was propped in the corner and he pulled out his only other clothes and then hunted for something to eat. He found paints, canvas, more books, but—apart from a couple of tins—no food. No wonder she was too thin.

Did she have anyone to help her? How the hell did she manage, if she had the same effect on everyone she got close to?

Grabbing his rucksack, Connor headed out. As he stooped to step out through the gap in the wall, pain hit him like a drill to his skull. He swayed, and then balanced himself with a hand against the rough stone as the pain receded. Gritting his teeth, he raised his head and searched the surrounding area.

She was hurrying away from him and with each step the pain became more bearable. Finally, when no more than a dull ache remained, she turned. Too far away to see her features clearly, he sensed the tension in her rigid body. He wanted to reassure her, but how could he when he couldn't even get close except as an animal?

He raised his hand and waved, then headed off in the opposite direction.

Had he gone for good?

Her chest hurt, and she blinked back tears. She hated feeling like this. She'd accepted long ago that she would never have a normal life. Never *be* normal. She was a freak. That's what the guards back at the Agency had called her. And they were right.

But then this man, or wolf, or whatever he was, had hardly been normal.

What had she thought?

That they could be freaks together?

She snorted. Hardly.

After watching until he disappeared from sight, Keira headed back inside. Collapsing on the bed, she hugged her knees to her chest and buried her face in the pillow, where the scent of wolf clung to the soft cotton. The hollow feeling in her belly reminded her she needed to make a trip to one of the outlying farms and see if she could steal some food.

When her mother had been alive, she'd dropped off food and other supplies, batteries and books, paints... Now she was gone, and Keira had to fend for herself, but each trip was fraught with the fear of discovery. And the danger that if she was seen, then the rumors might reach the Agency.

Had they already?

She took one last deep breath before pushing herself upright. And she saw his note.

Who are you?

Lightness filled her. He wouldn't have asked if he hadn't meant to come back. She found a pencil under a pile of clutter and wrote her response.

I'm Keira.

Connor came to a standstill as he realized he had no clue where he was going. He'd been booked into The King's House hotel, but while it might be scenically situated in the middle of nowhere, he needed shops. Where he'd gotten off the train yesterday was no good either, it consisted of three houses, a hotel and the train station.

He pulled a map out of his rucksack and figured out where he stood. The moor wasn't all that big, just over twenty miles across, although it seemed to go on forever.

His best bet looked to be the town of Kinlochlevin. It would take him a couple of hours to get there, but hopefully he could hire a car. There was no road across the moors, but at least he'd shave some distance off the journey back. And he could pick up a phone and get some supplies.

A light drizzle started to fall as he walked and by the time he reached the town, the rain had soaked him to the skin.

It was actually more of a village than a town and mostly catering to the tourist trade by the look of the place. This early in the year, he had no problem getting a room in the hotel and the young girl behind the desk promised him an early lunch or a late breakfast once he had dried off.

An hour later, with some food inside him, he felt almost human. Ironic really.

The girl, who'd left reception to serve his breakfast, was extremely doubtful he would find a cell phone for sale anywhere in town. She offered him the use of the office phone, and also promised to arrange for a rental car, though she claimed it would have to come from Fort William and so would probably take a couple of hours.

Connor took up her offer of the phone, and carried his coffee into the office and waited patiently for her to leave. This wasn't the sort of phone call anyone could listen to.

He slumped into the chair behind the desk and punched in Sebastian's number. "Hi," he muttered.

"Hey, you sound almost human," Sebastian said. "Must be the Scottish air."

"Yeah, or the Scottish rain—there's a lot of that."

"What do you need?"

Conner decided to get straight to the point. "I've found her."

"Found who?"

"Anya's sister."

"What?" The complete disbelief in Sebastian's voice confirmed that his alpha hadn't really expected anything to come of Connor's trip.

"Well, I'm presuming she's Anya's sister, though she has more of a look of Tasha." He remembered those strange golden eyes. Eyes, which could see into your mind and then boil your brain alive.

"Wait a minute," Sebastian said. "Don't go anywhere—I'm going to get Anya."

Connor sipped his coffee while he waited. Anya was Sebastian's mate. She and her sister, Tasha, were the two newest members of the pack. Connor had found himself watching them closely over the last few months. Unlike him, they had fully accepted the change and he struggled to understand why. How could they accept being one of the monsters?

But then, he was a doctor and therefore supposed to save lives. Impossible, when the mere scent of blood woke his beast and made his hunger rise. It was another thing Sebastian had said would improve if only he would give in and accept his wolf. But he couldn't risk it, not after—

He cut off the thought. Despite the intervening years, he still wasn't able to think about that night.

"You're on speaker," Sebastian said dragging Connor back to the present.

"Connor, tell me." Anya sounded animated. "You've found something? What? Where? When? Can I come?"

"Yes, I've found something. A woman. On Rannoch Moor. Yesterday. And no."

"No?"

"No, you can't come."

"What's going on, Connor?" Sebastian asked. "How do you know?"

"She's telepathic, but way more powerful than Anya or Tasha. There's something wrong with her. She can't control it, and anyone who gets close, gets their brain fried. I presume that's how the rumors started."

"I take it you got close."

"Yeah, and I shifted. I think it's the only thing that saved my life."

"That powerful?"

"And more."

"Did she see you shift?" Sebastian asked.

"Yes, but she's not telling anybody. She doesn't see anyone, lives in total isolation."

"We have to come and get her," Anya said.

"You can't. I think she'd run and hide and we might never find her again."

"So what do we do?"

He'd thought carefully about this and knew what he wanted to attempt. "I want to come back. Get the implant fitted. I think with the shielding, I'll be able to get close to her, talk to her. She'll trust me."

"Why?"

"Maybe because she likes big shaggy dogs."

Sebastian chuckled. "You're sure this isn't just your need to save the world coming out?"

"Perhaps. But isn't that what you wanted when you sent me here? Take my mind off my suicidal tendencies."

"And has it worked?"

He thought about his answer. "Maybe."

"Are you heading back here today?" Sebastian asked.

"No. Probably early tomorrow morning. I want to ask around, see what the rumors are, how much people know."

"Okay. I'll make sure we're ready for you. And we'll see you sometime tomorrow."

Two hours later, Connor left the bar on the edge of the loch, his stomach warm from the whisky he had drunk. He'd failed to find a cell phone in town—as predicted—but he had got some information on the rumors. The locals had been more than willing to talk in exchange for a dram or two, and as he'd expected, there had been others asking about the "strange beast of Rannoch Moor".

A sense of urgency filled him. Common sense told him the woman on the moors had survived alone for a long time. Nothing was going to happen in the next few hours. But he couldn't shake off the fear that the Agency might find her.

The rain had stopped though the day was gray and overcast as he headed back to pick up his car. He was searching the street in front of the hotel when something hard jabbed him in his side and a tall figure barred his way.

The sharp musky scent of werewolf hit him a moment later.

Chapter Three

Connor glanced down. The dull metal of a gun barrel pressed into his ribcage.

Two men blocked his path. Slowly, he raised his gaze to the faces of his attackers, stared into their eyes, and saw fear.

They feared him.

Part of him hated that. But another part liked it. A lot. His wolf knew he could take them.

Unfortunately, not if they shot him first.

A low growl trickled from his throat and the pistol jabbed him again. For a moment, he thought about pushing it; hadn't this been what he wanted for so long? An end to his existence. An end to the fear he might lose control, take another life.

"What do you want?" His tone was reasonable under the circumstances.

"The boss wants to see you."

They led him to a café on the main street. The place appeared normal, even quaint with red checked tablecloths and pictures of Loch Levin on the walls. They didn't linger—or offer him coffee—but led the way up a narrow staircase and halted at a door on the first landing. Connor's guard holstered his gun, tapped lightly, and pushed open the door. The swirl of power within the room brought Connor's wolf to full attention.

The air was heavy with the feral scent of werewolf. Connor's attention settled immediately on the man who stood at the far end of the room. The focus of attention for everyone, Connor guessed he must be the alpha. A woman stood before him, slender and beautiful, with long blond hair. Her whole body trembled under the gaze of the dark-eyed man.

"Your tribute, Maura?"

"I couldn't, I don't..." She swallowed and took a deep breath. "I don't have it."

The alpha nodded and two men closed in on her.

Panic flared in her eyes. "No, please. Next time. I'll have it next time. I promise. I—" Her words were cut off as the men grabbed her by the arms and she stood breathing hard. A sense of expectancy filled the room and the air crackled with imminent violence. Connor glanced around noting whose eyes gleamed with anticipation and who looked away. But no one moved to stop whatever was about to happen, and Connor took an instinctive step forward.

"Don't move," the man behind him said in a low voice.

"Fuck you," Connor snarled. Even if it got him beaten up, he wouldn't stand by and watch this. As he took another step, strong hands gripped his arms on either side and held him in place.

Everyone had turned his way and the alpha's dark gaze crawled over him. A slow smile curled his lips as he nodded to the men holding the woman.

The crack of bone sounded loud in the room followed by a high pitched scream, cut off abruptly as a hand slammed over her mouth. A moment later, she sagged into unconsciousness.

Connor knew the woman would heal when she shifted, but the casual use of violence told him a lot about how this pack was run. This was what he'd expected of a werewolf pack but never found in Sebastian's.

"Put her in the bedroom," the alpha said. "She can pay off her tribute another way."

The two men half dragged the woman away and his attention turned to Connor. The men holding him let go and prodded him in the center of his back so he took an involuntary step forward. Inside, his wolf snarled, but Connor bit down his instinctive response as he studied the other man.

He had the appearance of a Romany, with black hair pulled into a ponytail, swarthy skin and eyes so dark they were almost black. "I'm Logan," he said. "And you are?"

"Connor. Dr. Connor McNair."

"A doctor. Impressive. And what are you doing in town, Doctor?"

"I'm here on holiday."

Logan's eyes narrowed as though the concept of a werewolf as a tourist had never occurred to him.

"This is my territory." He shrugged as if losing interest. "You have a day to leave. If you stay longer, you swear a blood oath to me and my pack and you never leave. How does that sound?"

"Like a total pile of shit," Connor replied.

Without warning, someone punched him in the gut. Pain exploded and he doubled over. When he straightened, Logan raised an eyebrow.

Smug bastard.

"Hey," Connor muttered. "You're spoiling my holiday."

Why didn't he shut up? The thought crossed his mind as he was punched a second time. Only stubbornness kept him on his feet as something ruptured inside and agony flooded his body. It took him a moment to get the pain under control and he gritted his teeth and slowed his breathing. Like the woman, he would heal when he shifted. Provided he got out of here alive, and that probably depended on him keeping his big mouth shut.

Was it a death wish? He didn't think so. Inside him, his wolf was urging him on. Telling him he could take the alpha.

His wolf was a bloody aggressive bastard.

Connor didn't know where he got it from, because he'd always been one to back down out of a fight. In fact, he didn't think he'd ever been in a fight in his whole life before the change. Now, so often, he craved the release of letting go. Of giving in to the ferocity living within him. It was part of what terrified him so much—the desire for violence.

Closing his eyes, he pictured a woman, with long dark hair and golden eyes. The image soothed him. He straightened and nodded once.

"I'm leaving today."

Logan studied him a minute longer as though he didn't quite understand what was going on. Maybe he sensed Connor's wolf was more of a match for his own and was reconsidering the idea of letting him go.

It took every ounce of willpower he had, but Connor forced his wolf down, and hunched his shoulders as he'd seen the submissives do, even in Sebastian's pack.

Logan pursed his lips but nodded. "You get this one warning. Now go. If we see you again, you die."

Keira spent the day roaming the moor on Dubh, the black pony having miraculously appeared soon after the werewolf had left. She couldn't blame Dubh, she reckoned ponies and wolves were prey and predator and it was only common sense.

In the afternoon, she perched on a rock, which gave her a view for miles in all directions. Dubh grazed the rough grass while Keira stared out over the rugged landscape of the moors.

This place was her prison, but she loved it anyway, and a sense of peace and fatalism seeped into her.

The truth was, she had no choices. This was her life. If she involved anyone else with her problems, she might very well get them killed. If she didn't kill them herself, first. Maybe her wolf-man would come back. If he did, she would allow herself one more night of his company

As the sun sank low on the horizon, she returned to the keep, jumping down from Dubh as they got close, and sending the pony on his way with a pat on the rump.

What if the man didn't return?

She climbed the ruined tower and perched on the highest part. Finally, she saw him in the far distance. He moved at a fast walk despite being weighed down by bags and other things. He had a rucksack on his back, a shopping bag in one hand, and a bottle of camping gas in the other.

He wouldn't try and get close would he?

She gnawed on her lower lip. He was still safe. As he drew closer, she stood up and waved her arms.

He must have seen her because he dropped the bags and the bottle and waved back. Then he kicked off his boots and took off his clothes. And she wished he was nearer. He was as beautiful as a man, as he'd been as a wolf.

Finally, he stood naked, and she swallowed but didn't look away as an unfamiliar warmth stealing over her body. As she watched, he folded his clothes, placed them in a plastic bag, and tucked them under a nearby bush. Even from here, she felt the shiver of magic—or whatever it was—in the air. Then he vanished and the huge black wolf stood in his place.

She scrambled down the tower and ran across the moor toward him. He stayed where he was and she collapsed to her knees and hugged him around the broad neck, digging her fingers into the silky fur. A warm, wet tongue licked her cheek and she burst into tears.

Again.

It occurred to her how tenuous her hold on her emotions really was. She teetered on the edge of total breakdown and she had to get a grip. She allowed herself one more sniffle and then wiped her face on his fur and leaned away.

The wolf sat back on his haunches and grinned. Well, maybe it wasn't a real grin but close enough. He rose to his feet and crossed to the rucksack. It looked heavy, bulging, but he picked it up in his jaws and trotted toward the house. Keira sat for a moment watching the slow wave of his plumed tail. Then she scrambled to her feet, picked up the shopping bag in one hand and the camping gas in the other, and hurried after him.

Once inside, she put the bag and gas down, and lit the candles in the wall sconces around the room. The wolf stared down at the note she had written. He glanced over his shoulder and wagged his tail, then gestured toward the rucksack. Keira crossed to where it lay propped on the floor. She pulled open the fastener and found a piece of paper on the top. Picking it up, she read the untidily scrawled words.

My name is Connor and I'd like us to be friends.

She blinked; he'd hardly want to be her friend if she burst into tears every few seconds. Instead, she bent down and investigated the remaining contents of the rucksack.

Chocolate. Fruit. Tins of soup. Steaks. A bottle of whisky. A huge cake.

Her mouth watered and her stomach rumbled. Very slowly, she unwrapped a bar of chocolate and placed a piece in her mouth. She stood there, her eyes closed as she savored the intense flavor. When she opened her eyes the wolf was watching her, head cocked to one side. She broke off a square of chocolate and held it out to him and he took it delicately from her fingers.

"Hello, Connor," she murmured.

Turning away, she busied herself emptying the rucksack and shopping bag, nearly swooning as she discovered coffee and milk. He must be a mind reader to know of her cravings. Unable to resist, she set up her small kettle on the camping stove and left it to heat while putting things away on the makeshift shelves.

She'd cook a dinner, a proper dinner. Steak and salad, then cakes for dessert. Would a werewolf want his steak cooked or raw? A smile tugged at her lips at the thought.

She had a friend.

At least for tonight.

That night Connor didn't allow himself to sleep. Keira appeared nowhere near as tired as she'd been the night before and he didn't fancy waking up to find his brain melting. Instead, he lay beside her, listening to the sound of her breathing.

He realized something. Always before, he'd found his human self totally submerged when he was in wolf form, but this time he could think clearly. He made a mental note to ask Sebastian whether this was normal.

When he knew dawn was close, he rose from the bed, grabbed his rucksack in his teeth, and padded outside and back to where he'd left his clothes. He took a deep breath and shifted.

Once he'd dressed, he sat on a tussock of heather and took out his notebook and pen.

Keira,

I have to leave but I will be back.

He sat back and chewed the end of his pen while he thought about what to tell her. He didn't want to mention the Agency. Not until he knew more of her story, and he didn't think she was ready to tell him yet. She had talked nonstop last night while she cooked and ate. But nothing really of any importance and nothing of the past or how she had come to live here alone on the moors.

Watching her eat, he reckoned he'd felt the first moment of happiness since he'd been attacked six years ago. He suspected Sebastian was right and it was his goddamn savior complex coming back to life. And he knew that could only cause him pain. He was no savior; he was a monster. He went back to the letter.

You might not know it, but you have sisters, and they've been searching for you. They heard rumors and sent me to investigate. They want to help you. I need to return to London, but I'll be back in two days.

That was the quickest he reckoned he could do the journey both ways and fit in the operation to have the shielding implant. The operation was a simple one. Even so, he knew two days was pushing it. But he remembered Keira's tears when he'd arrived back last night and couldn't bear the idea of leaving her longer than he had to.

He needed to add one more thing.

Keep out of sight—there may be others who heard the rumors. Connor.

He thought about taking the note back but when he glanced up, she was standing in front of the keep, one hand shading her eyes from the rising sun. He lifted the note and waved it toward her, placed it on the ground and weighed it down with a rock. Then he turned, picked up his rucksack, and set off. It was at least five miles to where he had left the car, and he wanted to be back in London by nightfall.

Keira watched until he'd disappeared across the moor and couldn't help wondering whether she would ever see him again. The sun was just rising; for once, the sky was clear and the light sparkled on the water of the loch. She walked slowly toward the point where he'd stowed his clothes.

A piece of paper rested on a tussock of heather under a piece of rock. She was almost scared to reach for it. But at his first words, she relaxed and the tension inside her eased. She sank down to the grass and read the rest.

She had sisters?

She'd known she wasn't the only one. Back at the Agency, they'd told her there were others, but she'd never been allowed to meet them. Keira reckoned they'd probably been "terminated" as they'd planned to do to her. Either that or they now worked for the Agency. But perhaps some had escaped as she had done.

Could she trust them?

Maybe this was all a trap. But if Connor had wanted to kill her or even take her back to the Agency, he'd had plenty of opportunities.

And at the end of his note, he'd said there might be others after her. That had to be the Agency. Who else would care? She pressed her fingers to her forehead trying to ease the pressure. Should she go away? Head further north, lose herself in the Highlands?

But she was so tired of running and hiding.

Maybe the time had come to face up to what she was. Perhaps there was someone who could help her get control, even reverse whatever they had done to her all those years ago.

And for some reason, she trusted Connor.

She'd wait and hope that somewhere in the world, there were people who didn't want her dead.

Chapter Four

They arrived the afternoon Connor left.

A man and a woman.

Keira had seen them from a distance and known instantly they weren't the usual hikers. They were hunting for something—probably her—crisscrossing the moors, constantly alert. The woman appeared vaguely familiar, medium height and slender, with long dark hair, but from her safe distance, Keira could tell nothing more.

They didn't come near her the first day, but all the same, she hadn't returned to the keep to sleep. She didn't want to be trapped inside if they found her. Instead, she grabbed a sleeping bag and spent an uncomfortable night wedged in a rocky outcrop. It had started to rain just before dawn and she was cold, wet, and tired by the time the sun came up.

They returned that morning and found the keep around midday. Bel-Bel, her tame magpie had swooped down on them. They must have taken that as a sign there was no one around, because they circled the place once and then left.

Keira spent a second night outside and was close to exhaustion by dawn. But at least this morning, she was dry.

She rose to her feet and stretched, her muscles sore from the uncomfortable position. As she stared out over the moor, she became instantly still. The sun had burned off the last of the early morning mist revealing a solitary figure striding toward the keep.

Connor.

Relief rolled through her and she realized that despite his note—which was still in her pocket and which she read at regular intervals—she hadn't really believed he would return.

She raised a hand and waved. He stopped walking and lifted his own hand to shade his eyes. She'd forgotten how stunningly gorgeous he was. Tall and lean, and even in human form, he moved with the lithe grace of an animal. His black hair was glossy and fell over his forehead. He wore faded jeans that hugged his narrow hips and long legs, and a black sweater with the sleeves pushed up. A rucksack hung over one shoulder but he carried no shopping bags this time. Maybe he didn't plan to stay.

She waved again, and he started walking toward her.

What was he doing?

He was getting too close. She started to back away.

"Keira, wait."

She stopped at the sound of her name. How long since she'd heard it spoken?

"Don't go. I think I'll be okay, just stay where you are."

Okay? How could he be okay?

Then she realized how close he'd gotten and her fists clenched at her sides. She studied his face for signs of pain, but he showed nothing. Her feet itched with the need to run, but she held herself in place, hardly daring to breathe as though if she moved now, everything would fall apart.

Finally, he came to a halt only a foot away.

And she stood staring at him, her mind refusing to function. He seemed real. So why wasn't he rolling about in agony?

"How?"

He lifted his hand and touched the side of his head, behind the left ear. "I've got an implant. It stops telepaths from being able to read your mind. The Agency developed it—"

"You work for the Agency?"

Her panic must have shown.

"No. Never," he said quickly. "The people I... work with, they discovered the technology when they rescued your sister, Tasha, from one of the Agency's labs."

She found it hard to take in. For the first time in over five years, she stood close enough to touch somebody. And she couldn't resist. Her hand reached out of its own accord and her fingertip stroked his cheek. His skin was warm.

At least she wasn't crying; she was way beyond tears.

He stood like a statue while she touched him. Edging closer, she pressed her palm against the soft wool of his sweater, felt the steady thud of his heart.

His hands came up almost tentatively and rested on her shoulders. It occurred to her that she knew nothing about this man. Except he could turn into a wolf and somehow he could stand beside her and not scream in pain. It was enough.

More than enough.

She took the last step, which brought her up against his body. He was much taller, so her head tucked in beneath his chin. Breathing in, she caught a wild musky scent, which reminded her of his wolf. His arms came around her and pulled her tight against him, and for long minutes they stood wrapped close together. She thought she felt his lips brush her hair, but she wasn't sure.

If she turned her head slightly, she could taste him; kiss the skin of his throat. She'd never kissed a man. And up until five minutes ago, she'd been convinced she'd go to her grave without ever kissing a man.

Why was she even thinking about kissing?

Finally, his hands tightened on her arms and he put her slightly away from him. He stared down into her face, examining her. What did he see? She hadn't looked into a mirror in years. Occasionally, she caught a glimpse of her reflection in the still water of the loch, but never clearly. Now she wished she'd combed her hair—at least at some point in the last six months. When her mother had been alive she'd encouraged Keira at least to try and maintain a semblance of a normal life, normal routines. But since her mother had died, she'd almost given up. What did it matter what she looked like when only the animals of the moor ever saw her? And they didn't care.

His brows drew together in a frown. "You look a mess."

Well, what had she expected—romantic words? She'd read too many books. All the same, it didn't seem fair—she'd been standing here thinking how stunning he was and he'd been thinking she looked a mess.

His hand came up and he brushed her long hair away from her face and stroked her cheek beneath her eyes. "You're exhausted and malnourished. Haven't you been eating or sleeping?"

"No and no. What are you—a doctor?"

She'd meant the question to be sarcastic, but his lips curved into a smile. "Actually, yes."

"Oh."

"Why? I left you food. Why haven't you been eating? And what are you doing out so early?"

His scolding nearly broke her. She bit her lip and pulled herself together. She should tell him. "There were people here—the day before yesterday. They arrived not long after you left."

His brows drew together. "Hikers?"

She shook her head. "No. They were searching, systematically. And one of them—the woman—seemed familiar."

"You think they were from the Agency, looking for you?"

Could she trust him with her secrets? And would she be putting him in danger if she did?

"I can help you, Keira."

"Why? Why would you want to help me? Who are you and how do you know about the Agency."

"I told you in my note, I know your sisters. And they've been looking for others like them since they escaped the Agency."

She wanted to believe in him so badly. But she had relied on nobody but herself for so long she was finding it hard. Too much emotion, together with the lack of sleep and food, finally caught up with her and she swayed.

Connor tightened his hold on her arm and held her up. "Come on, let's get you to bed."

"I'd rather stay out here. I don't want to be stuck inside if they come back."

She thought he would argue, tell her she was being paranoid, but in the end, he shrugged and glanced around, his gaze resting on her sleeping bag. He nodded toward it. "Okay, get in then and get some sleep. I'll keep watch."

He shrugged off the rucksack and put it on the ground and then crouched down and rummaged inside. He brought out an apple, a bar of chocolate, and a thermos flask.

"In." He pointed at the sleeping bag, and she sat down and wriggled into it, then took the food he offered. He watched as she ate the chocolate and washed it down with hot coffee.

There were so many questions she wanted to ask, but waves of sleep were washing over her, dragging her under. She placed the empty cup on the ground beside her and snuggled down. Connor crouched by her head and stroked a hand over her hair. "Go to sleep. I'll wake you if anyone comes near."

She watched for a minute longer as he pulled a set of binoculars out of the rucksack then moved to the highest point and started to scan the surrounding area.

Then closing her eyes, she slept.

Keira slept for eight straight hours. Connor alternated between scanning the area for any signs of life and sitting on a nearby rock watching her sleep. He also tried his cell phone; he needed to contact Sebastian to tell him he'd arrived and Keira was safe. But the phone was dead—he suspected it was more than the lack of a signal. But he saw no one and by midday, he relaxed a little. Chances were, if they hadn't found anything in the last two days, they would have given up.

For once, the sun shone, the sky arched deep blue above them, transforming the moor. No longer the dark and depressing place he'd first seen.

He turned his attention to the sleeping woman. She was beautiful, though way too thin, the bones in her face sharp under pale skin. Her hair was dark, not black as he'd first thought, but deep dark brown with glints of ruby. Her brows were elegant arches, her lips soft in sleep, full and tender. Watching her, he felt something tug at his heart. A mixture of compassion and guilt.

He'd spent the last few years bemoaning his fate. Up until the attack, nothing in his life had ever caused him problems. For as long as he could remember, he'd wanted to be a doctor—like his mom—and save people. He'd sailed through med school and been well on his way to his dream of being a top surgeon when he'd been bitten.

He hadn't even been on duty in the ER that night, just passing through when he'd heard the commotion. Everyone else had had the sense to get out of the way, they'd all been running out of the room as he'd run in. Afterward, he hadn't remembered much.

It had been the end of his career as a surgeon. The end of any career as a doctor as far as he could see. The smell of blood raised a hunger in him he couldn't control. Though Sebastian claimed that was his own stubborn fault; if he would accept his wolf, then his control would grow.

He hadn't wanted to accept anything about his new situation. Instead, he'd wallowed in self-pity because his perfect life had been fucked up. He'd spent years rejecting what he was, refusing to even acknowledge it more than he absolutely had to.

But here was this young woman. He could only guess what she had gone through in her early years, but he doubted her childhood had been happy or normal. And her life must have been almost impossible since she'd fled the Agency, never to be able to approach another person for fear of hurting them.

But she'd made some sort of life for herself out here. She hadn't given up and immersed herself in self-pity as he had.

He went and sat beside her, his back resting against the rocky outcrop. As though she sensed his presence, she rolled onto her side and curled up against him one hand resting on his thigh and a sense of peace stole through him.

When she finally opened her eyes, the sun was high in the sky. She shifted onto her back and blinked, then came awake suddenly and bolted upright.

"Shh," he murmured. "It's okay. Everything is all right."

Wonder filled her eyes. He didn't think anyone had ever looked at him quite like that before and it made him feel inadequate. Unworthy.

"Hello," she said.

"Hello. How do you feel?"

"Better. Hungry."

"Well, get up and I'll heat you up some food. I think we're safe—there's been no sign of anyone all day."

He got to his feet and held out his hand to her. As she slipped her palm in his, a tingle passed up his arm. Her eyes widened and he knew she had felt it as well. He tightened his grip and pulled her up.

After pushing everything back into his rucksack, he slung it over his shoulder, picked up the sleeping bag, and headed toward the keep. They didn't speak on the way and once inside he busied himself sorting out the food he'd brought with him; rich beef stew ready to warm up. He set up the camping stove and placed the pan on to heat. Glancing up, he found her staring at him.

"What?" he asked.

Keira shook her head. "Nothing. I'm just not used to…" She waved a hand at the food cooking, the other provisions he'd set on the small table.

"Relax then. Sit down, have a glass of wine."

She peered down at herself and winced. "I think I'll go wash up. If that's okay?"

She was actually a little...crumpled. And grubby.

"Of course." It occurred to him as she disappeared to wonder where she actually went to wash. In the loch, he presumed and shivered a little at the thought. He hoped she wouldn't wander far despite seeing no sign of anyone all day. It also occurred to him that he was an idiot to worry; she'd lived here alone quite safely until he'd come along. All the same, he couldn't prevent a quick check. He went outside, and around the back of the keep. Keira stood poised on the edge of the loch.

Naked.

Her figure was slender and perfect; her legs long, her breasts small but full and long dark hair fell down her back to cover the curve of her ass.

A stab of desire hit him straight in the groin, taking him by surprise.

He hadn't felt desire in a long time. After the attack, he'd gone a little crazy, slept with just about every woman he could find. He'd later learned that sex was needed to trigger the first shift, and if he'd kept his dick in his pants then it would never have happened. But obviously, he hadn't known the finer details of being a werewolf back then.

He hadn't felt the urge again since he'd found out. Until Keira.

He couldn't turn away, feeling like some sort of voyeur as she raised her arms above her head, the action lifting her breasts. White skin and dark red nipples. His breath caught in his throat; he'd never seen anything quite so beautiful.

Only when she dived into the water did he move.

Shit, he'd bet that water was icy. Maybe he should have a dip himself. Instead, he waited for the sting of desire to subside then headed back inside.

Chapter Five

Keira had known he was watching her; she'd caught him out of the corner of her eye.

Did he like what he saw? She wasn't ugly. At least she didn't think so. But it was unlikely he would find her attractive. She was skinny—too skinny—he'd said so.

She swam a few strokes and then ducked under and rubbed at her hair. She hadn't had shampoo since her mother's visits, but if she scrubbed hard enough it might come clean.

After five minutes in the chill water, she was shivering. She climbed out, dried herself, pulled on panties, jeans and her favorite pink T-shirt, then sat on a rock to let her hair dry in the sun.

Part of her didn't want to go back. Right here and now, life was about as good as it had ever been. But once she went back inside, she suspected that would change. Real life would rear its—usually ugly—head and she would have to consider the future.

"Keira?"

She glanced up as he called her name.

"The food is ready."

She nodded, gathered up her things, and headed back to the keep. Connor handed her a chipped mug of red wine as she came in and she sipped it cautiously. She wasn't used to alcohol. But the flavor was warm and mellow on her tongue.

Why the hell not?

She downed the contents in one gulp and held out her mug for more.

He raised an eyebrow but refilled it from the bottle.

He'd set up the food on the small table. It smelled fabulous, rich and full of herbs. For a few seconds, she savored the scent, and then she picked up her spoon and started to eat.

And didn't stop until the bowl was empty.

She sat back and sighed.

Connor had been sitting on the bed, now he got up refilled her bowl, topped up her mug, then took a bowl of his own and sat back down.

By the time she had finished the second helping, she was replete, the wine a warm buzz in her belly and brain. "Thank you."

He grinned. "My pleasure. There's cake somewhere."

"Later."

She watched as he finished his food rather more delicately than she had done. They were going to have to talk soon, and she still wasn't certain of how much she could safely tell him. She thought of the copious notes she had made over the years—at least the early ones. Her mother had encouraged her to write down everything she remembered, names, places, happenings. None of it made any sense to her, but the notebooks were all piled up behind a loose rock in the wall of the keep.

They'd thought that if the Agency ever caught up with her, there might be something in there they could use as leverage to keep her alive. But she wouldn't even know how to separate the useless facts from the important stuff.

No use putting this off any longer.

"Who are you?" she asked.

He placed his bowl on the floor and leaned against the wall, his long legs stretched out in front of him.

"My name is Connor McNair. I am...I was a doctor. Six years ago a werewolf bit me and my life changed forever."

She heard the bitterness in his voice. "Don't you like your wolf?"

"What's to like? He's a beast, an animal."

"He stayed with me those nights, looked after me. He didn't hurt me."

Connor shrugged. "Anyway, afterward I became part of a pack—"

"Of werewolves?"

"Yes. The pack is run by a man called Sebastian Quinn. He's the alpha. He also works with a group of other—" he paused as if unsure how to go on and then shrugged again "—other beings. It's run by a vampire."

"What?" Was he kidding her? Though she supposed if werewolves were real then why not vampires?

"A year or so ago, Jack—that's the name of the vampire—infiltrated one of the Agency's research laboratories and rescued your sister, Tasha."

"Tasha is telepathic—like me?"

"Maybe not as strong, but yes. She's also a werewolf—she'd been attacked when she was a teenager and been a prisoner ever since. When she escaped, Tasha discovered there were others like her who had been created by the Agency, and she's been searching for you ever since."

She had a sister who was a werewolf and she'd been looking for her? She wasn't alone in the world. Even though she would probably never meet Tasha, Keira's heart ached; there was someone out there who cared whether she lived or died.

"Six months ago, they found Anya," Connor continued. "She'd been working as an assassin for the Agency—they sent her after Sebastian. But she'd started to suspect the Agency weren't the good guys they'd made themselves out to be. Anyway, she's with us now. But she was dying—the Agency had done something to her, given her poison, and without the antidote each day, she would die. Sebastian had to change her to save her life. She's Sebastian's mate."

"Mate? As in married?"

"Sort of, I suppose. Tasha and Anya sent you a message." He reached across and picked up a small tablet computer. "I'm afraid it doesn't work."

"No, I have a bad effect on technology. Pretty much like I do on people."

Something occurred to her. The Agency had done something to her as they had to Anya. She wasn't sure what, but maybe if Connor turned her into a werewolf then he could save her as well.

"Can you change me?" she asked.

Shock flashed on his face followed closely by rejection. "I could never turn someone else into a monster."

"You're no monster."

"You don't know what I am or the things I've done. I'll never do that to anyone."

"Not even to save their life."

"Are you dying?"

"No."

She remembered back to the first time she had seen him, and the anger that had rolled off him in waves. The self-hatred. Why did he hate his wolf so much? He'd been beautiful to her.

"Are you really a doctor?" she asked.

"I am. It was all I ever wanted to be."

"Why?"

"My mother's a doctor. When I was seven, we were in an accident. A train crash. We were unhurt but all around us people were screaming. My mom stayed so calm and she helped them. I guess it made a big impression on me."

"Where is she now?"

"She's in Africa working in a refugee camp."

"What about your father? Is he a doctor as well?"

Connor shook his head. "He was a Spanish waiter she met on holiday in Malaga."

So that was where he got the black hair and olive skin. "Did they marry?"

"No, they were too different, but strangely they've always been good friends. He runs a tapas bar in London now. I'll take you there one day."

Ha, like she would ever get to London. She could imagine the chaos she would cause.

"Enough of me," he said. "Tell me how you came to be here."

She might as well start from the beginning. "I was born in one of the Agency's laboratories in Devon. My 'mother' cared for me for as long as I can remember. She wasn't really my mother, but she came to love me."

Keira thought for a moment trying to get the past straight in her head. "I first became telepathic when I was eleven. After that, apart from my mother, I didn't see many people. I guess they were scared I would read them—there was nothing like this shielding back then. But I grew stronger and after that, I was sedated most of the time." She paused and drained the last of her wine. "I don't remember much for about a year. Then they must have decided to do something, maybe try and cut off my powers or put in some sort of trigger so they could switch them on and off. But it went wrong, and I lost all control."

It had been a horrible time. She'd felt as though her head would explode with all the people around her and all the information flooding in. In the end, they'd sedated her again.

"When I came to, I was here. They'd ordered my termination, but my mother sneaked me out of there instead. She risked everything for me and I probably killed her."

"Hey," Connor said. "Whatever happened to her, I'm sure it wasn't your fault."

"She died of brain cancer six months ago. You're a doctor—can you tell me I didn't play a part in that?"

She'd thought he would give her some platitude. Instead, he ran a hand through his thick hair.

"I honestly don't know. But it's not a forgone conclusion, and even if you did cause it, then it's still not your fault. You didn't do this to yourself."

It was a good answer and she wished she could dismiss her guilt so easily. "Why do you hate your wolf?"

His eyes widened at the change of subject and for a second, she thought he wasn't going to answer. Then he took a deep breath. "The first time I shifted, I killed someone."

She'd presumed it must have been something like that. What could be worse for a man who had dedicated his life to saving people?

"Who?"

Connor stood and paced; immediately her home seemed tiny. Finally, he turned back to face her.

"One of the pack. Sebastian had sent them to watch me the first full moon after the attack. He'd presumed they would be able to control me. I'd refused to join the pack. I wanted nothing to do with them. I guess I was in denial, didn't really believe I would shift. They were supposed to get me to a safe place— which they did—and contain me—which they didn't. They couldn't. I killed one of them and almost killed the second."

"And you blame yourself?"

"Why the hell wouldn't I blame myself?"

She gave him a small smile. "Because it's not your fault. You didn't do this to yourself."

He opened his mouth, no doubt to argue, and then snapped it shut again. He paced some more. Finally, he stopped and a wry smile tugged his lips.

"Yeah, we're a couple of life's victims."

Maybe she was, but anyone less like a victim than Connor McNair, she had never seen. He was so big and powerful. He was still pacing, the muscles of his shoulders bunching as he moved. Then he stopped, and stretched, raising his hands above his head, baring a strip of olive skin at his waist. Heat flickered to life inside her and she couldn't take her eyes from him. Her mouth went dry. She'd never felt like this; restless and confined. As though part of her wanted to move but the rest wanted to stay exactly where she was and fill her eyes with him.

He turned suddenly and caught her staring.

"What?" he asked.

When she didn't answer, his gaze dropped from her face, to slide over the rest of her. She peered down. Her nipples pressed against the thin cotton of her T-shirt and she fought the urge to wrap her arms around herself, hide from him. She glanced back up; he was watching her, a dull flush across his cheekbones, his dark eyes heavy lidded. Then he shook himself and looked away.

She ran a hand through her hair; it was almost dry now. Usually, when she felt like this, she'd go for a gallop on Dubh, but she reckoned the pony had made himself scarce when Connor had arrived.

"You want to go for a walk?" she asked.

"Walk?"

"You know, that thing you're doing backwards and forwards right now, but outdoors."

"Why not?"

Outside, the sun was still shining and she raised her face to the warmth.

"You know," Connor said. "When I first arrived here, I thought this was the most depressing place I'd been in my entire life."

"And now?"

"Now... it's growing on me."

Maybe he would stay a while.

He took her hand. In her whole life, she couldn't ever remember walking hand in hand with anyone. His palm was warm and hard against hers and he stroked her hand with his thumb almost absently as they strolled. Tingles shivered along her arm at his touch.

His legs were much longer than hers, but he slowed his pace to match her, and they walked together easily.

"What do you want from life?" he asked.

The question startled her. She'd actually been contemplating how to ask him to kiss her. She'd never really considered what she wanted before. It seemed foolish when her choices were so limited. Why torment herself with what could never be?

Now she made herself think about the answer. What did she really want?

"I don't want to be alone anymore." But that wasn't enough. "I want to feel safe, and I don't want to hurt anyone else."

He nodded. "I want you to come back with me."

At his words, she halted, her brows drawing together. "Back where?"

"To London."

She stared into his face. "How can I go to London? I hurt anyone I get close to. You felt what I did to you. I can't stop it."

"Just hear me out. I'd sedate you for the journey. Sebastian is building a room, based on the implant technology. We think when you're inside, you won't be able to reach out to anybody. You won't hurt anybody."

She chewed on her lower lip forcing down the hope threatening to bubble up and overtake all her good sense. Her mother had told her not to trust anyone, but she'd already trusted Connor with many of her secrets. Could he really make it safe for her to be around people?

"What have you got to lose?" he asked.

Hope? And hope was such a dangerous thing. If she tried this and failed, how would she ever face coming back to this lonely existence? "And then what?" she asked.

"Then we find out what they did to you, and we reverse it."

"You think that's possible?"

"I don't know. I won't make promises I can't keep, but there's a chance, and isn't it worth the risk? You can't keep living like this. There will be more rumors and one day the Agency will find you." He turned so he faced her fully, took her other hand in his, and squeezed gently. "Please come back with me, Keira."

She searched his face. "Why do you care?"

The question seemed to take him aback. He thought for a moment then shook his head. "I don't know. All I know is I can't walk away and leave you here alone and unprotected. For six years, I've not cared about anything or anyone. For some reason you've brought me back to life."

"So I'm just one more person to save then?"

"Perhaps we're supposed to save each other," he said. "The last couple of days are the first times I've woken up and not thought about killing myself."

She squeezed his hands in return. Maybe he was right. She'd felt his self-hatred, had been drawn to it. Perhaps in helping her, he would also find something redeemable in himself.

"You're the first person I've cared enough about to want to save since I was changed. So if you don't come, then I reckon I'll have to move in with you."

She blinked at his words, determined not to go all soppy. "I'll come."

"Good."

"But, Connor, you won't let me hurt anyone will you? You'll stop me any way you have to?"

"If the worst happens and the room doesn't work, we can keep you sedated while we run the tests. It won't be as easy but we can do it."

"Okay. So when do we go?"

"In the morning, I think. I drove through the night and I could do with some sleep."

Some of her tension seeped away as she realized she had a brief reprieve. Whatever he said, she wasn't convinced his plan would work. But she had this night with Connor before she had to face the world.

She knew what she wanted from him. But would he give it to her?

A little fire burst into life low down in her belly. She'd seen him naked that first morning when she'd woken beside him. He'd been aroused, but maybe that was the way men were in their sleep. He'd been magnificent, though the memory of his size sent a tremor of unease through her.

"What are you thinking?"

She glanced up to find Conner scrutinizing her, a slight frown on his face.

"I was thinking that I want you to kiss me."

Shock flashed across his face. "Why?"

She barely resisted rolling her eyes. "Because you're gorgeous, and I've never been kissed. And tomorrow…well tomorrow, I don't know what might happen. But in case it all goes horribly wrong, I'd like to be kissed first."

And a whole lot more than kissed if she had her way, but she'd break him in to the idea slowly. He was still studying her, and she frowned. "Come on Connor, I bet you kiss women all the time. What's the big deal?"

"I haven't kissed a woman in six years."

Why did that make her feel good? "Then maybe it's time."

She sensed the moment he gave in, and her breath left her in a long sigh. He took a single step, which brought him up close. Then he released her hands and raised his to frame her face. Warmth flowed through her from his touch. His thumb brushed over her lower lip and her mouth tingled. Without thinking, she parted her lips and her tongue licked at his skin. He tasted of salt.

He tipped her head back, and she stared up at him. His eyes were dark like bitter chocolate, but with little flecks of gold. She held his gaze as he lowered his face to hers. His lips were warm and hard as they touched her, lightly at first. He began to draw back, and she lifted her hands and wrapped them around his neck, sliding them into the silky softness of his hair, holding him against her.

"Kiss me, Connor," she murmured. "Kiss me like it might be the only chance we ever have."

His mouth slanted over hers, harder this time. She closed her eyes and sank into the sensation. He pulled her closer, until she felt him hard against the length of her body. As he stroked her lips with his tongue, she forgot about everything but the taste of him, the sensation of his lips on hers. Then his tongue was pushing slowly inside her mouth like warm, wet velvet. He licked along the sides of her tongue, the roof of her mouth, and heat flooded her, pooling between her clenched thighs. She held on as her knees shook and still his tongue thrust into her. She needed more. Much more, and a whimper rose up in her throat. His hands slid down over her back to cup her bottom and pull her harder against him. And still he kissed her, until her head swam and body ached for him.

Finally, he drew back and she sucked in air.

Staring up, she saw his eyes were feral and his wolf lurked just beneath the surface, but she experienced no fear, only a savage delight that she could make him lose control.

He was breathing hard as he stepped back from her.

"Please, Connor."

He shook his head. "I daren't. If I lose control, shift…"

"You've spent two nights with me as a wolf. They are the only times I've felt safe since I came here. I trust you. Trust yourself."

His dick throbbed with need and inside, his wolf howled.

How had he let this go so far? His hands fisted at his side as he fought for control.

She stared at him with those huge golden eyes pleading, her lips swollen from his kisses. Then holding his gaze, she gripped the hem of her T-shirt and pulled it over her head. His gaze dropped without thought. She was so beautiful, her breasts surprisingly full on her slender frame. Her nipples, dark and taut with the need he too felt. His hand came out slowly, hovered close to her.

"Please, Connor."

At her words, he gave in. The tension seeped from his body and his fists uncurled. Reaching out, he cupped one breast in his hand. Her skin was so pale against his. She'd gone still as he touched her, and now, as he ran the pad of his thumb over one taut peak, a shudder ran through her. Breathing in, he scented her arousal. He lowered his head and took the tip in his mouth, licked her with slow strokes of his tongue. Her hand held his head against her, and the fast thud of her heart drummed loud in his ears. He bit down gently. Her back arched and a gasp left her throat.

He picked her up in his arms and carried her back to the keep. She kissed him as he lowered her onto the bed, her hands in his hair. Pulling free, he straightened and stood staring down at her. Her lashes lifted and she gazed back.

"Don't leave me," she whispered.

"I won't."

He leaned down and tugged off her boots, then unfastened her jeans and peeled them down over her long legs, leaving her naked. At the sight, his cock pulsed and he tried to rein in his need.

She was a virgin. He had to go slowly, but every cell roared to take her, make her his. She watched him through half-closed eyes, her lips slightly parted, her breasts rising and falling with her rapid breaths. The air filled with the scent of her need and his hunger rose until he thought he might explode.

Quickly, he stripped off his sweater, kicked off his boots and almost tore off his jeans.

Her gaze followed the movements until he stood before her naked. She came up on her elbows, her eyes widening.

"Holy crap," she muttered.

The words did nothing for his control.

Slowly. I need to take this slowly.

She was perfect, her body long and slender, her breasts full and pointed, the nipples tight, her belly flat with sable curls at the base. As he stared, she arched her back and opened her legs, his eyes drawn to those curls. The flesh between her thighs gleamed with moisture. She wanted him, and the last of his control vanished. He had to taste her.

He fell to his knees, his hands gliding up her legs to drag them apart. He kissed his way up her inner thigh, breathing her in. She lay perfectly still and he glanced up the line of her body. Her hands were fisted at her side, her eyes closed.

He brushed one finger over her sex and her lids flew open. Holding her gaze, he parted the folds and his finger slowly pushed into her. She was so tight and slick.

His balls ached with the need to be deep inside, but he was determined to give her pleasure first. He withdrew his finger then slid it lightly upward and she jerked in reaction. He thrust inside her again, and then repeated the process. A sigh eased from her. Then two fingers, and she pushed back against his hand asking for more. Finally, he parted the folds of her sex, exposing the swollen nub. Leaning in close, his mouth caressed her. He kissed her sex as he had kissed her mouth earlier, as though he would never get enough. His tongue pushed inside, tasting the salty sweetness of her, then up over the tight little bud. She strained against him, her thighs widening as if to get him even closer. He played her with his teeth, grazing them across her sensitive flesh, and a small scream escaped her. Her hands were in his hair now holding him tight against her. She was so hot and wet and he could sense she was close by the tension in her muscles and the way her hips rose rhythmically as he filled her slick heat with his tongue. He shifted to concentrate on her clit, running his tongue over and over her. Then he sucked her into his mouth, bit down gently and she fell apart.

As she screamed her release, a scalding wave of molten pain poured through his mind. He felt the moment the implant gave way and his brain exploded in agony.

Some part of him knew she was still screaming. In panic now, but he couldn't concentrate on anything but the red hot agony threatening to tear him apart.

He threw himself backward onto the floor. He was dying. The blood vessels in his brain exploding. With the last of his consciousness, he called his wolf.

Too late.

His wolf rose to the surface and then blackness.

Chapter Six

Keira dragged herself across the floor to where he lay.

The room filled with a wild keening noise. She knew it came from her, but couldn't make herself stop. Her world had changed from pleasure beyond anything she had ever imagined to a nightmare of fear.

He lay so still. She couldn't feel anything from him and panic threatened to overwhelm her. Why couldn't she have left well alone? She had almost begged him to make love to her and now she had killed him.

She ran her trembling hands over his silky fur.

"Please," she murmured. "Please, Connor, be alive."

If he was dead, then so was she.

His body was still warm. She crawled around him and put her face close to the great jaws. For a moment, she felt nothing. Despair flooded her. She was beyond tears, but dry, heaving sobs racked her.

She hugged him, burrowing her face in his coat.

And against her cheek, she felt the faintest of heartbeats.

She didn't move for a long time. The day faded, the night drew in around her, and the cold crept into her body. The only warmth came from the great beast she held. Finally, when his heartbeat improved to a steady thud, she crawled onto her hands and knees and pushed herself to her feet.

The wolf didn't move as she pulled on her clothes. After adding a sweater on top of her T-shirt, she still shivered as though with cold. She knew it was deep inside her.

It had felt so good; she hadn't imagined it could be like that. His mouth on her, inside her.

Right up until the moment she had nearly killed him.

She still wasn't sure he'd be all right.

Stepping softly around the keep, she pulled things out of their places and considered them. Some she discarded, others she tucked into a small rucksack. After twenty-two years, she possessed little that had any meaning to her. Her hand hovered briefly over the hollow in the wall where she'd hidden her notes, but then passed it by. Maybe one day, she would tell someone of them, but not yet.

She placed the rucksack close to Connor, scribbled a note, and laid it on top.

I'm sorry.

Then she picked up her sleeping bag, left the keep, and took herself off to a safe distance. She dozed on and off through the long night but woke as the sky turned tangerine with the sunrise. Cold and stiff, she wrapped the bag tight around her as she stared at the entrance to the keep, willing Connor to appear. She didn't dare go back and check him in case he awoke while she was close, but her nerves were ripped to shreds by the time he finally emerged.

He was fully dressed and carried her rucksack in one hand. So the plan must still be on and he wasn't going to abandon her. She wouldn't have blamed him. As he came out of the shadows around the Keep, she saw how ill he looked, his skin tinged green under the olive, dark shadows beneath his eyes. But he was alive.

She stood so he would see her and not come too close.

He stopped. "Are you all right?"

She couldn't hear the words from this distance, but she understood their meaning.

Yeah, as all right as anyone could be when their first orgasm was probably also their last because it had nearly melted their almost lover's mind. Christ, she was messed up. But she nodded her head and forced a smile.

His smile in return looked equally forced, probably because he was wincing at the same time. She hoped she hadn't done any irreparable damage.

He put the rucksack on the ground and straightened. Raising one hand, he held up a piece of paper, a small brown bottle, and a mug. He placed them next to the rucksack and then strode off in the opposite direction. When he'd reached a safe distance, Keira headed back with her sleeping bag in tow. She picked up the note and read it slowly.

I'm sorry, too. That wasn't how I envisaged the evening ending.

Take two of the pills. They will knock you out for the journey. I'll see you when we get there.

And Keira, don't worry. Somehow, we'll sort this out. You're not alone.

Connor

PS then lie down before you fall down

She almost smiled at his attempt at lightness, but didn't quite succeed. This was the moment of truth. If she took those pills, she put herself totally in Connor's hands. Did she really trust him enough? Or would she wake up deep in some Agency laboratory. She glanced up to where he sat perched on a rock, watching her. Her heart ached. She'd never expected a happy ever after, but these last days she'd begun to hope for something more than her life had been. And her hopes all centered on this man.

Yes, she trusted him.

She stared at the bottle, rattled it, then slowly unscrewed the top. She shook two pills into her palm. They were small, white, and totally innocuous in appearance. Before she could think anymore, she popped them in her mouth, swallowed, and took a gulp of water from the mug. Then she lay down and curled on her side so she could watch Connor as the darkness stole over her.

The drug acted fast, too fast; he was disappearing from her vision as the shadows encroached on her mind. Finally, he was all she could see, and then the light went completely.

Connor felt like shit. He couldn't remember feeling this bad in his entire life. Except for the actual moments when Keira had just about melted his brain. A constant hammering battered his skull from behind his left ear. The implant had gone, whether it had melted, or come loose and vanished when he shifted, he didn't know. He'd have to check when he got back to London. He wished he had some pain killers, but since when did a goddamn werewolf get headaches?

It had occurred to him as he watched Keira unscrew the bottle, that it might have been a better idea to get her to walk the five miles to where he'd parked the vehicle and take the pills there. Obviously, his brain wasn't working as it should, and it was too late now. Under normal circumstances, carrying her would have been easy; she weighed almost nothing. But these were hardly normal circumstances. Anyway, it was too late.

The pills would take only minutes to work. She lay on her side, her head pillowed on her hands, her gaze fixe on him.

For a second, the memory of how she had tasted, how she had felt... the softness of her skin, overrode the pain in his skull. His cock twitched, which was amazing. Half an hour ago, he'd been ready to swear off even thinking about sex for the rest of his long and miserable life.

He felt the moment she slept, the pain in his head receded slightly. He waited another five minutes and then got slowly to his feet and approached her cautiously. Crouching down, he brushed the long hair from her face, and a wave of tenderness swept over him. She was deep under, and he lowered his head to kiss her lightly on the lips.

He gathered everything up, pulled the sleeping bag from under her, and carried them back to the keep. He didn't want to leave any signs in case the people searching for her returned. When he left the keep, he made sure the branches covered the opening. No one looking at the place would see it as anything more than a ruin.

Finally, he went back to her, put her rucksack over his shoulders, and picked her up in his arms. It was a long, hard five miles and he was glad of the reviving effect of the drizzle that started to fall half way through the journey. But at least his head cleared on the way, and he was pretty sure there'd be no permanent damage.

He was starting to feel a little more optimistic by the time the truck came into sight. Then he swore under his breath. Two men leaned against the vehicle, watching his approach.

His first thought was—Agency. But as he got closer, he recognized them. The taller man was one of the werewolves who had picked him up in Kinlochlevin. The other had been in the room with the alpha. It seemed a lifetime ago but was in fact only four days. He had a gun in the bottom of his rucksack—a gift from Sebastian. Unfortunately, his rucksack was back at Keira's keep. Besides, he would hardly have been able to draw the weapon with his arms full of unconscious woman.

He swore again then decided to ignore them while he put Keira in the vehicle. He juggled her into one arm and pulled his keys from his pocket. The men straightened but didn't speak as he opened the back and laid Keira down on the seat. He'd come prepared and had a cushion for underneath her head and a blanket for over her. She appeared tiny and pale curled up on the seat. He checked her pulse but it was steady and he sighed, slammed the door, and turned back to the two men.

"Is she dead?" the tall one asked.

"Of course she's not bloody dead." He was going to add—what do you take me for? A stupid question under the circumstances. Was he going to have to fight? And was there any point if they were armed?

"Look, I don't want any trouble. I'm on my way out of here and you won't see me again."

The shorter man moved forward. He had sandy hair and shrewd pale blue eyes. As he stepped up close, Connor's wolf awoke and without even thinking, a growl trickled from his throat.

The two men exchanged glances but made no aggressive moves.

Connor frowned. "What is it you want?"

The blond man nodded and the other spoke. "We want you to fight Logan."

Shock hit him in the gut. Whatever he'd been expecting, it wasn't this. "What? Why?"

"You saw what he's like. He's evil. But he's old and powerful. None of us can go up against him."

"And you think I can?" The disbelief was clear in his voice.

The taller man nodded toward the other. "Pete is the second strongest in the pack. And your wolf just faced him down and told him to piss off."

"He did?"

Pete's brows drew together. "Do you know anything?"

"Let's suppose I don't."

"How long since you were changed?"

Connor glanced at the vehicle, eager to get away. Keira wouldn't stay under forever and he needed her safely inside that room before she woke. But he suspected talking was the best way to get through this.

"Six years."

"Only six? Shit, I've never come across a wolf so strong at six."

Connor scowled. He didn't want to be fucking super-wolf.

"We've spoken to the others," Pete said. "No one will shoot you if you challenge Logan."

"Well, that's comforting, but I'm not challenging anyone." He nodded toward the back of the car. "I have a sick woman and she needs help."

Pete shrugged. "We had to try. We won't stop you. But if you change your mind..."

"I won't."

They stepped away as he opened the driver's door. Connor hesitated and turned back to them. "Why don't you all go up against him? You could take him if you worked together."

"It's not the way it's done. There would be no one strong enough to lead the pack. We would be in chaos. Look, if you change your mind, you'll find us in the big walled house at the northern end of the moors."

Connor shook his head. "I'm not the man you need."

He climbed in and turned on the engine, but couldn't get the image of the woman out of his mind, the one whose arm had been broken. But he was no pack leader. They would have to sort out their own problems. Right now, he had enough of his own. But he was aware of them watching him, and he couldn't drown out the little niggle of guilt that nagged until way after they had disappeared from sight.

Chapter Seven

"You look like total shit." Sebastian peered in through the open window of the vehicle.

He'd appeared as soon as Connor pulled up in the underground garage. Anya and Tasha were close behind, but they were pretty much ignoring Connor as they tried to see into the back of the truck.

Tasha frowned. "She is in there, isn't she?"

Connor nodded.

"Why didn't you phone?" Anya asked. "We were about to set off to search for you."

"Your sister has a habit of frying cell phones, and computers, and probably anything else she gets close to."

"Including people, if you're anything to go by." Sebastian studied him through narrowed eyes. "So the implant didn't work?"

Connor twitched uncomfortably. He glanced from Anya to Tasha and away again. He supposed he was going to have to tell them what had happened at some point. They needed to know the facts if they were going to help Keira and maybe the girls would have an insight into what had gone wrong. But he really wasn't up to the whole "we were fine until she came" conversation. He wasn't sure he ever would be, but he'd work himself up to it.

"To a point," he said eventually when it became obvious they were all waiting for an answer.

"What point?" Sebastian persisted.

Connor frowned. "Later." The word came out more as a growl than he'd intended. Sebastian quirked an eyebrow but nodded.

"Is the room ready?" Connor asked.

"Well, it's done as we discussed. I hope it will be enough."

So did he.

Connor rubbed his forehead, the headache had faded through the long day, but it was still an unpleasant memory. Now exhaustion tugged at his mind, his eyes ached, and his stomach growled for food.

He climbed out of the truck and stretched, trying to ease the kinks from his shoulders.

"Hey, did I mention you look like shit?"

"Yeah."

"Why don't you go upstairs and get some food and rest and we'll see to her." He nodded toward the back of the vehicle.

"No." Again, the word came out harsher than he'd planned. What the hell was wrong with him? But he needed to see Keira was safe and all right before he could rest.

Sebastian pursed his lips. "Is there something you're not telling us?"

"Like what?"

Sebastian shrugged. "Never mind. We can talk later. For now, let's get her out of there and settled."

Connor moved to the back of the vehicle and opened the door, trying to ignore the women attempting to peer around him. He checked Keira's pulse; it was steady, but she was still deep under. He picked her up gently and held her cradled against his chest. Her lips were slightly parted, and she was breathing lightly but evenly, and that wave of tenderness washed over him again.

Mine.

The word whispered through his mind and his arms tightened. He looked up to find all three watching him, their faces blanked of expressions. Sebastian, he presumed on purpose. But he suspected Tasha and Anya were "speaking" to each other.

He cleared his throat. "Lead the way."

He followed them out of the garage, down another two flights of stairs to one of the lower levels. Finally, Sebastian led him through a door into an antechamber and then into the room itself. It was small, with a narrow cot bed, a table, a single chair, a fridge in the corner, and a tiny bathroom.

"It was the best we could do in the time," Sebastian said.

But obviously, someone—Tasha and Anya presumably—had gone to some effort to brighten the place up with a scarlet bedspread and matching cushions. There were pictures of horses on the walls and a bright woven rug on the floor. Flowers in a vase. Still, it was hard to hide that it was essentially a small, windowless metal box.

A camera hung from the ceiling in one corner of the room, pointing at the bed. He supposed it was a necessity, but he hated the thought of other people watching her sleep.

Tasha ran in front of him and stripped down the bedspread. He laid Keira on the soft cotton sheets, tugged off her shoes, and then pulled the blanket over her. She immediately curled onto her side and snuggled into the pillow.

He wished he could lie next to her and hold her, be there for her when she woke, but he knew it was impossible, and he forced himself to turn away.

Once outside, the exhaustion dragged at him as he realized he'd done it. She was here and safe for the moment.

The outer room had been set up like an observation station, with a desk and monitor, a couple of chairs and a small sofa pushed against the back wall. He rifled in the desk, found a piece of paper and a pen, and scribbled a quick note so she wouldn't feel so alone when she awoke.

I'll be close by.

Connor.

Then he went back into the room and placed the note on the table where she would see it when she woke. When he came back out, they were all still there. He got the distinct impression they'd been talking about him.

Anya came to stand beside him and rested her hand on his arm. "Connor, go to bed," she said. "We'll watch out for her."

He knew it was sensible. He glanced at the monitor—someone had switched it on—and saw Keira still sleeping. He had no clue how long she would stay that way. "Don't go in there if she wakes," he said. "And come and get me if there's any change. And—"

"Connor, go to bed."

He glanced at Sebastian who regarded him with an expression of wry amusement that Connor wasn't sure he liked. Actually, he was sure—he hated it.

Closing his eyes, he counted to ten, and forced the tension from his muscles. When he opened his eyes, they were all still watching him.

"I'm going to bed," he announced, turned around and stalked from the room.

She was warm and dry. Positively cozy—all she had ever asked for when living on the moors.

The bed was soft and the pillow deep and she snuggled down for a moment longer. She didn't want to open her eyes, she was so comfortable, but something tugged at her memory.

Connor.

Making love.

Nearly killing him.

Taking the pills.

Her eyes opened. She was no longer on the moors, that much was clear. She lay on a bed in a small room, with no windows. For a few seconds claustrophobia threatened to overtake her. She'd spent a year in a cell when she had first become telepathic and the nightmares still haunted her from that time. She breathed in deeply and forced the panic down. Someone had left a bottle of water on the table and she drank, trying to get rid of the dry, sour taste in her mouth. Then she saw the note. Picking it up, she ran her hands across the script. Was he close?

She examined her surroundings some more. A fridge stood in the corner, hopefully with some food—her stomach rumbled at the thought. And a camera hung in the corner of the room, but at least they'd made no attempt to hide it. Were they watching her even now? Was Connor watching her?

She pushed off the blanket and swung her feet to the floor. Her legs shook a little, but she locked her muscles and managed to stand. A couple of shaky steps took her to the small bathroom, and she leaned over the sink and splashed her face with water.

A mirror hung above the sink and for the first time in years, she stared into her own face.

She was pretty. Sort of. Her face was too thin, but she was okay, not horrible anyway, and her eyes were unusual.

Back in the bedroom, she studied her new home. A huge bunch of flowers stood on a shelf by the door, all sorts, mixed colors. Leaning down, she breathed in the sweet scent. A note was propped underneath.

Welcome, love Tasha and Anya

Her sisters.

"She's awake," Sebastian said. "Perhaps we should call Connor."

"I'm here." Connor stepped into the room and closed the door behind him. Anya sat at the desk, watching the monitor, Sebastian stood behind her. Tasha was curled up on the sofa, yawning.

Connor crossed the room and stared down at the screen. Keira sat on the bed, a plate of food perched on her knee. He wanted to go to her, comfort her, and tell her she wasn't alone, but that would be stupid. And painful.

He'd known she was conscious. Something had startled him awake. Could he sense her even through these walls? Not a headache but a slight buzz in his brain.

"So tell me what happened with the implant," Sebastian said.

Connor sighed. As he'd suspected, he was no more prepared to talk about it now than he had been before. He'd been thinking about what happened, and he reckoned it was probably safe for Sebastian to go in there. He didn't like the idea, but she needed to talk to someone, and Sebastian was shielded. Neither of the girls were; they didn't want to block their telepathy. Sebastian should be okay as long as he didn't try and make love with Keira, and he wouldn't do that because Anya would kill him. And she was an assassin and good at it. Or Connor would kill him. Either way he'd be dead.

"I think it melted," he answered Sebastian's question.

"So they don't work with her, even double strength?"

"No it worked at first, but it's buggered now."

"So it's unsafe for me to go in there?" Sebastian asked.

God, he was persistent. Connor shifted uneasily. He so didn't want to have this conversation. He took a deep breath, shoved his hands in his pockets. Opened his mouth, saw Anya and Tasha waiting expectantly for his words, and closed it again. Perhaps he should talk to Sebastian alone.

Sebastian frowned. "Come on, Connor. What happened?"

He could do this. "It was fine, no problems, we talked—I'll go through that later. Then…"

He watched as Keira took a bite of her sandwich, licked the crumbs from her lips and heat flickered along his nerves.

"Then later on, we were making love, and she came, and my brain exploded." He said the words as quickly as possible then waited for the fallout. It never came. Nobody appeared in any way shocked. In fact, Tasha nodded.

"Tasha reckoned that's what happened," Anya said.

Sebastian grinned. "I said not likely, you're such a miserable bastard. But at least you were making a good job of it."

"Fuck off," Connor growled.

"So I should be okay?" Sebastian said.

"Just don't get her excited, because it fucking hurt."

"Did it force you to shift?"

"Yeah, I'd have been dead otherwise. I was very nearly dead anyway."

"You like her don't you?" Tasha murmured.

He turned at the question and shrugged; it was nobody's business but his and Keira's. He'd had to tell them about the making love, because of the implant, that didn't mean he had to expose the rest of how he was feeling.

"Of course he likes her," Anya replied when he said nothing. "You saw how he looked at her."

Okay, so maybe nobody else realized it wasn't their business.

"We could wait for Jack," Tasha said. "He could always keep me out of his mind."

"No, I'll go in." Sebastian replied. "Perhaps we'll save the vampire for when she's more settled. Jack can be a little...overwhelming."

Connor took up position behind Anya as Sebastian disappeared behind the first set of doors. A few seconds later, he appeared in the room. Keira almost jumped.

"Is there audio?" Connor asked.

"Yes, just a second." Anya pressed a few keys and Sebastian's voice came through clearly.

"I'm Sebastian Quinn."

"Is Connor all right?" Keira asked.

"He's fine." He nodded at the camera. "He's in the next room watching over you."

Sebastian approached the bed slowly as if uncertain. He glanced up at the camera. "I'm okay, I think. I can feel something, like a buzz, but it's manageable." He turned back to Keira, pulled up the small chair and sat by the bed. "Welcome," he said. "I won't stay for long, but I wanted you to know you're not alone."

"What's going to happen to me?"

"We'll do some tests. See if we can work out what was done to you. Maybe we can reverse it, or somehow help you control it."

"Do you think that's possible?"

Connor recognized the hope in her voice, and he prayed they would find some way to help her. Tomorrow when they were both stronger, they would start the tests.

Sebastian shrugged. "I honestly don't know, but we'll try."

She nodded and Sebastian got up. "There's paper and pens in the drawer over there. Make a list of questions and we'll get answers for you. Now I suggest you sleep. We'll start work tomorrow."

"Okay. Will you tell Connor…" she trailed off. "Never mind."

She curled on her side as Sebastian left the room. Her eyes were open and she stared at the closed door, where he'd disappeared. She appeared so small, hunched on the bed. Connor couldn't bear to think of her alone in a strange place. Almost without conscious thought, his tugged his T-shirt over his head.

Tasha whistled, but Connor ignored the sound. Being a werewolf had almost cured him of any modesty. They usually stripped before they shifted—it saved having to replace their clothes every time.

Sebastian came through the outer door as he kicked off his boots.

"What the hell are you doing?"

"She shouldn't be alone. Not on her first night."

"You're going to shift?"

Sebastian sounded shocked, but then Connor had never shifted except when he had no choice. He nodded and pulled off his jeans.

Closing his eyes, he willed his wolf to the surface. He shivered as the magic rippled through him. Then he was standing on all fours. His senses more acute, he could scent the others in the room and the metallic smell of the walls. It made him uneasy; he wanted to be outside, back on the moors. Wolf had liked the moors.

His claws made clicks on the tiles as he headed for the door. Sebastian opened it for him, then the inside door and he stepped into the small room.

Keira gasped as he appeared and then a smile curved her lips. He padded across the floor and leapt lightly on the bed. The narrow cot was hardly big enough for the both of them, but she scooted over and he stretched out beside her so their bodies touched all the way along.

He lifted his head to face the camera and curled his upper lip in a snarl. The green light turned to red. He laid his head down and she turned onto her side and wrapped her arms around his shoulders, pressed her face into his neck.

A sense of peace stole over him. He closed his eyes and slept.

Chapter Eight

"Can you reverse it?" Sebastian asked.

Connor pressed his fingers to his eyes trying to ease the pressure. His head ached constantly. He knew it was Keira, however hard he tried to deny it.

And he wasn't the only one affected.

Headaches. Nausea. They were all suffering.

Only the vampires were immune.

After a week, he knew Keira was beginning to despair.

He held up the X-ray of her brain and pointed to the dark patch of scar tissue. "I doubt they knew exactly what they were doing," he said. "They probably just blasted a laser at her brain to see what would happen and then decided to dispose of her when it didn't work."

Sebastian traced a finger down the film. "So what does it all mean?"

"That there's fuck all we can do."

"You can't operate?"

Connor ran a hand through his hair pressing his skull. "We don't know enough about that section of the brain to even try. We could do irreparable damage. And besides, the scarring is too bad."

"Maybe once we've all moved out, she can stay without doing too much harm. Might give the people in the neighboring buildings a headache, but they won't know the cause."

"And she might give them all brain cancer." Connor had to point out.

"You think she caused her mother's cancer?"

Connor didn't want to consider it but he knew he had to. "I don't know, but it's a distinct possibility. For us it's okay, each time we shift we clear anything. But for humans…"

"Send her back to Scotland?"

No way was Connor letting her return to the moors to live out her life alone. "That's not an option."

"You know there is one thing you could try," Sebastian said, his tone bland.

Yeah, Connor knew. He'd been trying not to think about that particular route. He'd always sworn he would never change anyone. But things were different now.

"Would it work?" he asked.

"There are no guarantees."

God, Sebastian could be annoying. "But what do you think?"

"I think if she survives, then it will work. I've seen amputees regain their limbs after they shift. Blind people see again. So yes, I believe it would heal the damage to her brain."

Connor latched on to one thing. "If she survives?"

"Many don't. Some go insane and have to be killed. Some just don't recover from the wound."

"Thanks," Connor muttered.

"You need to be aware of the dangers if you go ahead with this. You both need to be aware."

"What are the chances?"

"With normal humans only about one in ten survive. But you're strong and that's important."

"Would she be better off with you doing it?" Connor's wolf nipped at his insides at the thought of Sebastian touching her, but he had to ask.

Sebastian shook his head. "No. You might not want to admit it but you're as strong or stronger than me and you're much younger."

His wolf settled.

"The other factor in her favor is both her sisters survived," Sebastian said. "She has to be very close genetically. I think there's a good chance. But will *she* accept it?"

"She asked me already. In Scotland. Back then, I didn't want to. I still don't know whether I have the right to do that to anyone."

Sebastian gave a casual shrug. "So send her back to the moors."

"No."

Sebastian leaned back against the wall, arms folded across his chest. He appeared vaguely amused, which pissed the hell out of Connor.

"You do know even if it works, she has to have sex before she'll shift," Sebastian said.

Shit, he'd forgotten all about that bit. When a human was attacked, they wouldn't change until after they had sex, and then they'd shift at the next full moon after that. Or before if they wished. But they had no choice when the full moon came around. Connor hadn't known about the sex thing when he'd been bitten. Hell, he hadn't known about the werewolf thing. Why would he have? If he'd known, he might never have had sex again.

But he remembered the days after the attack. Once he'd recovered, he'd gone around with a constant hard on. At the time, he'd reckoned it had been some sort of survival reaction. He'd nearly died, but he hadn't, so he wanted to screw every acceptable woman he came across as a celebration of life. That's how he'd excused it anyway. Apparently, the urge was normal. Something else he hadn't known.

"And it's not going to be you," Sebastian continued.

The words dragged Connor from his less than pleasant memories. "The hell it isn't."

It certainly wasn't going to be anyone else.

"She won't heal entirely until she shifts for the first time, and until then you can't get near her. I think her best bet is a vampire. They're the only ones who aren't affected. Not Jack—Tasha might stake him first. But Keira can pick one of the others."

Connor growled. "Any one of them fucking bloodsucking leeches touches her and I'll rip their fucking throats out."

Sebastian grinned. "Hey, did you know you're actually starting to sound like a werewolf?"

"Piss off." He had the distinct impression Sebastian was baiting him.

"Seriously though," Sebastian said. "How are you going to do it? Maybe you could drug her—though I'm not sure it will work if she's unconscious."

He so did not want to be talking to Sebastian about having sex with Keira. But the alpha had a point. "I need another implant."

"Yeah, because that worked *so* well last time."

"I'll be careful." All he had to do was make sure she didn't enjoy it. She'd been fine right up until the point she came. He just had to ensure she didn't come. He'd make it up to her later.

"And I thought you'd decided against another implant."

"I had. And now I've changed my mind." He hoped his tone made it clear the conversation was over.

Finished.

Sebastian shrugged. "So, I'll go put it to her. See what she says."

"I'm coming."

"You are?"

Connor was already stripping.

Keira glanced up as the outer door clicked. She fixed a smile on her face.

Trying to feel optimistic was getting her down. As was this place. She longed to be able to talk to Connor face to face. Though she supposed she did talk to him, every night when he came to her in wolf form. Only trouble was, she wanted him to answer back and apart from the odd growl when he disapproved of something she said, she didn't get much response.

Her sisters had also spent time with her in their wolf form. Tasha was a beautiful slinky red wolf with golden eyes so like Keira's own. Anya was silver blond with dark eyes. Keira wanted to talk to them so badly. They were gone now. They'd written her a wonderful letter, but said they couldn't block her out and it hurt.

She hurt everyone.

Connor and Sebastian were working hard, doing tests, trying to find a way to help her. But she also knew that so far they had come up with nothing.

When the inner door opened, she was surprised to see Sebastian. He'd stayed away since their first meeting. She suspected that despite the implant, she gave him a headache.

She'd been expecting one of the vampires and had braced herself accordingly. She hated to admit it, but they terrified her. Jack was okay. She reckoned because he was older and better able to hide what he was. With some of the younger ones, you could almost see them sniffing at her neck. Or maybe it was just her overactive imagination.

Behind Sebastian padded a huge black wolf. Connor. Her fake smile faded to be replaced by the real thing. He came to a halt by her chair and sat on his haunches, resting his great head on her lap. She stroked him while she waited for Sebastian to speak.

He perched on the edge of her bed, his expression solemn. Keira glanced from one to the other.

"Tell me," she said.

It was bad news. She knew it. She was killing everyone. Or dying. Or…

"Hey, it's not that bad. We just want to talk to you about something."

"You do? About what?" She still couldn't shake the conviction the "something" wasn't good.

"How would you feel about becoming a werewolf?"

For a moment, she thought she'd misheard. Since that first time she'd mentioned it to Connor and he'd reacted so negatively, she hadn't considered it again. Or she'd tried not to.

She'd asked Jack about it, but he'd said she needed to talk to one of the wolves. It wasn't his place to give out pack information. That was all very well, but the only wolf she spent time with was Connor, and he wasn't talking.

"Connor said it wasn't an option."

"He was maybe a little hasty. I'm not going to lie. It might kill you or send you crazy. Only around ten percent of people successfully make the transition. And we have no guarantees it will reverse whatever was done to you."

She forced a weak smile. "If you're trying to convince me, you're doing a crap job."

"I don't want you to think this is the easy path. You need to consider the choices."

"I have choices?"

"You can stay here for now. Later, we'll set up somewhere similar but away from so many people. And maybe a bit nicer. We can continue to research, we might eventually come up with an answer."

It would still be a prison though. She thought about a lifetime in a tiny room, the years passing, and the hope gradually fading to nothing.

"Or you could return to Scotland."

For a moment, she was filled with the need to be out on the wide open moors. To feel the rain on her face.

"We won't abandon you. You won't be alone. We'll set up some system where we can keep in contact, provide you with food…whatever you need."

But she knew she couldn't go back to her old life. The thought of the loneliness, of living with the fear the Agency would find her. Or that she would inadvertently kill some unsuspecting stranger.

"You haven't mentioned one choice," she said.

"What's that?" Sebastian asked.

"You could put me down like the Agency planned to do all those years ago."

A low growl came from Connor and she forced herself to stare into his dark eyes. Even as a wolf, she was able to read his emotions so clearly. He was pissed off.

"Maybe it would have been better," she said. "My mother might be still alive."

He nipped her hand.

"Ow."

Sebastian leaned back in his chair, his eyes narrowed, lips pursed. "I can see why Connor likes you now—no doubt you wallow in self-pity together." Then he sighed and ran a hand through his hair. "I've done my share of wallowing, but in the end, it does no good. You have to decide if you want to survive. But I think you did that a long time ago."

He was right. Even at her darkest moments, she hadn't wanted to die.

"What does Connor think?" she asked. He'd been so against even the idea of her becoming like him.

"Connor wants you to survive."

He licked her hand.

"You know," Sebastian said. "I think you saved Connor's life."

The wolf snarled revealing a sharp white fang. Sebastian ignored him.

"I did?"

"When I sent him to Scotland, he was bordering on suicidal. I don't think he would have killed himself, but he was searching for a way out, and for a werewolf there's always a violent way to die if you want it enough. But he's changed, and I think that's because of you. You've given him a reason to go on. Made him see his wolf as something that can do good, instead of only evil."

Keira hated to think of Connor in so much pain. But she'd sensed it herself that first day on the moors. It had been what drew her to him. What would happen to him if she did this and failed? Would he go back to being angry at the world? But if she didn't attempt it, would he feel the need to stay with her? Tie himself to the pathetic sort of life, which was all she would ever have. Come and sleep with her each night as a wolf. Never to talk. Never to hold each other. Never to make love.

She stroked his head absentmindedly while she considered her "choices". But inside her, a wild exhilaration was awakening. She tried to make herself concentrate on the risks. One in ten didn't sound like good odds. And what if she went insane? But then that might happen anyway—who knew what was going on in her head?

Or what if she allowed herself to hope and nothing changed?

Still, the little spark wouldn't die. Instead, it burned brighter. If she did this, she'd finally be part of something. Have a family. Maybe even see where this thing with Connor would take them. But what if he hated all werewolves? Would he also hate her if she changed?

She thought about asking, but he'd hardly be likely to tell her the truth. Instead, she turned to Sebastian. "What would *you* do?"

"I'd go for it. And I know Anya and Tasha feel the same."

"You've discussed it?"

"We have, but we didn't want to bring it up until Connor reached the same conclusion on his own."

"What if he never did?"

"Then sooner or later we would have offered you the opportunity anyway."

Keira closed her eyes for a moment and searched deep inside her mind. Yes, she was scared. But she wanted this so much it was like an ache in her heart.

She blinked. "I'll do it."

Sebastian released his breath and she realized he'd been in no way sure of her answer. Connor nipped her again and she took his face between her hands and kissed the top of his head. Then drew in a deep breath. "Though I'm not entirely sure what 'it' is. How does this work?"

"Usually a person is attacked, maybe by a rogue wolf or in Tasha's case a wolf was paid to attack her."

"Really? Why?"

"The Agency wanted her out of the way, but they also liked the idea of a werewolf to study."

"What about Anya?"

"I changed Anya. It was the only way to save her life after the Agency poisoned her."

"You attacked her?"

"I bit her."

She looked at him. Sebastian was gorgeous, tall and lean with blond hair down to his shoulders and the wickedest blue eyes she had ever seen. He had an easy way about him, relaxed and laidback, which no doubt hid what he really was—a powerful alpha werewolf. But despite him being stunning, she wasn't sure she wanted him that close. "Would you bite me?"

A low growl came from Connor and Sebastian grinned. "I think I'll leave the biting to someone else. But make no mistake—this is going to hurt. It's not exactly a scientific process, but for the best chance, I reckon the wound needs to be pretty severe. Are you sure you can you do that?"

The question was aimed at Connor. He nodded his huge head though she sensed he wasn't happy. She peeked at his teeth and realized they would have to sink into her flesh, draw blood... she shivered.

Sebastian must have seen her reaction. "We could drug you, I suppose. I doubt that would interfere."

"Did you drug Anya?"

"No, but she was so close to death, she wasn't aware of what was going on."

Keira shook her head. "I've been drugged before. I don't want that."

He shrugged, but appeared pleased by her answer. "It usually takes about a week to recover from the wound—if you do recover."

"And if I don't? How long will I have?"

"You'll be dead within days. If you're lucky."

Keira decided not to go there. "Then what? Then I'll be a wolf, be able to change?"

Sebastian stood up and shoved his hands in his pockets. "There's one more thing you need to do."

Why did he seem uncomfortable? What was worse than being bitten by a wolf?"

"You have to have sex," he said.

For a few seconds, she thought she'd misheard. "Sex?"

"You won't shift until you've had sexual intercourse. And you won't heal until you shift."

"So I have to have sex?"

He nodded.

"With another werewolf?" She glanced at Connor and he licked her hand. But how could she? She had almost killed him last time. She'd melted the implant. Nearly melted his brain.

"No," Sebastian replied. "It doesn't have to be a werewolf. One of the vamps could do it."

Connor growled.

"She needs to know the options," Sebastian said to him. "If this works you'll have plenty of time to do what you like. But not if you're dead."

Connor tugged away from her and went to stand in front of Sebastian. He growled some more.

Sebastian sighed. "Yeah, I'll tell her."

"Tell me what?"

His lips quirked. "That if you have sex with one of those blood sucking leeches, Connor will rip their throat out."

Relief washed through her. She so did not want to have sex with a scary vampire. She wanted to make love with Connor. But right now, he couldn't even be in the same room as her without shifting so she wasn't sure how they were going to accomplish the deed.

She glanced from the wolf to Sebastian as a horrible thought occurred to her. "Hey, it has to be with a human, right?"

Sebastian's lips quirked again. She was glad *he* was finding this amusing.

"Yeah, it has to be with a human or in human form."

"Well, that's a relief." She chewed on her lower lip then shrugged helplessly. "So, how…"

"He's going to have another implant."

"Is that safe?" She knew if it had been totally safe then he would have done it by now. So obviously not.

Sebastian didn't meet her eyes. "Connor reckons he can be careful."

"Whatever that means," she muttered.

Careful she didn't enjoy herself too much, she reckoned. She had a flashback to the feel of his warm mouth between her thighs, his tongue stroking her. She squirmed as she relived the moment she had come apart and then everything had gone to hell.

Perhaps *not* enjoying herself might not be such a big issue. Her insides shriveled up at the memory. Her pleasure centers locking down. It made her sad in a way. But if this worked then it would be worth some sacrifice.

"When? When do we do this?"

Sebastian glanced from her to Connor and back again. "Why not now?"

Chapter Nine

"Why not?" she murmured as the door closed behind Sebastian.

Actually, she could think of a whole load of very good reasons. Starting with—she was scared.

Glancing down, she caught Connor's dark gaze. She wondered how much persuasion it had taken Sebastian to get him this far. And how badly her brain was messed up. Pretty bad, she supposed if Connor had agreed to try and change her. He would have explored every other possibility before they had come to this.

"Is it so bad being a wolf?" she asked.

He didn't answer, but turned away and paced the room. It took him two steps to reach the wall and he swiveled and came back. She could see the frustration in his eyes, and the fear. He was scared as well. She just wasn't sure what he feared. That they would fail or that they'd succeed.

No, she wasn't being fair. He wanted her to live. That he would even consider doing this was a testament to how much. She crouched down and took his face between her hands.

"Whatever happens, thank you for finding me, trying to help me. It means so much."

He nodded.

How the hell did they do this? Should she just stand and wait? Would he leap at her?

He padded to the bed.

"Where?" she asked.

He tilted his head to the bed. She gave a sigh. "I mean where will you bite me?"

His dark gaze wandered down over her body, then up again to settle on the spot where her neck met her shoulder. She winced as if she could already feel his teeth sinking into her flesh. Then she dragged her T-shirt over her head. She'd better do this quickly before she lost her nerve. Tossing the shirt on the chair, she shuffled closer to the bed.

She knew all about pain. She occasionally suffered almost blinding headaches. How much worse could this be?

Time to find out.

She lay down, and then came up on one elbow. "Hey, is this going to be messy?"

He nodded.

"Maybe, I should get a towel or something."

He shook his head then leapt lightly onto the bed beside her.

Keira could hear the thud of her heart and feel the blood pulsing through her veins. A light sweat broke out on her skin.

I can do this. I can do this.

Connor inched up the bed on his belly until his hot breath fanned across her bare shoulder.

Every one of her muscles locked up tight, anticipating the pain.

"Maybe those drugs weren't such a bad idea," she muttered.

Connor raised his head and backed off slightly, a question clear in his eyes.

"I'm kidding," she said and took a deep breath. "I think. Just do it."

And she closed her eyes tight.

She heard the crunch of bone before she felt the pain, like a delayed reaction. Her lids flew open as blood sprayed from the wound and splashed across the white sheets and grey walls.

So much blood.

Then the pain came, washing over her in a tidal wave of red hot fire. It drove every thought from her mind leaving her with nothing but the teeth tearing at her flesh, the thick heavy stench of blood filling her nostrils. Her back arched and she screamed.

She hadn't meant to fight back, but she couldn't help herself, her hands clawing at the great beast, her legs kicking out.

The pain built inside her, until she knew something had to give. Behind her closed lids, great flashes of red and black played across her mind. The darkness was coming for her, closing on her, and she welcomed it as an end to the pain.

She was dying.

She'd failed.

And she wanted to tell Connor it wasn't his fault.

Connor released his grip and backed away. He jumped off the bed and stood, head hanging low. Then he willed the change to come over him. Finally, he stood over her. Her shoulder was a mangled mess and the room looked like an abattoir. For once, the scent and sight of blood didn't arouse his hunger.

She was unconscious, and he was glad. He'd nearly failed at the last minute when she'd screamed and he'd known how much he was hurting her. Instead, he had closed his ears to the sound and did what he had to do.

He spat and then swallowed the nausea rising up in his throat.

Leaning down, he felt the pulse in her throat, it was way too fast, but still strong, and some of the tension seeped from him.

He went to the small bathroom and threw up, then rinsed his face. He had to get himself together. He was a doctor. Time to behave like one.

He found Sebastian in the outer room and ignored his expression of pity as he dragged on his clothes. Sebastian nodded toward the doctor's bag on the floor beside him.

"Clean the wound but don't try and close it or cover it. If she's going to come through this, then it will heal itself."

"How long until we know?"

"It varies. All we can do is keep her comfortable. Also, I've arranged for the implant. Go up to the medical center when you've seen to her."

Connor nodded absently, picked up the bag, and turned back.

"You did the right thing," Sebastian said.

"Maybe."

He returned to the room and stared down at her for a second. She appeared so tiny. Her top half was bare but for the black bra, stark against her pale skin. The wound was still seeping. He'd made a mess, but he wasn't very experienced at biting people. Maybe he should have let Sebastian do the job after all. Sinking down beside her, he stroked her hair from her face. Her skin felt clammy to the touch, but she turned her face into his palm.

He cleaned the wound quickly. The sheets needed changing, but he couldn't risk moving her. She was becoming restless and he had to get out of there before she regained consciousness. Leaning close, he kissed her lightly on the lips and then got to his feet.

His life had been a nightmare for so long. He'd fought what he was every inch of the way, hating what he had become. And now he'd done the same to someone else. Only time would tell if he'd been right to attempt this, or whether it was one more thing he would come to regret bitterly.

"She's going to make it."

Connor had been dozing in the chair by the bed, but Sebastian's words made him come instantly awake. He jumped to his feet. "What?"

Sebastian nodded to where Keira lay on the bed. It had been three days since Connor had bitten her and her condition had remained unchanged. Her waking moments had been almost unbearable for him; she'd screamed and tossed, aware of nothing but pain. She hadn't recognized him and he'd spent much of the time holding her down to stop her damaging herself. Luckily, she'd been unconscious most of the time, though Sebastian had refused to say whether that was a good or bad sign. Connor didn't remember suffering like this. The pain had been bad but his wounds had healed quickly.

"She'll be all right," Sebastian said

"You're sure?"

Sebastian peeled back the sheet covering her shoulder. Connor saw the change immediately. The wound had been angry, seeping, refusing to close. Now, the skin surrounding the bite glowed pink and healthy, the edges knitting together. He peered into her face; her eyes were closed, dark lashes fanning her pale cheeks, but her breathing was even, and she was resting comfortably.

Connor closed his eyes for a moment as relief threatened to take him down. Then he sank into the chair behind him, put his head in his hands, and pressed his fingers to his eyes. He'd been so sure he'd failed. That he'd killed her and would have to live with that forever because dying would have been the easy way out.

"She'll wake soon," Sebastian said. He rested a hand on Connor's shoulder. "I'll leave you, but you did good. You both did. Say welcome to the pack for me."

Connor didn't move until the other man had left the room. Then he stood slowly and stretched. He found the change from despair to hope almost too much to cope with. Maybe he'd been a miserable bastard for too long. Or perhaps that was merely his nature.

He kicked off his shoes and stretched out on the bed besides Keira, his touch tentative at first, but when no sounds of pain came from her, he pulled her into his arms, tucked her head under his chin, and was asleep in seconds.

Keira blinked open her eyes. For a second, she panicked. Something wrapped around her tight, taking her back to those times at the Agency when she had woken strapped to a metal table not knowing what they were going to do to her.

Then she breathed in and recognized the scent of her favorite werewolf. It came back to her slowly. The bite. The agony.

She was still alive and she felt...good.

Had it worked?

She twisted her neck expecting to feel pain, but there was nothing, maybe a slight tingle. She pulled her hand free and ran it over her shoulder; the skin was raised and tender, but the wound had closed.

Turning her head, she looked straight into Connor's open eyes, deep dark brown with flecks of gold. He smiled, a slow lazy smile, and the muscles in her stomach clenched. He was plastered against her, and this close it was impossible not to feel the steely hardness of his erection pressing against her thigh.

She shifted slightly and his smile faded.

He pulled away and came up on one elbow. "How do you feel?"

"Good." She forced herself to ask the question. "Am I going to be all right?"

"Yes. According to Sebastian, you'll be fine now."

Reaching up, she ran her hands over his skull, feeling for the slight raise where the implant had been inserted.

"You got the implant?"

He nodded. "I could have waited to see if..."

"...if I survived."

"Yeah, but I wanted to be with you when you woke."

"I'm glad." She bit her lip. She'd come this far, and now it was all starting to get real. She was finally accepting there might be a chance of some sort of normal life for her. Though it occurred to her that her concept of "normal" had changed radically if she considered life as a werewolf in any way qualified. "What happens afterward?"

"Afterward?"

"If it all works. Where do I go? Do I stay with the pack? Is that what happens?"

"Things are a bit unusual right now since the Agency destroyed the pack house."

"The pack house—where's that?"

"An hour or so outside London. It's an estate, walled, safe for us to run. Sebastian has sent some of his people back already. But I've never stayed there. I've always preferred to live on my own."

"And what about now? You don't want to stay with the pack?"

"I thought you might move in with me. See how it works."

Relief flooded her; he wanted her with him. For a moment there, she'd thought he'd meant to leave her with the pack and go on with his solitary existence. "Of course, I'll come with you. I owe you my life, but more than that, I want us to be together."

He shrugged. "I thought if we were alone, we might be able to have some sort of normal life. Most of the time anyway. I know we'll have to shift at full moon and it's better to join the pack for that. But otherwise… I might even be able to go back to being a doctor, not a surgeon, but I could do something."

Obviously, he was still in denial over what he was, and sadness flickered through her. But maybe she asked too much of him.

Connor pulled away. "I'll go get you some food."

At his words, her stomach rumbled. She was starving, but she didn't want him to go. They still needed to do something and heat pooled low down in her belly.

That wasn't good. She wasn't supposed to get turned on by the thought.

Connor's eyes narrowed as though he sensed a change in her. He scrambled from the bed. "You probably want a shower," he said backing away.

Yeah, she did. She guessed she wasn't at her most desirable right now. Or maybe he didn't fancy her any more, now she had joined the monster brigade. She watched him go, but she had a feeling the longer they put it off the harder the next part was going to be.

When he got to the door, she called to him. "Connor?"

"Yes?"

"Thank you."

Since that first time when she'd woken next to him, she hadn't got close enough to Connor to tell whether he had an erection or not. For the last two days, he'd kept his distance. Well, as much as possible in a ten foot by ten foot room. Keira was still confined in here until after she'd shifted the first time, when hopefully the damage to her brain would be repaired and she'd have some control. That was the theory anyway.

Connor spent most of his time with her. They talked, listened to music, talked some more. About everything apart from the fact they needed to make love. He didn't touch her, but he watched her constantly.

"Sebastian says it's full moon tonight," she said.

"I know."

"He says it's the easiest to change at full moon for the first time."

"I know. He told me as well."

She gritted her teeth together. "We need to talk about this, Connor."

"We do?"

"I understand if you're scared and you don't want to do it with me. Or if you just can't—I know I hurt you last time."

"I'm not scared."

He was being obtuse. "Perhaps I should ask Jack if I can borrow one of his vampires."

Ha—that had got him. His eyes narrowed. He put his book down slowly. Rose to his feet.

"I lied. I am scared. Scared I'll mess it up. I know I have to do this, but I want it to be good for you and I can't make it good, because…"

"Because if you do, I'll probably blow your brain."

"Yeah. I've put it off because I wanted to wait until full moon for your first shift and I thought if we made love once it would be harder to keep my hands off you."

She liked that.

He took a step toward her. "And I know it's your first time, but I also know I can't do anything to make it easier for you. I can't risk it. Last time, I nearly died. This time I'm not sure I would survive."

"And I'm guessing you dying on me might be a little more traumatic than me not…you know…"

"Coming apart in my arms. You were beautiful."

"Yeah, if only I hadn't melted your brain afterward."

A small smile tugged at his lips. He took a step closer so the heat radiating from his body warmed her skin. "Well, keep that in mind," he said. "If you feel anything—anything at all—tell me to stop."

He looked sexy as hell in his black jeans and black T-shirt. And she couldn't help it; at the thought of what they were going to do together, her sex grew hot and heavy, damp with need.

His nostrils flared and he closed his eyes for a moment. "I've never tried *not* to make a girl come before."

She didn't want to hear about him and other girls. "I'll recite poetry in my head, or do my times tables or—"

He cut her off with a glance, grasped the hem of her T-shirt and tugged it over her head. Then his hands went to her waist, unsnapped her jeans, and stripped them from her together with her panties. In seconds, she was naked.

For a moment, he stared down at her, his expression hot with need. She flicked her gaze down his long lean body and saw the line of his erection pressing against his jeans.

Her mouth went dry and her sex flooded with moist heat. She pressed her thighs together as a pulse started its insistent throb at her very core.

"Two times two is four," she muttered.

His quick laugh interrupted her, and then the amusement vanished from his face. He stared at her with pure masculine lust and her breath caught in her throat, her nipples tightening almost painfully. She remembered the feel of his lips on her breasts, between her thighs and tried to banish the thought.

He pushed her back against the small cot so she toppled onto her back and lay staring up at him. He appeared huge from this angle and as she watched, he unzipped his jeans and his erection sprang free.

He came down on his knees between her legs, nudging them further apart. Her hips lifted from the bed of their own accord and she closed her eyes and tried to think of something else. Vampires.

Pretend a vampire lay on top of her. About to shove inside her.

But she knew his scent now as though it were her own, and a moan of need escaped her lips.

Then he was nudging at the opening to her body, parting her sex and pushing inside.

"Christ, you're wet. And tight. And Jesus... that feels so good."

And he filled her with one stroke.

Keira lay there, feeling the fullness of him, fighting the urge to wrap her legs around him, rub up against him. She could feel the swollen nub at her core, so sensitive, if she shifted slightly...

His hands went to her hips and he held her in place. "Next time." His words were a dark sensual promise.

Then he balanced on his elbows and withdrew. The drag of him against her flesh was exquisite.

Vampires. There was a particularly scary one called Seth—her skin prickled and shivers ran through her whenever he was close. She screwed her eyes shut and brought up his face in her mind.

Then Connor thrust into her hard and her lids flew open. His face was a mask of concentration. He withdrew, then entered her again. He was big, this was new, and the feeling bordered on pain. She tried to hold on to that as his speed increased until he was slamming into her.

She focused on his face, tried to ignore the ripples of pleasure tugging at her spine. His expression grew fierce, predatory, his eyes almost feral, his lips gritted together in a hard line.

Then finally, his back arched, he shoved into her one last time and flooded her with his seed.

Chapter Ten

"I'm sorry," he muttered five minutes later. "But that was so fucking good." Pushing himself onto his elbows, he glanced down. "Shit, I didn't even take my shoes off."

He really couldn't get worked up about it though. His whole body exuded a sense of wellbeing. He knew he shouldn't feel this good, but he couldn't help it.

He'd been sort of dreading this. Now the relief that he wasn't writhing on the floor in agony almost equaled the pure bliss radiating from his still throbbing dick.

It had been a long time.

He turned his attention to the woman at his side. So far, she hadn't said anything. She'd been a virgin and this had hardly been a great introduction to making love. Except for him. For him it had been great. But he needn't have worried; when he looked into her face, he saw his own relief reflected there.

He shifted closer, leaned down over her, and kissed her lightly on the lips. "Next time will be better." Then he kissed her again. Kissed her how he'd wanted to kiss her before they'd made love but hadn't dared. His mouth slanted over hers, he parted her lips with his tongue and pushed inside.

She moved restlessly against him, her hands coming up to slide into his hair, pull him closer and his cock twitched. All set for another go.

Not going to happen.

Not yet at least.

He pulled free. For a second, her fingers tightened in his hair and then she released him. Tugging the sheet over her, she sat leaning against the wall.

She picked up his hand and played with his fingers. "I never thought I would get this with anyone."

"This?"

"Just being close. Touching. You've given me so much, and I want you to know—even if it doesn't work—it will still have been worth it."

"It will work."

The truth was he had no clue whether it would or not. But then, he had no clue how the whole werewolf thing worked. He'd questioned Sebastian, but really, no one knew. He suspected it involved magic, whatever that meant. As a doctor and a scientist, he'd never believed in magic. But then he'd never believed in vampires or werewolves either and he'd been totally wrong there. Maybe magic was just another science they didn't yet understand. He would start investigating when this thing with Keira was resolved.

"So what happens now?" she asked.

Connor glanced at the clock on the wall. "Any moment now, the moon will rise." Already, he could feel the tug of the full moon, stirring a wild excitement in his blood. "Then you shift. I can't take you out of here until then. But as soon as you change, I'll drive us out to the forest where you can run."

"Will it hurt? Shifting I mean?"

Connor remembered back to his own first time. The fear and confusion, the pain as though his body was being ripped apart, his bones smashed into splinters. Of course, he'd been in total denial and he suspected that's why it had hurt so badly.

"No, it shouldn't hurt."

"What must I do?" she asked.

"Relax. This is magic, let it flow through you."

Keira held herself immobile and closed her eyes.

"Good girl," Connor murmured.

He saw the moment the magic took over, and the creature within her roared to be free. For a moment, she held it at bay. Then she opened her eyes and they gleamed feral. The change came over her smoothly, no pain as she accepted her beast. Then she vanished, and in her place stood a dark brown wolf, with deep golden eyes.

Connor felt a moment of regret for the woman she had been and would never be again. She was one of them now.

One of the monsters.

But even as the thought crossed his mind, he pushed it aside. Keira could never be a monster. Whatever this changed in her, she was intrinsically the same person.

Did that mean so was he?

Had he been wrong all this time? Could it be that he didn't have to be evil after all?

The door opened. For a moment, she stood poised in the opening. Low in the sky, the fat yellow moon hung heavy and the magic shifted inside her. She leapt to the ground and stood on all fours sniffing the air. The world was changed. Twisting her head, she stared at the rich dark chocolate fur covering her back. She lifted each paw in turn, placing it down with exaggerated care, her sharp claws digging into the soft earth.

Breathing in, she caught a wild feral scent. She turned as a huge black wolf appeared behind her, his tail wagging frantically.

Connor.

The name whispered through her mind and she took a step toward him, touched her nose lightly to his and then jumped back with a yip when she found it cold and wet.

She gazed around her. Everything was sharply defined. Her ears swiveled, to pick up the sound of the wind in the treetops above her, and somewhere far off an owl hooted. She opened her mouth and tasted the rain on her tongue. The scents of the night filled her nostrils, the rich damp earth, leaf mold, the musky aroma of strange wolves. Her muzzle twitched, and she searched the edges of the clearing.

They came out of the trees.

Wolves.

At their head, stalked a huge silver wolf with dark blue eyes. Keira's legs trembled with excitement as he approached. Behind him trotted two smaller wolves, silver and red.

Her sisters.

Then others. Until they surrounded her in a circle. In unison, they raised their heads to the sky and howled. And Keira threw back her head and joined them. Wild excitement tugged at her. She needed to move, to run, to...

She found Connor at the edge of the circle, watching her from his dark wolf eyes, his black plumed tail waving. He caught her gaze, yipped once then turned and headed into the trees. The circle parted and she followed, stepped through and into the shadows.

She raced through the dark forest, the pads of her paws making no sound on the soft leaf-littered floor. Smoothly, she twisted her way between the gnarled trunks of the oaks, chasing the sable wolf. As the trees thinned, she picked up speed, running ever faster, until she was aware of nothing but the wind flowing past her. All her tension, the loneliness that had plagued her for so long fell away beneath the relentless stretch and release of muscle and sinew. A wild exhilaration filled her. She didn't falter as she reached the edge of the forest, and she was racing out in the open under the full moon.

Without warning, a huge form slammed into her from the side, pushing her to the ground, knocking the air from her lungs. She rolled, then jumped to her feet, shook herself, a growl rising up in her throat.

The black wolf faced her, hackles raised. When he saw he had her attention, he growled softly then looked back towards the dark shadows of the forest. She knew he wanted her to return to safety, but she didn't want safety. For the first time in so long, she was wildly alive, filled with joy. Laughter bubbled up in her mind but could find no release, and she sank to her haunches, threw back her head, and howled.

She woke in the first light of dawn. The moon had set and the rising sun painted the sky in pinks and orange. She was back in human form, lying under a huge oak tree, naked. But warm and cozy with Connor's strong arms wrapped around her. All her senses were acutely aware. Above her, the breeze rustled the canopy, and the scent of damp earth and warm musky werewolf filled her nostrils.

And something else.

She pulled free and sat up. Connor stirred in his sleep but didn't awaken.

Something teased at her mind and she rose slowly to her feet as two figures stepped out of the forest. Tasha and Anya.

Wonder filled her as she realized how close they were and neither was in pain.

It had worked. She was free.

She walked slowly toward them, then she was enfolded in their arms as she blinked back hot tears.

"It worked," Tasha said.

She nodded. "I guess."

"Can you hear us in your head?" Anya asked.

For a moment, fear froze her brain, then she reached out tentatively, opening her mind and a whole deluge of images poured in. Too many to make sense of.

Shaking her head, she laughed. "Yes, but perhaps I need a little practice."

"We'll help you. We just wanted to check you were okay. And bring you some clothes. You get used to being naked after a while but it takes a little time." Tasha dropped the bundle she was carrying and then peered past Keira to where Connor still lay sleeping.

"I guess we'll leave you then," Anya said. "You probably have things to do." She grinned. "But when you get back we need to talk. Serious girl talk."

"That sounds wonderful—I've never done girl talk."

"We'll see you later then."

"You will. And thank you," Keira said. "For looking for me."

"It was our pleasure."

Keira turned back to Connor. He was awake and watching her out of half-closed eyes. His gaze dropped to her body and her nipples tightened in anticipation of the dark promise in his eyes.

He held out a hand. She closed the distance between them.

"Good morning."

She mingled her fingers with his and he tugged so she collapsed to the soft ground beside him.

"Are you okay?" he asked.

"I'm wonderful. It worked, Connor. I'm healed."

"That's good." His eyes darkened to black as he focused on her face. "Very good."

He pulled her to him and rolled her so she lay beneath him and his hardness pressed against her belly.

"I owe you an orgasm," he murmured against her lips.

Chapter Eleven

At his words, every muscle in Keira's body locked up tight. She was cured. Totally cured. So why couldn't she banish the fear that she would hurt him again?

He must have sensed her tension, because he came up onto his elbows and cupped her face between his big warm hands. "What is it, *querida*?"

"Querida?"

"It means darling in Spanish." He stroked the hair from her face. "Tell me..."

"I'm scared."

"So am I. Scared I won't please you."

There wasn't much chance of that. Just looking at him pleased her. "I keep remembering the first time. I thought I'd killed you."

A shudder ran through her. "Maybe you should just do it quickly. Not worry about me."

A rueful smile curved his lips. "Then I'd owe you two orgasms and that would hardly be fair." He nudged a knee between her thighs, pushed up against her sex so a jolt of pleasure shot through her. "Just relax," he murmured.

Keira gave a shaky laugh. "I don't think I can."

"Well, I'm going to have to try really hard to get you over that." His voice was a low husky purr. The sound sent quivers trembling across her skin, as one hair-roughened thigh massaged her, rotating against her most sensitive spot, eliciting a delicious friction.

He lowered his head and nibbled her lower lip, then stroked her with his tongue. Her mouth opened beneath his, and he pushed inside. She gave up thinking for a while, her fears melting beneath the intensity of his touch. His lips caressed her cheek, then the soft spot below her ear and lower, to scatter kisses across her breasts. Her nipples tightened as he drew closer, teasing her with his mouth and tongue.

"Breathe," he whispered against her skin and she drew in a shuddering gasp of air just as his lips closed over her nipple. A bolt of pure pleasure flashed to her groin. Her sex grew hot and heavy, moist with need. The last of her fear was slipping away, the tension seeping from her as her insides turned molten and her belly filled with hot liquid heat.

Connor moved to her other breast, bit down gently on the taut peak, and then soothed her with kisses. Keira was squirming beneath him now; she'd never felt anything like this. Well, not since that first time...

The thought doused the fires burning within her. She went still.

As though he sensed her unease, Connor raised his head to stare into her face. "We'll just take it very, very slowly." His hand slid down between their bodies, ruffling the curls at the juncture of her thighs. She stopped breathing again as he delved between the drenched folds of her sex. His clever fingers drew lazy circles around her clit, driving every thought, every fear from her mind until she was aware of nothing but his hands, his mouth, his big body poised above her.

His erection pressed scalding hot against her thigh and suddenly she needed him inside her. "Please, Connor."

He shifted, positioning himself. "This is for you." And he eased into her.

Last night, when he'd taken her, Keira hadn't allowed herself to think about what was happening, had concentrated on anything but the fact that he was deep inside her. Now her body shuddered under the realization that they were joined as one. He was big and he filled her, stretching her, completing her.

He stared down at her, his eyes dark with desire. "Okay, I lied. This is for me as well—that feels *so* good."

He moved slowly, withdrawing almost to the tip, then pushing back inside. At the end of each stroke, he rotated his pelvis against her core. Her clit was swollen with need and so sensitive that each grind of his hips had her hovering on the edge.

She opened her legs wider, wrapping them around his waist. She'd lost the ability to think, all she knew was the swell of pleasure rising and falling, each time taking her higher than the last.

Then he slid his hands beneath her, clasped the globes of her bottom, and ground her against him. She came in an explosion of pleasure, arching her back. He leaned down and swallowed her cries with his kiss, as his body went rigid and he spilled himself inside her.

For a second, she froze, waiting…

And nothing. No screams of agony.

She had no time to savor the relief as Connor rocked her against his still hard shaft, and she came again. Happiness mingled with the exquisite pleasure.

She was cured.

Connor lay behind her, his body pressed along the whole length of her back, hot and hard. One long muscular leg was hooked across hers and one arm wrapped around her. She peered down, her gaze captured by the sight of his huge hand cupping her breast, his olive skin dark against her paleness. His fingers were long, sprinkled with short black hair. As she watched, they tightened on her, sending a spasm of intense pleasure shooting from her breast to her belly, and then lower, so she writhed against him.

The sun was directly overhead, and she'd lost track of who owed who orgasms a long time ago. They'd made love, and talked, and dozed in the warm sunlight. Then woken to make love again.

Now she felt him harden behind her, his cock nudging her bottom. His leg shifted to slide between hers, parting her thighs so he could push inside slowly. His fingers plucked at her nipples then stroked down over her belly, into the damp curls at the base. Then lower to find the swollen bud at her core. He massaged her lightly in time with his strokes. She was so sensitive and the pleasure built quickly, like a great swelling of sensation, filling her with warmth and light. She relaxed into it, letting the feelings take her over until they exploded in a starburst of light behind her closed lids.

He came a moment later, pulsating inside her.

His breath feathered her skin, as he kissed the back of her neck, his teeth nipping at the spot where he'd bitten her all those days ago.

It seemed like another lifetime.

"I love you," he whispered the words in her ear.

A wave of happiness washed over her. She didn't know where they would go from here. Their relationship had formed too fast, under such extreme conditions. But right now, it was enough. The moment was perfect.

She pushed herself up, needing to see his face when she spoke her reply.

His eyes held such tender passion that her heart ached. She rested her palm on the curve of his cheek, stared into his beautiful eyes.

"I—"

Her words were cut off abruptly as a small red dot appeared on Connor's chest.

"What is it?" he asked.

She swallowed and nodded downward.

"Shit."

Don't move, Keira.

The voice spoke inside her head. And she went instantly still.

And tell your friend not to move.

"Connor, don't move."

She sat totally still. The red dot never wavered from Connor's heart. She peered sideways as four people stepped out from the trees to their left.

A woman flanked by three men. Dressed in a black pant suit, with dark glasses covering her eyes, something seemed familiar about her. Was this the woman who had been hunting her on Rannoch Moor? Keira thought it must be, but as before, she couldn't shake the idea it was more than that.

The woman came to a halt in front of them, a smile curving her crimson lips, a pistol gripped in one hand. She waved the other and the red dot vanished. Keira breathed again.

"Sorry to disturb you," the woman said. "But at least we waited until you'd finished."

"Who are you?" Keira asked.

The woman took off the glasses revealing dark golden eyes and arched brows. "My name is Darla."

"Shit, you're twins," Connor muttered.

The woman grinned. "I'm guessing you're right, though those bastards back at the Agency never let on. They could have warned me—not that it makes a difference." Her gaze wandered down over Connor's naked form. "Nice."

She strolled across the clearing, picked up the bundle of clothes, and tossed them over. "I suggest the two of you get dressed. Pity to cover him up, but I want out of this place and quick. I'm not expecting any company, but I'm not a country lover and fresh air does nothing for me."

Keira's mind reeled. She had a twin sister.

Who worked for the Agency.

And was a complete bitch.

She searched the woman's face. It was no surprise she hadn't recognized her the other day. She'd been at a distance, plus Keira hadn't seen her own reflection in years. And this glossy woman was like a pampered thoroughbred racehorse next to Keira's muddy underfed pony. She became acutely aware she was naked, her hair tangled, and she reeked of sex. What a time to get self-conscious about her appearance.

All along, she'd known the Agency would destroy her if they ever found her. How could she have forgotten them so completely? Now she'd got Connor taken as well. She had no doubt they would kill him without a second thought. But probably not before they tortured him to find out if he knew anything—if she had passed on any of her secrets.

"You don't have to do this," Connor said in a low voice that wouldn't carry to the men who stood about ten feet away. "You can come back with us. We'll help you get away from the Agency."

"Now, why would I want to get away from the Agency? They've been good to me."

Conner got to his feet and pulled on his pants. "Because they tried to kill your sisters, and as soon as your usefulness is over or they see you as a threat, they'll turn on you."

"Well, I'd better make sure I stay useful then."

Keira forced herself to function. Pushing herself to her feet, she took a deep breath and tried to control the shaking of her limbs. She dragged on the jeans and T-shirt. "How did you find me?"

"I sensed you back in Scotland. But I couldn't hone in on you. Rather than waste time in that godforsaken place, I set up satellite surveillance on the area. We caught you leaving, but afterward, we lost you. And then not a flicker from either of you."

She waved the pistol in the direction they had come from to indicate they should start walking.

"Then I got a message last night that your doctor friend had been spotted by another surveillance unit, driving through London. After that it was easy."

"Do you know what they'll do to me?"

"Do I seem the type to care? Look, sweetie, I've learned that you trust no one in this life. You're alone in this world. You think your new boyfriend there wouldn't turn on you in a moment if he thought it would save his life?"

Keira looked at Connor, and he smiled a slow smile that told her so much.

"You're wrong," she said. "He'd die for me."

Darla shrugged. "No doubt he will. And probably soon. Now, let's go."

Keira pushed her fears aside. Somehow, she needed to get Connor out of this mess alive. She wouldn't allow him to die because of her. Once they got inside the Agency, their chances of getting out were around zero. She had to find a way to avoid that.

It seemed as though Darla knew little of what was going on. Did she know they were werewolves? Could they shift and escape in the confusion. But she could almost feel the guns trained on them, and she pushed the idea aside. For the moment, at least.

After a fifteen minute trek through the woods, they came to a black van. Darla indicated the open back door.

"Wait," Keira said.

Darla gave an exaggerated sigh. "What?"

"You know once we get inside the Agency we're as good as dead."

"So?"

"I don't want to die."

"Well, isn't that a goddamn pity. Neither do I. So if you're after some sympathy, you're looking in the wrong place."

"Not sympathy. I may have something to trade."

"Now what could you possibly have?"

"Why do you think they're still after me after all these years? Why did they want me dead in the first place?"

"I don't know, but are you going to get to the point?"

"I have secrets. Information they don't want to get out. I've written it all down."

Darla sighed. "Do you really think they'll care?"

"Can *you* really risk that they won't?"

"Shit." Darla pulled a phone from her pocket and walked a little away so they couldn't hear her words. Turning back, she shoved the phone in her pocket.

"So where are these notes?"

"I hid them on the moor."

"Why did I guess that was coming?" Darla pursed her lips and cast Keira a black look. "Hey, sis, you know what, I'm beginning to dislike you."

"The feeling is mutual. But take me back and I'll get you them. But only once Connor is safe."

She knew this was stupid. Why would they let him go? Or they'd let him go and then hunt him down and kill him afterward. But she couldn't think of anything else and at least this might give him a chance. Especially if they didn't know about the werewolf thing. If they divided the group, then there might be more of a chance that Connor could take his guards.

"Give me a minute alone with him. We need to set up a signal so I'll know he's really safe."

"You are aware they'll just go after him and kill him once you're dead," Darla pointed out in a reasonable tone.

Keira flinched at the callousness of the words, but forced a shrug. "He can take care of himself."

"Go ahead then."

She dragged Connor a few feet away and turned so her back was to the group. "They'll split us up."

"I don't like it."

"Connor, if you get the chance you have to escape. There's no hope for me—as long as I'm alive the Agency will keep coming."

"Why? What is it they think you know?"

"I don't know. I've never known."

"Don't give up. Somehow we'll get through this."

"Of course we will."

It was hard to believe that only half an hour ago, she'd been thinking how perfect everything was. She should never have forgotten that she didn't believe in happy endings. Connor cupped her face, leaned down, and kissed her.

"Come on, you two," Darla snapped. "We're on a schedule here."

Keira bit her lip as they cuffed her hands in front of her then watched as they did the same to Connor. She scrambled into the back of the van after him and Darla gave her one last disgusted look.

"Crap," she muttered. "We're heading back to the most desolate place God ever made."

They were going home.

Keira realized she hadn't told Connor she loved him. She turned, but as she opened her mouth, a needle pricked her arm and the darkness swallowed her.

Chapter Twelve

Connor's mouth tasted like paint stripper. He pushed himself up on his elbows—awkward in the handcuffs—and retched. Nothing came out, and he realized he hadn't eaten in twenty-four hours.

First, he'd been too keyed up, then he'd been too busy making love to Keira, and finally, he'd been unconscious.

Shit. How long had he been out for?

And where was Keira?

Panic tore at his insides. Connor forced the emotion down; he needed to keep a clear head. He blinked a couple of times to clear his vision, still blurred from whatever drug they'd given him. His limbs felt heavy but he was coming around fast. Drugs didn't work the same on werewolves.

He lay on a carpet with fat pink roses. A matching pink sofa sat to his side facing an empty fireplace. Where the hell was he? Rain spattered against the window, the view outside wreathed in mist. He guessed he must be back in Scotland. So hopefully Keira was somewhere near.

A door opened and a pair of boots entered his line of sight. He peered up and recognized one of the guards who'd been with them in the forest. He frowned down at Connor. Probably expected him to be out a lot longer.

"Water?" Connor's voice was a raspy croak.

The man studied him for a second then reached into his pocket and brought out a key, he unfastened the cuff and looped it through a radiator pipe on the wall beside Connor. Then refastened it around his wrist, gave a tug, and left the room. He came back a minute later with a glass. Connor grasped it awkwardly. The water tasted wonderful. Afterward, he cleared his throat and struggled into a sitting position leaning back against the sofa, his handcuffed hands on his lap. "So what happens now?"

"We wait for a call."

"And then?"

The man shrugged.

One thing was clear, they were unaware of the werewolf thing or there would have been more than one man guarding him.

He heard a sound from the next room. Two men. Still no problem. But that left at least six people guarding Keira. With so many, he didn't dare do a full on attack. They'd kill her before he took them all out.

He needed help.

But first, he had to get out of here.

"Any chance of some food?" he asked.

He waited until the guard left the room and then concentrated on his hand. He'd never done this before, but he'd seen Sebastian do it. Magic shivered through the air. His skin rippled, faded, and reformed into a claw. He slipped it through the handcuff and willed it back to normal.

The soft sound of murmured voices drifted in from the next room. Connor rose silently and stepped lightly across the floor in his bare feet. He stood by the side of the door. When it opened, he held his breath, waiting until the man was fully in the room. He clipped him lightly on the jaw, measuring the force, knowing with his extra strength he could easily kill with one punch. Connor grabbed him as he fell and lowered him gently to the floor. He rifled through the pockets, found car keys, which he transferred to his own, and a small silver key for the cuffs. After dragging the man across the room, he fastened him by the cuff and then straightened.

One more to take down.

He pulled the pistol from the underarm holster and crossed the room. At the door, he hesitated, then peered out into a hallway. A second door stood open opposite where Connor stood. He spotted the guard with his back to him, fixing food at the counter. He raised his head, caught sight of Connor's reflection in the darkened window, and whirled around.

Connor aimed the pistol and the man stopped. He seemed to weigh up his options and then kept coming. He moved fast, but not as fast as Connor. He raised the pistol and smashed it into the guard's skull. This time he allowed his opponent to crash to the floor on his own. There was no one else to hear.

He went through his pockets and found a cell phone.

Sebastian picked up at the first ring. "Where the hell are you?"

"Scotland."

"What the fuck are you doing in Scotland?"

"The Agency has Keira. She told them she has information hidden up here."

"I take it you got free."

"They separated us. I've taken down the two guards left with me, but I'm guessing there are at least six still with Keira. I'm not sure where I am—wait a second." Connor opened the outer door and glanced outside. The house stood alone, but he recognized the moors to his right. He reckoned he was in one of the farmhouses at the edge of Rannoch Moor. "I'm a few miles from where I think Keira is taking them."

"You can't go in alone," Sebastian said. "You could take them out but probably not before they kill Keira."

Frustration gnawed at him. "I know."

"Just a moment." Connor heard him talking to someone in the background. He spoke again a minute later. "Jack reckons we can be there in less than two hours in the helicopter."

"It's still too long. But come anyway. You have the coordinates for Keira's old home?"

"Yeah, we'll head straight there. What about you—don't do anything stupid, Connor."

"I won't. I've thought of somewhere I can get help."

"And that would be?"

"The local pack."

"I thought you said they were assholes."

"The alpha is an asshole, the rest I don't know. But I'm about to find out."

Sebastian was silent for a second. "If you challenge him, don't hesitate. It's a fight to the death, Connor. It can be nothing else."

"I know."

Connor found the house exactly where Pete had told him it would be—at the northern end of the moor. In some ways it reminded him of Sebastian's home, a large sprawling building set in its own grounds with a six foot wall around the perimeter. But where Sebastian's had always felt welcoming, this had a depressing, dark aspect.

He drew up at the wrought iron gates and waited as the guard came around to speak to him.

"What do you want?"

"I'm here to see Logan," he answered.

"Name?"

"Dr. Connor McNair."

He waited, tapping his fingers on the wheel while the guard spoke into his phone. Impatience built inside him. He didn't even know if Keira had these secrets she'd spoken of. She'd never mentioned them before. Maybe it had been a story to give them more time. Give him a chance to survive, while she sacrificed herself.

But how long would it buy them?

It would take them a while to reach Keira's keep; they would have to walk the last few miles. He was hoping he'd make better time—if he survived this next meeting.

The guard turned back to him, nodded and the gates glided open. Connor drove through, along the tree-lined drive and pulled up in front of the house. As he turned off the engine, the front door opened and a man stepped through and onto the terrace. Connor recognized him immediately.

He climbed out and walked slowly toward the other man.

"Did you know you have no shoes on?" Pete asked as Connor came to a halt in front of him.

Connor glanced down. To be honest, he'd totally forgotten. He got straight to the point. "I need your help."

"Mine personally?"

"No. The whole pack."

Pete shrugged. "Then you'll have to ask Logan. And I'm warning you, he's not particularly helpful."

"I could offer him money."

"He has plenty."

It had been worth a try. "Let me talk to him."

Pete rested his hand on Connor's arm before they entered. "One thing—if he does accept your challenge, he'll move fast. He knows you're strong."

Connor's wolf became instantly alert as soon as he stepped into Logan's presence. The alpha sat on a chair at the far end of the room. The blonde woman from the previous meeting knelt at his feet, a leather collar around her throat, tied to a leash in Logan's hand.

Asshole.

Connor's wolf stalked inside the confines of his body. He wanted to be free. He wanted to fight, but Connor wouldn't go that route if he could avoid it. He'd always sworn he would never accept being one of the monsters, and this would be the last, final step down that road.

As he stopped in front of the other man, he tried for a passive pose, but wolf clawed at his insides making him wince. "I need your help."

Logan ignored the comment. "I told you what would happen if you were seen in my territory again. Unless you've come to pledge your allegiance to me?" He studied Connor out of narrow black eyes. "But I think it's too late for that. Pete, take him out the back and get rid of him."

Connor took a deep breath. He could do this. He had to do this. "I challenge you."

As the words left him, he knew he was saying goodbye to his old life and finally accepting the new. Relief flowed through him as he finally and fully accepted what he was.

Logan's eyes widened. "But I don't accept your challenge. Pete?"

Connor turned to look at the other man. Pete gripped his pistol in his hand. The weapon wasn't aimed at Connor but at the group of other men in the room. "Don't interfere," he said.

"You'll die for this," Logan snarled.

"Maybe."

Connor stood half turned away from the alpha, but he was expecting Logan's move. The man hurled himself at Connor, shifting as he flew through the air. Connor released his wolf and had already changed as Logan smashed into him. They went down in a flurry of claws and fangs. He rolled, coming up on all fours then hurled himself at the other wolf. Teeth snapped close to his face, but he didn't slow, getting a grip around the other's throat, his fangs sinking into flesh and bone.

Logan heaved him off with a scrabble of claws. Connor lost his grip, and he crashed to the floor.

For a minute, they circled, Connor growling as the metallic scent of fresh blood filled his nostrils.

Finish it.

Everything inside him screamed to end this now.

He leapt for Logan. This time, as his teeth sank into the flesh, he knew he had a death grip. Clamping his jaws closed, he held on, shaking the great black wolf, then pressing him down to the ground. He felt the spurt as his teeth severed the artery. Blood sprayed, blinding him for a moment and his mouth filled with the sweet coppery taste. And still he maintained his grip until the life went out of Logan, and he lay still.

Connor loosened his hold and backed away, sniffing at the body.

Then the wolf disappeared, and Logan lay on the ground naked, an open wound at his throat that spilled crimson on to the tiled floor. Logan was dead, and Connor threw back his head and howled as a tidal wave of exhilaration swept over him. For the first time, he knew what it was to be wolf.

Finally, he looked around the circle of men. They stared from him to Logan.

"There's not a mark on you," Pete murmured.

Connor stared into his eyes and growled.

"You need our help?"

Connor inclined his head.

"We're yours to command now."

Connor wasn't sure he wanted anyone to command, long term. But right now, he needed their help. All around him, the air filled with magic. The pack was shifting. More entered the room until there must have been thirty wolves.

Connor led them out into the night and then they were racing across the moor.

Darla shoved the phone in her pocket and turned to face Keira.

"There's no answer. Looks like your boyfriend's done a runner and left you to it."

The tension seeped from Keira's muscles. She'd known the only way Connor would survive this was if he escaped. Once she handed her secrets to Darla, she had no doubt the order would be given to kill him. Keira only hoped he would get far away from here before that happened.

Well, most of her hoped that, but she didn't really believe it. Connor would come after her and even if he'd got weapons from his guards, it was still one against six. The cuffs bound her hands in front of her and she was less than useless. Perhaps she could try to shift, but she wasn't sure how fast she would be. Likely not fast enough to save herself from a bullet.

No, her only hope of saving Connor was to hand the stuff over and get out of there as fast as possible.

Life wasn't fair. To have found Connor, to have seen a glimpse of another life, only to have them snatched from her. Darla would take her back to the Agency and sooner or later, they would complete what they set out to do so long ago and end her life. She suspected she'd come to hope for "sooner" in the time ahead.

"Come on, get this information, and let's get the hell out of here," Darla muttered and shoved her in the side.

The night was cloudy, no moon or stars broke through the solid darkness, and the only light came from the torches the guards carried. It had taken two hours walking and a lot of swearing to get to the place, but now they stood outside the keep. Keira led them around the side and then pushed away the branches covering the entrance. She ducked to enter, ignoring Darla who followed her inside.

"Now, where?" Darla snapped. Her temper had become shorter as the night progressed.

Keira crossed the room and nodded toward the wall. "Behind the stone."

She stepped aside as Darla tugged at the loose rock. "If I break a fingernail, I'll be pissed. And believe me you wouldn't like me when I'm pissed."

"I don't like you now."

"Ah, got it." She dropped the stone to the ground and pulled out the notebooks hidden behind it. She flicked through them. "What is this shit?"

Keira shrugged. "Everything I remember. Everything I got from people's minds back at the Agency. Presumably in there is the information they want me dead for."

"Interesting," Darla mused, flicking through the pages.

"I'll tell them if you read it. Then they'll kill you too."

Darla shot her a filthy look, but slammed the notebook closed. "Let's get out of here."

She led the way out and Keira followed her, casting a last look at the place that had been her home for so long. She doubted she would see it again. But as soon as she stepped out into the night, magic enveloped her, wrapping itself around her. Deep inside, her wolf stirred eager to be free. She paused, trying to identify where it came from, but the sensation surrounded her.

Connor?

Darla turned to her, eyes narrowed. "What is it?"

"Nothing."

Should she shift? Before she could make the decision, Darla grabbed her and shoved the gun to her throat. "Move a millimeter and I shoot." She turned to the guards. "Go check it out, see if anyone else is here."

"Can't you tell?" Keira asked, wincing as the gun jabbed her. She reached out with her inner eye and found only their little group close by. Darla obviously came to the same conclusion. Her tense figure relaxed and the gun eased off a little.

The guards came back. "There's no one out there."

"No, there isn't, is there?"

Keira felt her probing at her thoughts and slammed down a wall. Darla had tried once or twice to pry into her mind. So far, Keira had kept her out.

"What are you hiding?" Darla asked.

A sharp pain blasted her in the brain. Obviously, Darla hadn't tried very hard up to now. A hot poker probed Keira's mind, dropping her to her knees as the agony threatened to overwhelm her. She had to keep up the wall. She couldn't let Darla see the wolves inside her head.

"Let me in," Darla murmured. "And I'll stop."

Blood trickled from her nostrils as the pain kept up, unrelenting. Keira knew she should shift, but her wolf cowered somewhere deep inside her, and she didn't know if she had the power to call her. Darkness encroached on her mind, blotting out the light until all that remained was a pinprick. She knew if that went out she would be dead, and she fought to concentrate on the tiny spot. She collapsed to the ground on all fours, clumsy in the handcuffs, her fingernails digging into the soft soil.

Would Connor arrive only to find her already dead?

"Shit," Darla growled. "Stop being so fucking stubborn."

Then the night exploded around her. Guns and growls filled the air.

And the pain cut off abruptly.

Keira pushed herself up. Next to her, a huge black wolf crouched on top of Darla, its teeth close to her throat.

"Connor, don't kill her," Keira said.

The wolf backed away a little but kept one front paw resting on Darla's chest. Blood oozed from a wound at her shoulder, but she managed to turn her head to stare into Keira's eyes.

"Tell him to let me up or I'll burn your brain out," Darla snarled, her voice hoarse with pain.

Agony flooded Keira again. But this time she knew how it was done; she'd seen into Darla's mind, and she countered with a blast from her own.

Darla screamed and rolled onto her side away from her and the pain in Keira's head dimmed. The power pouring from her swelled and grew until Darla's screams shrank to whimpers and then nothing.

"Keira, it's okay, you can stop. She's unconscious." Hard hands gripped her shoulders, pulled her to her feet, and held her close. "Come on, stop. You don't want to kill her. She's your sister."

She forced the power back into her own mind and slammed the door, breathing hard as she stared down at the woman on the ground.

"Is she alive?"

Connor released her, crouched down and touched his hand to Darla's throat. "Just. But I bit her—she'll be a wolf if she survives."

"Not good." Darla as a werewolf was something she really didn't want to think about right now.

Connor straightened and turned back to her. He was naked and Keira had never seen anything so beautiful in her life. He held out a hand, and she slid her palm into his and allowed him to pull her close.

"I thought I was too late," he whispered the words against her skin. "I thought she'd killed you."

His voice was rough with remembered panic. She buried her head in his chest and reveled in the knowledge they were both alive and—for the moment—safe. But who knew how long that would last. Raising her head, she stared into his dark eyes. She needed to say this just in case...

"I love you, Connor."

He dropped a too brief kiss on her lips. "I love you too. Now, let's get out of here."

Letting her go, he turned back to Darla, rummaging in her pockets and producing a small silver key. He un-cuffed Keira and rubbed her wrists. "Are you okay?" Reaching up, he wiped her face with his finger. "You're bleeding."

Her head ached a little, but happiness bubbled inside her. "We're both alive and we're free. Right now, that's way more than enough. How about you?"

"I'm okay as well. More than okay. Fantastic."

Keira glanced around. The guards were all down. Dead she presumed. And there were wolves everywhere. Some paced, some sat on their haunches. All were focused on Connor. "Who are they?"

He followed her gaze. "They're my pack."

She heard the pride and acceptance in his voice. At last, Connor knew who and what he was.

"I've been thinking," Connor said. "How would you feel about coming back here to live? I don't mean in the keep. But we'd find somewhere close to the moors."

"I thought you hated the moors," she said but hope grew inside her. Those days and nights in the cell had made her realize how much she loved the wildness of Rannoch Moor.

He wrapped his arms around her and turned her so they faced to the east. Dawn was coming, the sun rising on a new day, streaking the sky with color, casting a warm, almost welcoming glow over the desolate moors.

"Let's just say, it's growing on me. In fact, I think it might be a bloody good place to live."

Epilogue

"So what do we do with her?" Sebastian murmured to the room in general.

Connor stared at the woman on the monitor and felt a rush of hatred. She had come so close to killing Keira. The memory still had the power to make his heart skip a beat.

At the same time, she looked so like her twin he couldn't completely separate his feelings.

How could two sisters be so different?

What had been done to Darla to make her as she was?

He'd studied genetics, but he also knew people were way more complicated than a few strands of DNA. As much nurture went into the forging a character as nature, and he reckoned Darla hadn't had much nurturing in her life. All the same, he found it hard to feel sorry for her.

Darla was awake but lay on the narrow cot in the room they had built for Keira, staring straight up at the ceiling, her face expressionless. She'd recovered from Connor's bite, now her wolf lay dormant inside her.

"Leave her here for now," Jack said. "We'll take care of her."

"Nothing like the company of vampires to make you consider the error of your ways," Sebastian said dryly. "Just make sure none of them screw her. I don't want her turning werewolf until we've decided what to do with her." He turned to Connor. "So what do you plan?"

"We're going back to Rannoch Moor. Apparently, everything that belonged to Logan is mine, including the house and the pack. And they're a mess." He wanted to ask Sebastian's help. He'd been in denial so long, he knew next to nothing about how a healthy pack should run, and he wanted to know. There were people relying on him now.

Anya nudged Sebastian in the side and he grinned. "I have to ask—do you want some company? Anya wants to spend some time with Keira—"

"And us," Tasha interrupted. "We want to come as well. Just for a little while."

That meant the vampire. He'd have to check the house had a basement. But the thought didn't upset him.

"And we would like to go through the notebooks with Keira," Jack said. "There must be names in there that will give us a lead on the Agency."

Connor realized that while he might be moving on to a new life, these people would always be his family, willing to answer if he called.

He had a future.

Keira's hand slipped into his and she squeezed. *They* had a future. One he'd never dreamed possible at the start of all this. And that was all due to the woman at his side. He pulled her closer.

Mine

The word echoed through his mind. His wolf approved.

The End

Did you enjoy this book? You can make a huge difference.

Honest reviews of my books help bring them to the attention of other readers. In fact, reviews are the most powerful tool in my arsenal, when it comes to getting attention for my books. If you enjoyed this book, I would be very grateful if you could spend five minutes leaving a review.

Thank you very much!

Nina xxx

Subscribe to my Newsletter.

Building a relationship with my readers is one of the things I love about writing. I occasionally send out newsletters with information about new releases, free stories, competitions and other news about my books.

If you'd like to subscribe to my newsletter then visit my website at www.ninacroft.com

(I never send spam and will never pass on your details. Check out my Privacy Policy on my website.)

About the Author

Growing up, Nina Croft spent her time dreaming of faraway sunnier places and ponies. When she discovered both, and much more, could be found between the covers of a book, her life changed forever.

Later, she headed south, picked up a husband on the way, and together they discovered a love of travel and a dislike of 9-5 work. Eventually they stumbled upon the small almond farm in Spain they now call home.

Nina spends her days reading, writing and riding under the blue Spanish skies—sunshine and ponies. Proof that dreams can come true if you want them enough.

Find out more about Nina at www.ninacroft.com

Also by Nina Croft...

The Sisters of the Moon series

Bound to Night
Bound to Moonlight
Bound to Secrets

The Storm Lords series

Remember Me
Return to Me
Release Me
Boxed Set (books 1 – 3)
Unwrap Me

The Order series

Bittersweet Blood
Bittersweet Magic
Bittersweet Darkness
Bittersweet Christmas

Daughters of the Morrigan series

The Prophecy
The Darkness
Witch's Moon
Bewitched Before Christmas

The Dark Desires series

Break Out
Deadly Pursuit
Death Defying
Temporal Shift
Blood and Metal
Flying Through Fire
A Diversion in Time (short story)

Dark Desires Origins series

Malfunction

Deception

Insurrection

The Beyond Human series

Unthinkable

Unspeakable

Uncontrollable

For information on all these and more, visit Nina's website at www.ninacroft.com

Printed in Great Britain
by Amazon